THE AIR-CONDITIONED NIGHTMARE

(Volume One)

The
AIR-CONDITIONED
NIGHTMARE

HENRY MILLER
A New Directions Book

ACKNOWLEDGMENTS
Many chapters of this volume have appeared in magazines and an-
thologies here and abroad. For permission to reprint we beg to thank
the editors of the following: "The Shadows"—*Town & Country;*
"Good News! God Is Love!"—*Horizon* (England); "Soirée in Hollywood"—*Horizon;* "My Dream of Mobile"—*View* and *Now* (England); "A Night with Jupiter"— *View;* "Vive la France"—*Hemi-
spheres, Fontaine* (Algiers), and *Tricolor;* "With Edgar Varèse in
the Gobi Desert"—*Poetry-London;* "Marin and Stieglitz"—*Twice a
Year;* "Preface" (abridged)—*The Quarterly Review of Literature
and Modern Reading* (England); "Automotive Passacaglia"—*Rocky
Mountain Review* and *To-morrow* (England); "Day in the Park"—
Interim; "The Soul of Anesthesia"—*The Illiterati;* "The Most Lovely
Inanimate Object in Existence"—*Harvard Advocate* and *Now* (Eng-
land); "Letter to Lafayette"—*Chimera;* "The Southland"—*The New
English Weekly* (England).

Manufactured in the United States of America

First published clothbound in 1945
First published as New Directions Paperbook 302 in 1970
New Directions Books are printed on acid-free paper
Published simultaneously in Canada by
Penguin Books Canada Limited

New Directions Books are published for James Laughlin
by New Directions Publishing Corporation,
80 Eighth Avenue, New York 10011

SEVENTEENTH PRINTING

"The greatest men in the world have passed away unknown. The Buddhas and the Christs that we know are but second-rate heroes in comparison with the greatest men of whom the world knows nothing. Hundreds of these unknown heroes have lived in every country working silently. Silently they live and silently they pass away; and in time their thoughts find expression in Buddhas or Christs; and it is these latter that become known to us. The highest men do not seek to get any name or fame from their knowledge. They leave their ideas to the world; they put forth no claims for themselves and establish no schools or systems in their name. Their whole nature shrinks from such a thing. They are the pure Sattvikas, *who can never make any stir but only melt down in love.* . . .

"In the life of Gautama Buddha we notice him constantly saying that he is the twenty-fifth Buddha. The twenty-four before him are unknown to history, although the Buddha known to history must have built upon foundations laid by them. *The highest men are calm, silent and unknown.* They are the men who really know the power of thought; they are sure that even if they go into a cave and close the door and simply think five true thoughts and then pass away, these five thoughts of theirs will live throughout eternity. Indeed such thoughts of theirs will penetrate through the mountains, cross the oceans and travel through the world. They will enter deep into human hearts and brains and raise up men and women who will give them practical expression in the workings of human life . . . The Buddhas and the Christs will go from place to place preaching these truths. . . . These Sattvika men are too near the Lord to be active and to fight, to be working, struggling, preaching and doing good, as they say, here on earth to humanity. . . ."

—Swami Vivekananda

CONTENTS

THE ILLUSTRATIONS

The portraits of Henry Miller, Abe Rattner, Edgar Varèse and Alfred Stieglitz were photographed by William Candlewood, Alfredo Valente, Robin Carson and Dorothy Norman respectively. The shots of a milltown and the Chicago slums are from the archives of the Farm Security Administration in the Library of Congress, taken by Arthur Rothstein and Russell Lee. Abe Rattner photographed Henry Miller in Jacksonville, and Weeks Hall supplied the picture of his home. Marin's painting "Maine Islands" is in The Phillips Memorial Gallery, Washington. Hilaire Hiler and Dr. Marion Souchon sent the publisher the photographs of their paintings, photographers not known.

Henry Miller at Big Sur, California—Spring, 1944

PREFACE

THE THOUGHT of writing a book on America came to me in Paris some years ago. At that time the possibility of realizing my dream seemed rather remote, for in order to write the book I would have to visit America, travel leisurely, have money in my pocket, and so on. I hadn't the slightest notion when such a day would dawn.

Not having the means to undertake the trip, the next best thing was to live it imaginatively, which I proceeded to do at odd moments. This preliminary journey began, I recall, with the inheritance of a huge scrap-book which once belonged to Walter Lowenfels who, on the eve of his departure from France, invited me to assist at the burning of a huge pile of manuscripts which he had spent years in producing.

Often, on returning to my studio at midnight, I would stand at the table and register in this celestial sort of ledger the innumerable little items which constitute a writer's bookkeeping: dreams, plans of attack and defense, remembrances, titles of books I intended to write, names and addresses of potential creditors, obsessive phrases, editors to harry, battlefields, monuments, monastic retreats, and so on. I remember distinctly the thrill I had when putting down such words as Mobile, Suwanee River, Navajos, Painted Desert, the lynching bee, the electric chair.

It seems a pity now that I didn't write an account of that imaginary journey which began in Paris. What a different book it would have been!

There was a reason, however, for making the physical journey, fruitless though it proved to be. I felt the need to effect a reconciliation with my native land. It was an urgent need because, unlike most prodigal sons, I was returning not with the intention of remaining in the bosom of the family but of wandering forth again, perhaps never to return. I wanted to have a last look at my country and leave it with a good taste in my mouth. I didn't want to run away from it, as I had originally. I wanted to embrace it, to feel that the old wounds were really healed, and set out for the unknown with a blessing on my lips.

On leaving Greece I was in a serene mood. If any one on earth were free of hatred, prejudice, bitterness, I thought it was myself. I was confident that for the first time in my life I would look upon New York and what lay beyond it without a trace of loathing or disgust.

It turned out that the boat was stopping at Boston first. That was unfortunate perhaps, but it was an excellent test. I had never been to Boston and I was rather pleased that Fate had played a trick on me. I was prepared to like Boston.

When I came up on deck to catch my first glimpse of the shore line I was immediately disappointed. Not only disappointed, I might say, but actually saddened. The American coast looked bleak and uninviting to me. I didn't like the look of the American house; there is something cold, austere, something barren and chill, about the architecture of the American home. It was *home*, with all the ugly, evil, sinister connotations which the word contains for a restless soul. There was a frigid, moral aspect to it which chilled me to the bone.

It was a wintry day and a gale was blowing. I went ashore with one of the passengers. I can't remember any more who he was or what he looked like, which is significant of the state of mind I was in. For some unknown reason we strolled through the railway station, a lugubrious place which filled me with dread, and which instantly revived the remembrance of similar stations in similar cities, all painful, harrowing recollections. What I remember most vividly about this Boston railway station were the enormous piles of books and magazines, looking just as cheap, vulgar, trashy as of yore. And the womb-like warmth of the place—so American, so unforgettably so.

It was a Sunday and the mob was out, reinforced by groups of rowdy students. The spectacle nauseated me. I wanted to get back to the ship as fast as possible. In an hour or so I had seen all I wanted to see of Boston. It seemed hideous to me.

Returning to the boat we passed bridges, railroad tracks, warehouses, factories, wharves and what not. It was like following in the wake of a demented giant who had sown the earth with crazy dreams. If I could only have seen a horse or a cow, or just a cantankerous goat chewing tin cans, it would have been a tremendous relief. But there was nothing of the animal, vegetable or human kingdom in sight. It was a vast jumbled waste created by pre-human or sub-human monsters in a delirium of greed. It was something negative, some not-ness of some kind or other. It was a bad dream and towards the end I broke into a trot, what with disgust and nausea, what with the howling icy gale which was whipping everything in sight into a frozen pie crust. When I got back to the boat I was praying that by some miracle the captain would decide to alter his course and return to Piraeus.

It was a bad beginning. The sight of New York, of the harbor, the bridges, the skyscrapers, did nothing to eradicate my first impressions. To the image of stark, grim ugliness which Boston had created was added a familiar feeling of terror. Sailing around the Battery from one river to the other, gliding close to shore, night coming on, the streets dotted with scurrying insects, I felt as I had always felt about New York—that it is the most horrible place on God's earth. No matter how many times I escape I am brought back, like a runaway slave, each time detesting it, loathing it, more and more.

Back in the rat trap. I try to hide away from my old friends; I don't want to relive the past with them because the past is full of wretched, sordid memories. My one thought is to get out of New York, to experience something genuinely American. I want to revisit some of the spots I once knew. I want to get out into the open.

To do anything you need money. I had arrived without a cent, exactly as I left the country years ago. At the Gotham Book Mart I found a little sum of money which Miss Steloff had collected for me from her patrons. It was a pleasant surprise. I was touched. Still, it was not enough to live on for any length of time. I would have to find more money. Perhaps I would have to take a job—a most depressing thought.

12

Meanwhile my father was dying. He had been dying for three years. I hadn't the heart to visit him empty-handed. I was getting desperate. Something would have to happen, something miraculous. It did. By accident I ran across a man who I thought was my enemy. Almost the first words out of his mouth were: "How are you fixed? Can I help you?" Again I was touched, this time to the point of tears.

In a few months I was down South at the home of an old friend. I spent a good part of the Summer there, then returned to New York. My father was still alive. I visited him regularly at his home in Brooklyn, talked about the old days in New York (the '80's and '90's), met the neighbors, listened to the radio (always that damned "Information Please!"), discussed the nature of the prostate gland, the peculiarities of the bladder, the New Deal which was still new to me and rather goofy and meaningless. "*That Roosevelt!*" I can hear the neighbors saying, as if they were saying "*That Hitler!*" A great change had come over America, no doubt about that. There were greater ones coming, I felt certain. We were only witnessing the prelude to something unimaginable. Everything was cock-eyed, and getting more and more so. Maybe we would end up on all fours, gibbering like baboons. Something disastrous was in store—everybody felt it. Yes, America had changed. The lack of resilience, the feeling of hopelessness, the resignation, the skepticism, the defeatism—I could scarcely believe my ears at first. And over it all that same veneer of fatuous optimism—only now decidedly cracked.

I was getting restless. My father didn't seem ready to die yet. God knows how long I might be marooned in New York. I decided to go ahead with my plans. The trip had to be made some time— why wait? Money again, of course. One needs money to travel around the country for a year or so. Real money, I mean. I had no

13

idea what it would require; I knew only that I must start soon or be bogged down forever.

Ever since my return from the South I had been visiting Abe Rattner's studio in my spare moments, trying to improve my skill as a water-colorist. One day I broached the subject of my forthcoming trip. To my surprise Rattner expressed a desire to accompany me. Soon we were discussing the kind of book we would do—a huge affair with color plates and so on. Something de luxe, like the beautiful French books which we were familiar with. Who would publish it for us we didn't know. The principal thing was to do it—then find a publisher. And if nothing came of it we would have had our trip anyway.

Little by little we evolved the idea of getting a car. The only way to see America is by automobile—that's what everybody says. It's not true, of course, but it sounds wonderful. I had never owned a car, didn't know how to drive one even. I wish now we had chosen a canoe instead.

The first car we looked at was the one we selected. Neither of us knew anything about cars; we just took the man's word for it that it was a good, reliable vehicle. It was, too, all things considered, though it had its weak points.

A few days before we were ready to shove off I met a man called John Woodburn of Doubleday, Doran & Co. He seemed unusually interested in our project. To my amazement a few days later I was signing a contract for the book at his office. Theodore Roosevelt was one of the signatories, if that's how you call it. He had never heard of me and was a little dubious about signing his name, it seems. But he signed it just the same.

I had expected a five thousand dollar advance and got five hundred. The money was gone before I ever left the Holland Tunnel. Rattner's contribution to the book was ruled out. It would

Abe Rattner

have been too expensive to print a book such as we had planned. I was embarrassed and chagrined, the more so because Rattner took it with such good grace. He had expected as much, no doubt. I, on the other hand, always expect the angels to pee in my beer. "The principal thing," said Rattner, "is to see America." I agreed. Secretly I nourished the hope that out of my future royalties I would be able to print Rattner's own version of America in line and color. It was a compromise, and I hate compromises, but that's America for you. "Next time you will be able to do as you please"— that's the song. It's a dastardly lie, but to palliate it you are given hush money.

That's how the trip began. We were in good fettle, nevertheless, when we left New York. A little nervous, I must confess, because we had only had about a half dozen lessons in driving at the Automobile School. I knew how to steer, how to shift gears, how to apply the brake—what more was necessary? As I say, by the time we started out for the Holland Tunnel we were in high spirits. It was a Saturday noon when we left. I had never been in the damned hole before, except once in a taxi. It was a nightmare. The beginning of the endless nightmare, I should say.

When we found ourselves aimlessly circling around in Newark I surrendered the wheel to Rattner. I was all in after an hour's driving. To get to Newark is easy, but to get out of it on a Saturday afternoon in the rain, to find the insane sky-way again, is another thing. In another hour, however, we were in open country, the traffic almost nil, the air tangy, the scenery promising. We were on our way! New Hope was to be our first stop.

New Hope! It's rather curious that we should have selected a town by that name as our first stopping place. It was a beautiful spot too, reminding me somewhat of a slumbering European village. And Bill Ney, whom we were visiting, was the very symbol of new hope, new enthusiasms, new deals. It was an excellent start; the air was full of promise.

New Hope is one of America's art colonies. I have a vivid recollection of my state of mind on leaving the place. It framed itself thus: *no hope for the artist!* The only artists who were not leading a dog's life were the commercial artists; they had beautiful homes, beautiful brushes, beautiful models. The others were living like ex-convicts. This impression was confirmed and deepened as I travelled along. America is no place for an artist: to be an artist is to be a moral leper, an economic misfit, a social liability. A corn-fed hog enjoys a better life than a creative writer, painter or musician. To be a rabbit is better still.

When I first returned from Europe I was frequently reminded of the fact that I was an "expatriate", often in an unpleasant way. The expatriate had come to be looked upon as an escapist. Until the war broke out it was the dream of every American artist to go to Europe—and to stay there as long as possible. Nobody thought of calling a man an escapist in the old days; it was the natural, proper, fitting thing to do, go to Europe, I mean. With the outbreak of the war a sort of childish, petulant chauvinism set in. "Aren't you glad to be back in the good old U.S.A.?" was the usual greeting. "No place like America, *what?*" To this you were expected to say "You betcha!" Behind these remarks there was of course an un-acknowledged feeling of disappointment; the American artist who had been obliged to seek refuge again in his native land was angry with his European friends for having deprived him of the privilege of leading the life he most desired. He was annoyed that they had allowed such an ugly, unnecessary thing as war to break out. America is made up, as we all know, of people who ran away from such ugly situations. America is the land par excellence of expatriates and escapists, *renegades*, to use a strong word. A wonderful world

16

we might have made of this new continent if we had really run out on our fellow-men in Europe, Asia and Africa. A brave, new world it might have become, had we had the courage to turn our back on the old, to build afresh, to eradicate the poisons which had accumulated through centuries of bitter rivalry, jealousy and strife.

A new world is not made simply by trying to forget the old. A new world is made with a new spirit, with new values. Our world may have begun that way, but to-day it is caricatural. Our world is a world of *things*. It is made up of comforts and luxuries, or else the desire for them. What we dread most, in facing the impending débâcle, is that we shall be obliged to give up our gew-gaws, our gadgets, all the little comforts which have made us so uncomfortable. There is nothing brave, chivalrous, heroic or magnanimous about our attitude. We are not peaceful souls; we are smug, timid, queasy and quaky.

I speak of the war because coming from Europe I was constantly besieged for an opinion about the European situation. As if the mere fact that I had lived there a few years could give my words pregnant meaning! Who can unravel the enigma embedded in such a wide-spread conflict? Journalists and historians will pretend to, but their hindsight is so disproportionate to their foresight that one is justified in being skeptical about their analyses. What I am getting round to is this—though I am a born American, though I became what is called an expatriate, I look upon the world not as a partisan of this country or that but as an inhabitant of the globe. That I happened to be born here is no reason why the American way of life should seem the best; that I chose to live in Paris is no reason why I should pay with my life for the errors of the French politicians. To be a victim of one's own mistakes is bad enough, but to be a victim of the other fellow's mistakes as well is too much. Moreover, I see no reason why I should lose *my* balance because a madman named Hitler goes on a rampage. Hitler will pass away, as did Napoleon, Tamerlane, Alexander and the others. A great scourge never appears unless there is a reason for it. There were a thousand excellent reasons for the emergence of the European and Asiatic dictators. We have our own dictator, only he is hydra-headed. Those who believe that the only way to eliminate these personifications of evil is to destroy them, let them destroy. Destroy everything in sight, if you think that's the way to get rid of your problems. I don't believe in that kind of destruction. I believe only in the destruction which is natural, incidental to and inherent in creation. As John Marin said in a letter to Stieglitz once: "Some men's singing time is when they are gashing themselves, some when they are gashing others."

Now that the trip is over I must confess that the experience which stands out most strongly in my mind is the reading of Romain Rolland's two volumes on Ramakrishna and Vivekananda. Let me quickly add a few other items . . .

The most beautiful woman I encountered, a queen in every sense of the word, was the wife of a Negro poet. The most masterful individual, the only person I met whom I could truly call "a great soul", was a quiet Hindu swami in Hollywood. The man with the greatest vision of the future was a Jewish professor of philosophy whose name is practically unknown to Americans though he has been living in our midst for almost ten years. The most promising book in progress was that of a painter who had never written a line before. The only mural I saw worthy of being called a mural was the one in San Francisco done by an American expatriate. The most exciting and the most intelligently chosen collection of modern paintings was the privately owned collection of Walter Arensberg, of Hollywood. The one person whom I found satisfied with his lot, adjusted to his environment, happy in his work, and representative of all that is best in the American tradition was a humble, modest librarian at U.C.L.A. (Los Angeles) named Lawrence Clark Powell. Here I must include John Steinbeck's friend, Ed Ricketts, of the Pacific Biological Laboratories, a most exceptional individual in character and temperament, a man radiating peace, joy and wisdom. The youngest and most vital man I came up against was seventy-year-old Dr. Marion Souchon of New Orleans. Of the working class the highest types seemed to me to be the service station men in the Far West, notably those attached to the Standard Stations. They are a different breed entirely from those in the East. The person who spoke the finest English was a guide in the Massanutten Caves in Virginia. The man with the most stimulating mind, among all the public speakers I can think of, was a Theosophist named Fritz Kunz. The only town which gave me a genuine and a pleasant surprise was Biloxi, Mississippi. Though there are hundreds of book shops in America only a dozen or so can be ranked with those on the Continent, among these notably the Argus Book Shop, New York, the Gotham Book Mart, New York, Terence Holliday's Book Shop, New York, and the Satyr Book Shop in Hollywood. The most interesting college I visited was Black Mountain College in North Carolina; it was the students who were interesting, not the professors. The most boring group in all communities were the university professors—and their wives. Particularly the wives. Jamestown, Virginia, impressed me as the most tragic spot in all America. The most mysterious region of the country seemed to me to be the enormous rectangular area found within the four states of Utah, Arizona, Colorado and New Mexico.

I had to travel about ten thousand miles before receiving the inspiration to write a single line. Everything worth saying about the American way of life I could put in thirty pages. Topographically the country is magnificent—*and* terrifying. Why terrifying? Because nowhere else in the world is the divorce between man and nature so complete. Nowhere have I encountered such a dull, monotonous fabric of life as here in America. Here boredom reaches its peak.

We are accustomed to think of ourselves as an emancipated people; we say that we are democratic, liberty-loving, free of prejudices and hatred. This is the melting-pot, the seat of a great human experiment. Beautiful words, full of noble, idealistic sentiment. Actually we are a vulgar, pushing mob whose passions are easily mobilized by demagogues, newspaper men, religious quacks, agitators and such like. To call this a society of free peoples is blasphemous. What have we to offer the world beside the superabundant loot which we recklessly plunder from the earth under the maniacal delusion that this insane activity represents progress and enlightenment? The land of opportunity has become the land of senseless sweat and struggle. The goal of all our striving has long been forgotten. We no longer wish to succor the oppressed and homeless; there is no room in this great, empty land for those who, like our forefathers before us, now seek a place of refuge. Millions of men and women are, or were until very recently, on relief, condemned like guinea pigs to a life of forced idleness. The world meanwhile looks to us with a desperation such as it has never known before. Where is the democratic spirit? Where are the leaders?

To conduct a great human experiment we must first of all have *men*. Behind the conception MAN there must be grandeur. No political party is capable of ushering in the Kingdom of Man. The workers of the world *may* one day, if they cease listening to their bigoted leaders, organize a brotherhood of man. But men cannot be brothers without first becoming peers, that is, equals in a kingly sense. What prevents men from uniting as brothers is their own base inadequacy. Slaves cannot unite; cowards cannot unite; the ignorant cannot unite. It is only by obeying our highest impulses that we can unite. The urge to surpass oneself has to be instinctive, not theoretical or believable merely. Unless we make the effort to *realize* the truths which are in us we shall fail again and again. As Democrats, Republicans, Fascists, Communists, we are all on one level. That is one of the reasons why we wage war so beautifully. We defend with our lives the petty principles which divide us. The common principle, which is *the establishment of the empire of man on earth*, we never lift a finger to defend. We are frightened of any urge which would lift us out of the muck. We fight only for the status quo, *our particular status quo*. We battle with heads down and eyes closed. Actually there never is a status quo, except in the minds of political imbeciles. All is flux. Those who are on the defensive are fighting phantoms.

What is the greatest treason? To question what it is one may be fighting for. Here insanity and treason join hands. War is a form of insanity—the noblest or the basest, according to your point of view. Because it is a mass insanity the wise are powerless to prevail against it. Above any other single factor that may be adduced in explanation of war is confusion. When all other weapons fail one resorts to force. But there may be nothing wrong with the weapons which we so easily and readily discard. They may need to be sharpened, or we may need to improve our skill, or both. To fight is to admit that one is confused; it is an act of desperation, not of strength. A rat can fight magnificently when it is cornered. Are we to emulate the rat?

To know peace man has to experience conflict. He has to go through the heroic stage before he can act as a sage. He has to be a victim of his passions before he can rise above them. To arouse man's passionate nature, to hand him over to the devil and put him

21

to the supreme test, there has to be a conflict involving something more than country, political principles, ideologies, etc. Man in revolt against his own cloying nature—that is real war. And that is a bloodless war which goes on forever, under the peaceful name of evolution. In *this* war man ranges himself once and for all on the side of the angels. Though he may, as individual, be defeated, he can be certain of the outcome—because the whole universe is with him.

There are experiments which are made with cunning and precision, because the outcome is divined beforehand. The scientist for example always sets himself soluble problems. But man's experiment is not of this order. The answer to the grand experiment is in the heart; the search must be conducted inwardly. We are afraid to trust the heart. We inhabit a mental world, a labyrinth in whose dark recesses a monster waits to devour us. Thus far we have been moving in mythological dream sequence, finding no solutions because we are posing the wrong questions. We find only what we look for, and we are looking in the wrong place. We have to come out of the darkness, abandon these explorations which are only flights of fear. We have to cease groping on all fours. We have to come out in the open, erect, and fully exposed.

These wars teach us nothing, not even how to conquer our fears. We are still cave men. Democratic cave men, perhaps, but that is small comfort. *Our fight is to get out of the cave.* If we were to make the least effort in that direction we would inspire the whole world.

If we are going to play the role of Vulcan let us forge dazzling new weapons which will unshackle the chains which bind us. Let us not love the earth in a perverse way. Let us stop playing the role of recidivist. Let us stop murdering one another. The earth is not a lair, neither is it a prison. The earth is a Paradise, the only one we will ever know. We will realize it the moment we open our eyes. We don't have to make it a Paradise—it *is* one. We have only to make ourselves fit to inhabit it. The man with the gun, the man with murder in his heart, cannot possibly recognize Paradise even when he is shown it.

The other night, at the home of a Hungarian friend, I fell into a discussion with him about the exile and the émigré. I had just been recounting to him my impressions of America, ending with the assertion that all the trip had done for me was to corroborate my intuitions. By way of answer he told me that I had probably loved America too much. A moment later he led me to his desk by the window and asked me to sit down in his chair. "Look at that view!" he said. "Isn't it magnificent?" I looked out upon the Hudson River and saw a great bridge twinkling with moving lights. I knew what he felt when looking out upon that scene; I knew that for him it represented the future, the world which his children would inherit. For him it was a world of promise. To me it was a world I knew only too well, a world that made me infinitely sad.

"It's strange," I said, "that you should bring me to this window. Do you know what I thought of as I sat there? I was thinking of another window, in Budapest, where I stood one evening and caught my first glimpse of the city. You hate Budapest. You had to run away from it. And to me it seemed like a magical place. I loved it instantly. I was at home there. In fact, I feel at home everywhere, except in my native land. Here I feel alien, especially here in New York, my birth-place."

All his life, he responded, he had dreamed of coming to America, to New York particularly.

"And how did you find it," I asked, "when you first looked upon it? Was it anything like you had dreamed it to be?"

He said it was exactly as he had dreamed it, even down to its ugly aspects. The defects hadn't bothered him: they were part of the picture which he had accepted in advance.

I thought of another European city—of Paris. I had felt the same way about Paris. I might even say that I loved the defects and the ugliness. I was in love with Paris. I don't know any part of Paris which repels me, unless it be the sombre, dull, bourgeois section of Passy. In New York what I like best is the ghetto. It gives me a sense of life. The people of the ghetto are foreigners; when I am in their midst I am no longer in New York but amidst the peoples of Europe. It is that which excites me. All that is progressive and American about New York I loathe.

As to whether I have been deceived, disillusioned. . . . The answer is yes, I suppose. I had the misfortune to be nourished by the dreams and visions of great Americans—the poets and seers. Some other breed of man has won out. This world which is in the making fills me with dread. I have seen it germinate; I can read it like a blue-print. It is not a world I want to live in. It is a world suited for monomaniacs obsessed with the idea of progress—but a false progress, a progress which stinks. It is a world cluttered with useless objects which men and women, in order to be exploited and degraded, are taught to regard as useful. The dreamer whose dreams are non-utilitarian has no place in this world. Whatever does not lend itself to being bought and sold, whether in the realm of things, ideas, principles, dreams or hopes, is debarred. In this world the poet is anathema, the thinker a fool, the artist an escapist, the man of vision a criminal.

* * *

Since writing the foregoing war has been declared. Some people think that a declaration of war changes everything. If only it were true! If only we could look forward to a radical, sweeping change from top to bottom! The changes brought about by war are noth-

24

ing, however, compared to the discoveries and inventions of an Edison. Yet, for good or ill, war can bring about a change in the spirit of a people. And that is what I am vitally interested in—a change of heart, a conversion.

We have a condition now which is called "a national emergency". Though the legislators and politicians may rant at will, though the newspaper tribe may rave and spread hysteria, though the military clique may bluster, threaten, and clamp down on everything which is not to their liking, the private citizen, for whom and by whom the war is being fought, is supposed to hold his tongue. Since I have not the least respect for this attitude, since it does nothing to advance the cause of freedom, I have left unaltered those statements which are apt to cause anoyance and irritation even in times of peace. I believe with John Stuart Mill that "a State which dwarfs its men, in order that they may be more docile instruments in its hands even for beneficial purposes, will find that with small men no great thing can really be accomplished." I would rather my opinions and appraisals were proved wrong—by the emergence of a new and vital spirit. If it takes a calamity such as war to awaken and transform us, well and good, so be it. Let us see now if the unemployed will be put to work and the poor properly clothed, housed and fed; let us see if the rich will be stripped of their booty and made to endure the privations and sufferings of the ordinary citizen; let us see if *all* the workers of America, regardless of class, ability or usefulness, can be persuaded to accept a common wage; let us see if the people can voice their wishes in direct fashion, without the intercession, the distortion, and the bungling of politicians; let us see if we can create a real democracy in place of the fake one we have been finally roused to defend; let us see if we can be fair and just to our own kind, to say nothing of the enemy whom we shall doubtless conquer over.

GOOD NEWS! GOD IS LOVE!

It was in a hotel in Pittsburgh that I finished the book on Rama-krishna by Romain Rolland. Pittsburgh and Ramakrishna—could any more violent contrast be possible? The one the symbol of brutal power and wealth, the other the very incarnation of love and wisdom.

We begin here then, in the very quick of the nightmare, in the crucible where all values are reduced to slag.

I am in a small, supposedly comfortable room of a modern hotel equipped with all the latest conveniences. The bed is clean and soft, the shower functions perfectly, the toilet seat has beer sterilized since the last occupancy, if I am to believe what is printed on the paper band which garlands it; soap, towels, lights, stationery, everything is provided in abundance.

I am depressed, depressed beyond words. If I were to occupy this room for any length of time I would go mad—or commit suicide. The spirit of the place, the spirit of the men who made it the hideous city it is, seeps through the walls. There is murder in the air. It suffocates me.

A few moments ago I went out to get a breath of air. I was back again in Czarist Russia. I saw Ivan the Terrible followed by a cavalcade of snouted brutes. There they were, armed with clubs and revolvers. They had the look of men who obey with zest, who shoot to kill on the slightest provocation.

Never has the status quo seemed more hideous to me. This is not the worst place, I know. But I am here and what I see hits me hard.

It was fortunate perhaps that I didn't begin my tour of America via Pittsburgh, Youngstown, Detroit; fortunate that I didn't start out by visiting Bayonne, Bethlehem, Scranton and such like. I might never have gotten as far as Chicago. I might have turned into a human bomb and exploded. By some canny instinct of self-preservation I turned south first, to explore the so-called "backward" states of the Union. If I was bored for the most part I at least knew peace. Did I not see suffering and misery in the South too? Of course I did. There is suffering and misery everywhere throughout this broad land. But there are kinds and degrees of suffering; the worst, in my opinion, is the sort one encounters in the very heart of progress.

At this moment we are talking about the defense of our country, our institutions, our way of life. It is taken for granted that these *must* be defended, whether we are invaded or not. But there are

27

things which ought not to be defended, which ought to be allowed to die; there are things which we should destroy voluntarily, with our own hands.

Let us make an imaginative recapitulation. Let us try to think back to the days when our forefathers first came to these shores. To begin with, they were running away from something; like the exiles and expatriates whom we are in the habit of denigrating and reviling, they too had abandoned the homeland in search of something nearer to their heart's desire.

One of the curious things about these progenitors of ours is that though avowedly searching for peace and happiness, for political and religious freedom, they began by robbing, poisoning, murdering, almost exterminating the race to whom this vast continent belonged. Later, when the gold rush started, they did the same to the Mexicans as they had to the Indians. And when the Mormons sprang up they practised the same cruelties, the same intolerance and persecution upon their own white brothers.

I think of these ugly facts because as I was riding from Pittsburgh to Youngstown, through an Inferno which exceeds anything that Dante imagined, the idea suddenly came to me that I ought to have an American Indian by my side, that he ought to share this voyage with me, communicate to me silently or otherwise his emotions and reflections. By preference I would like to have had a descendant of one of the admittedly "civilized" Indian tribes, a Seminole, let us say, who had passed his life in the tangled swamps of Florida.

Imagine the two of us then standing in contemplation before the hideous grandeur of one of those steel mills which dot the railway line. I can almost hear him thinking—"So it was for this that you deprived us of our birthright, took away our slaves, burned our homes, massacred our women and children, poisoned our souls,

28

broke every treaty which you made with us and left us to die in the swamps and jungles of the Everglades!"

Do you think it would be easy to get him to change places with one of our steady workers? What sort of persuasion would you use? What now could you promise him that would be truly seductive? A used car that he could drive to work in? A slap-board shack that he could, if he were ignorant enough, call a home? An education for his children which would lift them out of vice, ignorance and superstition but still keep them in slavery? A clean, healthy life in the midst of poverty, crime, filth, disease and fear? Wages that barely keep your head above water and often not? Radio, telephone, cinema, newspaper, pulp magazine, fountain pen, wrist watch, vacuum cleaner or other gadgets ad infinitum? Are these the baubles that make life worthwhile? Are these what make us happy, care-free, generous-hearted, sympathetic, kindly, peaceful and godly? Are we now prosperous and secure, as so many stupidly dream of being? Are any of us, even the richest and most powerful, certain that an adverse wind will not sweep away our possessions, our authority, the fear or the respect in which we are held?

This frenzied activity which has us all, rich and poor, weak and powerful, in its grip—where is it leading us? There are two things in life which it seems to me all men want and very few ever get (because both of them belong to the domain of the spiritual) and they are health and freedom. The druggist, the doctor, the surgeon are all powerless to give health; money, power, security, authority do not give freedom. Education can never provide wisdom, nor churches religion, nor wealth happiness, nor security peace. What is the meaning of our activity then? To what end?

We are not only as ignorant, as superstitious, as vicious in our conduct as the "ignorant, bloodthirsty savages" whom we dispossessed and annihilated upon arriving here—we are worse than they by far. We have degenerated; we have degraded the life which we sought to establish on this continent. The most productive nation in the world, yet unable to properly feed, clothe and shelter over a third of its population. Vast areas of valuable soil turning to waste land because of neglect, indifference, greed and vandalism. Torn some eighty years ago by the bloodiest civil war in the history of man and yet to this day unable to convince the defeated section of our country of the righteousness of our cause nor able, as liberators and emancipators of the slaves, to give them true freedom and equality, but instead enslaving and degrading our own white brothers. Yes, the industrial North defeated the aristocratic South —the fruits of that victory are now apparent. Wherever there is industry there is ugliness, misery, oppression, gloom and despair. The banks which grew rich by piously teaching us to save, in order to swindle us with our own money, now beg us not to bring our savings to them, threatening to wipe out even that ridiculous interest rate they now offer should we disregard their advice. Three-quarters of the world's gold lies buried in Kentucky. Inventions which would throw millions more out of work, since by the queer irony of our system every potential boon to the human race is converted into an evil, lie idle on the shelves of the patent office or are bought up and destroyed by the powers that control our destiny. The land, thinly populated and producing in wasteful, haphazard way enormous surpluses of every kind, is deemed by its owners, a mere handful of men, unable to accommodate not only the starving millions of Europe but our own starving hordes. A country which makes itself ridiculous by sending out missionaries to the most remote parts of the globe, asking for pennies of the poor in order to maintain the Christian work of deluded devils who no more represent Christ than I do the Pope, and yet unable through

30

its churches and missions at home to rescue the weak and defeated, the miserable and the oppressed. The hospitals, the insane asylums, the prisons filled to overflowing. Counties, some of them big as a European country, practically uninhabited, owned by an intangible corporation whose tentacles reach everywhere and whose responsibilities nobody can formulate or clarify. A man seated in a comfortable chair in New York, Chicago or San Francisco, a man surrounded by every luxury and yet paralyzed with fear and anxiety, controls the lives and destinies of thousands of men and women whom he has never seen, whom he never wishes to see and whose fate he is thoroughly uninterested in.

This is what is called progress in the year 1941 in these United States of America. Since I am not of Indian, Negro or Mexican descent I do not derive any vengeful joy in delineating this picture of the white man's civilization. I am a descendant of two men who ran away from their native land because they did not wish to become soldiers. My descendants, ironically enough, will no longer be able to escape that duty: the whole white world has at last been turned into an armed camp.

Well, as I was saying, I was full of Ramakrishna on leaving Pittsburgh. Ramakrishna who never criticized, who never preached, who accepted all religions, who saw God everywhere in everything: the most ecstatic being, I imagine, that ever lived. Then came Coraopolis, Aliquippa, Wampum. Then Niles, the birth-place of President McKinley, and Warren, the birth-place of Kenneth Patchen. Then Youngstown and two girls are descending the bluff beside the railroad tracks in the most fantastic setting I have laid eyes on since I left Crete. Instantly I am back on that ancient Greek island, standing at the edge of a crowd on the outskirts of Heraklion just a few miles from Knossus. There is no railroad on the island, the sanitation is bad, the dust is thick, the flies are everywhere,

31

the food is lousy—but it is a wonderful place, one of the most wonderful places in the whole world. As at Youngstown by the railroad station there is a bluff here and a Greek peasant woman is slowly descending, a basket on her head, her feet bare, her body poised. *Here the resemblance ends. . . .*

As everybody knows, Ohio has given the country more Presidents than any other State in the Union. Presidents like McKinley, Hayes, Garfield, Grant, Harding—weak, characterless men. It has also given us writers like Sherwood Anderson and Kenneth Patchen, the one looking for poetry everywhere and the other driven almost mad by the evil and ugliness everywhere. The one walks the streets at night in solitude and tells us of the imaginary life going on behind closed doors; the other is so stricken with pain and chagrin by what he sees that he re-creates the cosmos in terms of blood and tears, stands it upside down and walks out on it in loathing and disgust. I am glad I had the chance to see these Ohio towns, this Mahoning River which looks as if the poisonous bile of all humanity had poured into it, though in truth it may contain nothing more evil than the chemicals and waste products of the mills and factories. I am glad I had the chance to see the color of the earth here in winter, a color not of age and death but of disease and sorrow. Glad I could take in the rhinoceros-skinned banks that rise from the river's edge and in the pale light of a wintry afternoon reflect the lunacy of a planet given over to rivalry and hatred. Glad I caught a glimpse of those slag heaps which look like the accumulated droppings of sickly prehistoric monsters which passed in the night. It helps me to understand the black and monstrous poetry which the younger man distils in order to preserve his sanity; helps me to understand why the older writer had to pretend madness in order to escape the prison which he found himself in when he was working in the paint factory. It helps me to understand how prosperity built

Workers' homes in an American mill town

on this plane of life can make Ohio the mother of presidents and the persecutor of men of genius.

The saddest sight of all is the automobiles parked outside the mills and factories. The automobile stands out in my mind as the very symbol of falsity and illusion. There they are, thousands upon thousands of them, in such profusion that it would seem as if no man were too poor to own one. In Europe, Asia, Africa the toiling masses of humanity look with watery eyes towards this Paradise where the worker rides to work in his own car. What a magnificent world of opportunity it must be, they think to themselves. (At least we like to think that they think that way!) They never ask what one must do to have this great boon. They don't realize that when the American worker steps out of his shining tin chariot he delivers himself body and soul to the most stultifying labor a man can perform. They have no idea that it is possible, even when one works under the best possible conditions, to forfeit all rights as a human being. They don't know that the best possible conditions (in American lingo) mean the biggest profits for the boss, the utmost servitude for the worker, the greatest confusion and disillusionment for the public in general. They see a beautiful, shining car which purrs like a cat; they see endless concrete roads so smooth and flawless that the driver has difficulty keeping awake; they see cinemas which look like palaces; they see department stores with mannikins dressed like princesses. They see the glitter and paint, the baubles, the gadgets, the luxuries; they don't see the bitterness in the heart, the skepticism, the cynicism, the emptiness, the sterility, the despair, the hopelessness which is eating up the American worker. They don't want to see this—they are full of misery themselves. They want a way out: they want the lethal comforts, conveniences, luxuries. And they follow in our footsteps—blindly, heedlessly, recklessly.

33

Of course not all American workers ride to work in automobiles. In Beaufort, S. C., only a few weeks ago I saw a man on a two-wheeled cart driving a bullock through the main street. He was a black man, to be sure, but from the look on his face I take it that he was far better off than the poor devil in the steel mill who drives his own car. In Tennessee I saw white men toiling like beasts of burden; I saw them struggling desperately to scratch a living from the thin soil on the mountainsides. I saw the shacks they live in and wondered if it were possible to put together anything more primitive. But I can't say that I felt sorry for them. No, they are not the sort of people to inspire pity. On the contrary, one has to admire them. If they represent the "backward" people of America then we need more backward people. In the subway in New York you can see the other type, the newspaper addict, who revels in social and political theories and lives the life of a drudge, foolishly flattering himself that because he is not working with his hands (nor with his brain either, for that matter) he is better off than the poor white trash of the South.

Those two girls in Youngstown coming down the slippery bluff —it was like a bad dream, I tell you. But we look at these bad dreams constantly with eyes open and when some one remarks about it we say, "Yes, that's right, that's how it is!" and we go about our business or we take to dope, the dope which is worse by far than opium or hashish—I mean the newspapers, the radio, the movies. Real dope gives you the freedom to dream your own dreams; the American kind forces you to swallow the perverted dreams of men whose only ambition is to hold their job regardless of what they are bidden to do.

The most terrible thing about America is that there is no escape from the treadmill which we have created. There isn't one fearless champion of truth in the publishing world, not one film company devoted to art instead of profits. We have no theatre worth the name, and what we have of theatre is practically concentrated in one city; we have no music worth talking about except what the Negro has given us, and scarcely a handful of writers who might be called creative. We have murals decorating our public buildings which are about on a par with the aesthetic development of high school students, and sometimes below that level in conception and execution. We have art museums that are crammed with lifeless junk for the most part. We have war memorials in our public squares that must make the dead in whose name they were erected squirm in their graves. We have an architectural taste which is about as near the vanishing point as it is possible to achieve. In the ten thousand miles I have travelled thus far I have come across two cities which have each of them a little section worth a second look— I mean Charleston and New Orleans. As for the other cities, towns and villages through which I passed I hope never to see them again. Some of them have such marvelous names, too, which only makes the deception more cruel. Names like Chattanooga, Pensacola, Tallahassee, like Mantua, Phoebus, Bethlehem, Paoli, like Algiers, Mobile, Natchez, Savannah, like Baton Rouge, Saginaw, Pough-keepsie: names that revive glorious memories of the past or awaken dreams of the future. Visit them, I urge you. See for yourself. Try to think of Schubert or Shakespeare when you are in Phoebus, Virginia. Try to think of North Africa when you are in Algiers, Louisiana. Try to think of the life the Indians once led here when you are on a lake, a mountain or river bearing the names we borrowed from them. Try to think of the dreams of the Spaniards when you are motoring over the old Spanish Trail. Walk around in the old French Quarter of New Orleans and try to reconstruct the life that once this city knew. Less than a hundred years has elapsed since this jewel of America faded out. It seems more like a thousand.

Everything that was of beauty, significance or promise has been destroyed and buried in the avalanche of false progress. In the thousand years of almost incessant war Europe has not lost what we have lost in a hundred years of "peace and progress". No foreign enemy ruined the South. No barbaric vandals devastated the great tracts of land which are as barren and hideous as the dead surface of the moon. We can't attribute to the Indians the transformation of a peaceful, slumbering island like Manhattan into the most hideous city in the world. Nor can we blame the collapse of our economic system on the hordes of peaceful, industrious immigrants whom we no longer want. No, the European nations may blame one another for their miseries, but we have no such excuse—we have only ourselves to blame.

Less than two hundred years ago a great social experiment was begun on this virgin continent. The Indians whom we dispossessed, decimated and reduced to the status of outcasts, just as the Aryans did with the Dravidians of India, had a reverent attitude towards the land. The forests were intact, the soil rich and fertile. They lived in communion with Nature on what we choose to call a low level of life. Though they possessed no written language they were poetic to the core and deeply religious. Our forefathers came along and, seeking refuge from their oppressors, began by poisoning the Indians with alcohol and venereal disease, by raping their women and murdering their children. The wisdom of life which the Indians possessed they scorned and denigrated. When they had finally completed their work of conquest and extermination they herded the miserable remnants of a great race into concentration camps and proceeded to break what spirit was left in them.

Not long ago I happened to pass through a tiny Indian reservation belonging to the Cherokees in the mountains of North Carolina. The contrast between this world and ours is almost unbelievable. The little Cherokee reservation is a virtual Paradise. A great peace and silence pervades the land, giving one the impression of being at last in the happy hunting grounds to which the brave Indian goes upon his death. In my journey thus far I have struck only one other community which had anything like this atmosphere, and that was in Lancaster County, Pennsylvania, among the Amish people. Here a small religious group, clinging stubbornly to the ways of their ancestors in comportment, dress, beliefs and customs, have converted the land into a veritable garden of peace and plenty. It is said of them that ever since they settled here they have never known a crop failure. They live a life in direct opposition to that of the majority of the American people—and the result is strikingly apparent. Only a few miles away are the hell-holes of America where, as if to prove to the world that no alien ideas, theories or isms will ever get a foothold here, the American flag is brazenly and tauntingly flown from roofs and smokestacks. And what sorry looking flags they are which the arrogant, bigoted owners of these plants display! You would think that such fervid patriotism would be inconsonant with the display of a torn, blackened, weather-beaten emblem. You would think that out of the huge profits which they accumulate enough might be put aside to purchase a bright, new, gleaming emblem of liberty. But no, in the industrial world everything is soiled, degraded, vilified. It has become so to-day that when you see the flag boldly and proudly displayed you smell a rat somewhere. The flag has become a cloak to hide iniquity. We have two American flags always: one for the rich and one for the poor. When the rich fly it it means that things are under control; when the poor fly it it means danger, revolution, anarchy. In less than two hundred years the land of liberty, home of the free, refuge of the oppressed has so altered the meaning of the Stars and Stripes that to-day when a man or woman succeeds in escaping from the horrors of Europe, when he finally stands before the bar under our glorious national emblem, the first question put to him is: *"How much money have you?"* If you have no money but only a love of freedom, only a prayer for mercy on your lips, you are debarred, returned to the slaughter-house, shunned as a leper. This is the bitter caricature which the descendants of our liberty-loving forefathers have made of the national emblem.

Everything is caricatural here. I take a plane to see my father on his death-bed and up there in the clouds, in a raging storm, I overhear two men behind me discussing how to put over a big deal, the big deal involving paper boxes, no less. The stewardess, who has been trained to behave like a mother, a nurse, a mistress, a cook, a drudge, never to look untidy, never to lose her Marcel wave, never to show a sign of fatigue or disappointment or chagrin or loneliness, the stewardess puts her lily-white hand on the brow of one of the paper-box salesmen and in the voice of a ministering angel, says: "Do you feel tired this evening? Have you a headache? Would you like a little aspirin?" We are up in the clouds and she is going through this performance like a trained seal. When the plane lurches suddenly she falls and reveals a tempting pair of thighs. The two salesmen are now talking about buttons, where to get them cheaply, how to sell them dearly. Another man, a weary banker, is reading the war news. There is a great strike going on somewhere —several of them, in fact. We are going to build a fleet of merchant vessels to help England—*next December*. The storm rages. The girl falls down again—she's full of black and blue marks. But she comes up smiling, dispensing coffee and chewing gum, putting her lily-white hand on someone else's forehead, inquiring if he is a little low, a little tired perhaps. I ask her if she likes her job. For answer she says, "It's better than being a trained nurse." The salesmen are going over her points; they talk about her like a commodity.

They buy and sell, buy and sell. For that they have to have the best rooms in the best hotels, the fastest, smoothest planes, the thickest, warmest overcoats, the biggest, fattest purses. We need their paper boxes, their buttons, their synthetic furs, their rubber goods, their hosiery, their plastic this and that. We need the banker, his genius for taking our money and making himself rich. The insurance man, his policies, his talk of security, of dividends—we need him too. *Do we?* I don't see that we need any of these vultures. I don't see that we need any of these cities, these hell-holes I've been in. I don't think we need a two-ocean fleet either. I was in Detroit a few nights ago. I saw the Mannerheim Line in the movies. I saw how the Russians pulverized it. I learned the lesson. *Did you?* Tell me what it is that man can build, to protect himself, which other men cannot destroy? What are we trying to defend? Only what is old, useless, dead, indefensible. Every defense is a provocation to assault. Why not surrender? Why not give—give all? It's so damned practical, so thoroughly effective and disarming. Here we are, we the people of the United States: the greatest people on earth, so we think. We have everything—everything it takes to make people happy. We have land, water, sky and all that goes with it. We could become the great shining example of the world; we could radiate peace, joy, power, benevolence. But there are ghosts all about, ghosts whom we can't seem to lay hands on. We are not happy, not contented, not radiant, not fearless.

We bring miracles about and we sit in the sky taking aspirin and talking paper boxes. On the other side of the ocean they sit in the sky and deal out death and destruction indiscriminately. We're not doing that yet, *not yet,* but we are committed to furnishing the said instruments of destruction. Sometimes, in our greed, we furnish them to the wrong side. But that's nothing—everything will come out right in the end. Eventually we will have helped to wipe out or render prostrate a good part of the human race—not savages this time, but civilized "barbarians." Men like ourselves, in short, except that they have different views about the universe, different ideological principles, as we say. Of course, if we don't destroy them they will destroy us. That's logic—nobody can question it. That's political logic, and that's what we live and die by. A flourishing state of affairs. Really exciting, don't you know. "We live in such exciting times." Aren't you happy about it? The world changing so rapidly and all that—isn't.it marvelous? Think what it was a hundred years ago. Time marches on. . . .

A man of genius whom I know would like to be spared the ordeal of indiscriminate killing which they are preparing him for. He is not interested in putting the world to rights. He is interested in putting his thoughts down on paper. But then he has a good set of teeth, he is not flat-footed, his heart and lungs are sound, he has no nervous disorders. He is thoroughly healthy and a genius to boot. He never talks about paper boxes or buttons or new-fangled gadgets. He talks poetry, talks about God. But he doesn't belong to some God sect and therefore is disqualified as a conscientious objector. The answer is that he must get ready to be shipped to the front. He must defend our ideological principles. The banker is too old to be of service; the salesmen I was talking about are too clever; so the genius has to serve, though God knows, since we have so few of them, you would think we might be able to spare one now and then.

I hope that Walt Disney is exempted, because he's the man, though I doubt that he realizes it, to illustrate what I have to say. In fact, he's been doing it all along, unconsciously. He's the master of the nightmare. He's the Gustave Doré of the world of Henry Ford & Co., Inc. The Mannerheim Line is just a scratch on the surface. True, the temperature was abnormal—about forty degrees below zero on the average. (Amazing how men can be trained to kill in all kinds of weather. Almost as intelligent as horses.) But as I was saying, Disney has all kinds of temperature—a temperature to suit every fresh horror. He doesn't have to think: the newspapers are always on tap. Of course they're not real men and women. Oh no! They're more real than real men and women: they're dream creatures. They tell us what we look like beneath the covering of flesh. A fascinating world, what? Really, when you think about it, even more fascinating than Dali's cream puffs. Dali thinks too much. Besides, he has only two hands. Disney has a million. And besides hands he has voices—the voice of the hyena, the voice of the donkey, the voice of the dinosaur. The Soviet film, for example, is intimidating enough, but slow, ponderous, cumbersome, unwieldly. It takes time in real life to demolish all those concrete pill-boxes, cut all that barbed wire, kill all those soldiers, burn all those villages. Slow work. Disney works fast—like greased lightning. That's how we'll all operate soon. What we dream we become. We'll get the knack of it soon. We'll learn how to annihilate the whole planet in the wink of an eye—just wait and see.

The capital of the new planet—the one, I mean, which will kill itself off—is of course Detroit. I realized that the moment I arrived. At first I thought I'd go and see Henry Ford, give him my congratulations. But then I thought—what's the use? He wouldn't know what I was talking about. Neither would Mr. Cameron most likely. That lovely Ford evening hour! Every time I hear it announced I think of Céline—Ferdinand, as he so affectionately calls himself. Yes, I think of Céline standing outside the factory gates (pp. 222–225, I think it is: *Journey to the End of the Night*). Will he get the job? Sure he will. He gets it. He goes through the baptism—the baptism of stultification through noise. He sings a wonderful song there for a few pages about the machine, the blessings that it showers upon mankind. Then he meets Molly. Molly is just a whore. You'll find another Molly in *Ulysses*, but Molly the whore of Detroit is much better. Molly has a soul. Molly is the milk of human kindness. Céline pays a tribute to her at the end of the chapter. It's remarkable because all the other characters are paid off in one way or another. Molly is whitewashed. Molly, believe it or not, looms up bigger and holier than Mr. Ford's huge enterprise. Yes, that's the beautiful and surprising thing about Céline's chapter on Detroit—that he makes the body of a whore triumph over the soul of the machine. You wouldn't suspect that there was such a thing as a soul if you went to Detroit. Everything is too new, too slick, too bright, too ruthless. Souls don't grow in factories. Souls are killed in factories—even the niggardly ones. Detroit can do in a week for the white man what the South couldn't do in a hundred years to the Negro. That's why I like the Ford evening hour—it's so soothing, so inspiring.

Of course Detroit isn't the worst place—not by a long shot. That's what I said about Pittsburgh. That's what I'll say about other places too. None of them is the worst. There is no worst or worstest. The worst is in process of becoming. It's inside us now, only we haven't brought it forth. Disney dreams about it—and he gets paid for it, that's the curious thing. People bring their children to look and scream with laughter. (Ten years later it happens now and then that they fail to recognize the little monster who so joyfully clapped his hands and screamed with delight. It's always hard to believe that a Jack-the-Ripper could have sprung out of your own loins.) However. . . . It's cold in Detroit. A gale is blowing. Happily I am not one of those without work, without food, without shelter. I am stopping at the gay Detroiter, the Mecca of the futilitarian salesmen. There is a swanky haberdashery shop in the lobby. Salesmen love silk shirts. Sometimes they buy cute little panties too—for the ministering angels in the aeroplanes. They buy any and everything—just to keep money in circulation. The men of Detroit who are left out in the cold freeze to death in woolen underwear. The temperature in winter is distinctly sub-tropical. The buildings are straight and cruel. The wind is like a double-bladed knife. If you're lucky you can go inside where it's warm and see the Mannerheim Line. A cheering spectacle. See how ideological principles can triumph in spite of sub-normal temperatures. See men in white cloaks crawling through the snow on their bellies; they have scissors in their hands, big ones, and when they reach the barbed wire they cut, cut, cut. Now and then they get shot doing it—but then they become heroes—and besides there are always others to take their places, all armed with scissors. Very edifying, very instructive. Heartening, I should say. Outside, on the streets of Detroit, the wind is howling and people are running for shelter. But it's warm and cosy in the cinema. After the spectacle a nice warm cup of chocolate in the lobby of the hotel. Men talking buttons and chewing gum there. Not the same men as in the aeroplane—different ones. Always find them where it's warm and comfortable. Always buying and selling. And of course a pocketful of cigars. Things are picking up in Detroit. Defense orders, you know. The taxi driver told me he expected to get his job back soon. In the factory, I mean. What would happen if the war suddenly stopped I can't imagine. There would be a lot of broken hearts. Maybe another crisis. People wouldn't know what to do for themselves if peace were suddenly declared. Everybody would be laid off. The bread lines would start up. Strange, how we can manage to feed the world and not learn how to feed ourselves.

I remember when the wireless came how everybody thought —how wonderful! now we will be in communication with the whole world! And television—how marvelous! now we shall be able to

43

see what's going on in China, in Africa, in the remotest parts of the world! I used to think that perhaps one day I'd own a little apparatus which by turning a dial would enable me to see Chinamen walking through the streets of Peking or Shanghai or savages in the heart of Africa performing their rites of initiation. What do we actually see and hear to-day? What the censors permit us to see and hear, nothing more. India is just as remote as it ever was—in fact, I think it is even more so now than it was fifty years ago. In China a great war is going on—a revolution fraught with far greater significance for the human race than this little affair in Europe. Do you see anything of it in the news reels? Even the newspapers have very little to say about it. Five million Chinese can die of flood, famine or pestilence or be driven from their homes by the invader, and the news (a headliner for one day usually) leaves us unruffled. In Paris I saw one news reel of the bombing of Shanghai and that was all. It was too horrible—the French couldn't stomach it. To this day we haven't been shown the real pictures of the first World War. You have to have influence to get a glimpse of those fairly recent horrors. . . . There are the "educational" pictures, to be sure. Have you seen them? Nice, dull, soporific, hygienic, statistical poems fully castrated and sprinkled with lysol. The sort of thing the Baptist or Methodist Church could endorse.

The news reels deal largely with diplomatic funerals, christenings of battleships, fires and explosions, aeroplane wrecks, athletic contests, beauty parades, fashions, cosmetics and political speeches. Educational pictures deal largely with machines, fabrics, commodities and crime. If there's a war on we get a glimpse of foreign scenery. We get about as much information about the other peoples of this globe, through the movies and the radio, as the Martians get about us. And this abysmal separation is reflected in the American physiognomy. In the towns and cities you find the typical

American everywhere. His expression is mild, bland, pseudo-serious and definitely fatuous. He is usually neatly dressed in a cheap ready-made suit, his shoes shined, a fountain pen and pencil in his breast pocket, a brief case under his arm—and of course he wears glasses, the model changing with the changing styles. He looks as though he were turned out by a university with the aid of a chain store cloak and suit house. One looks like the other, just as the automobiles, the radios and the telephones do. This is the type between 25 and 40. After that age we get another type— the middle-aged man who is already fitted with a set of false teeth, who puffs and pants, who insists on wearing a belt though he should be wearing a truss. He is a man who eats and drinks too much, smokes too much, sits too much, talks too much and is always on the edge of a break-down. Often he dies of heart failure in the next few years. In a city like Cleveland this type comes to apotheosis. So do the buildings, the restaurants, the parks, the war memorials. The most typical American city I have struck thus far. Thriving, prosperous, active, clean, spacious, sanitary, vitalized by a liberal infusion of foreign blood and by the ozone from the lake, it stands out in my mind as the composite of many American cities. Possessing all the virtues, all the prerequisites for life, growth, blossoming, it remains nevertheless a thoroughly dead place—a deadly, dull, dead place. (In Cleveland to see "The Doctor's Dilemma" is an exciting event.) I would rather die in Richmond somehow, though God knows Richmond has little enough to offer. But in Richmond, or in any Southern city for that matter, you do see types now and then which depart from the norm. The South is full of eccentric characters; it still fosters individuality. And the most individualistic are of course from the land, from the out of the way places. When you go through a sparsely settled state like South Carolina you do meet men, interesting men—

jovial, cantankerous, disputative, pleasure-loving, independent-thinking creatures who disagree with everything, on principle, but who make life charming and gracious. There can hardly be any greater contrast between two regions in these United States, in my mind, than between a state like Ohio and a state like South Carolina. Nor can there be a greater contrast in these States than between two cities like Cleveland and Charleston, for example. In the latter place you actually have to pin a man to the mat before you can talk business to him. And if he happens to be a good business man, this chap from Charleston, the chances are that he is also a fanatic about something unheard of. His face registers changes of expression, his eyes light up, his hair stands on end, his voice swells with passion, his cravat slips out of place, his suspenders are apt to come undone, he spits and curses, he coos and prances, he pirouettes now and then. And there's one thing he never dangles in front of your nose—his time-piece. He has time, oodles of time. And he accomplishes everything he chooses to accomplish in due time, with the result that the air is not filled with dust and machine oil and cash register clickings. The great time-wasters, I find, are in the North, among the busy-bodies. Their whole life, one might say, is just so much time wasted. The fat, puffy, wattle-faced man of forty-five who has turned asexual is the greatest monument to futility that America has created. He's a nymphomaniac of energy accomplishing nothing. He's an hallucination of the Paleolithic man. He's a statistical bundle of fat and jangled nerves for the insurance man to convert into a frightening thesis. He sows the land with prosperous, restless, empty-headed, idle-handed widows who gang together in ghoulish sororities where politics and diabetes go hand in hand.

About Detroit, before I forget it—yes, it was here that Swami Vivekananda kicked over the traces. Some of you who read this m y be old enough to remember the stir he created when he spoke b fore the Parliament of Religions in Chicago back in the early N ineties. The story of the pilgrimage of this man who electrified t ie American people reads like a legend. At first unrecognized, re- ected, reduced to starvation and forced to beg in the streets, he was finally hailed as the greatest spiritual leader of our time. Offers of all kinds were showered upon him; the rich took him in and tried to make a monkey of him. In Detroit, after six weeks of it, he rebelled. All contracts were cancelled and from that time on he went alone from town to town at the invitation of such or such a society. Here are the words of Romain Rolland:

"His first feeling of attraction and admiration for the formidable power of the young republic had faded. Vivekananda almost at once fell foul of the brutality, the inhumanity, the littleness of spirit, the narrow fanaticism, the monumental ignorance, the crush- ing incomprehension, so frank and sure of itself with regard to all who thought, who believed, who regarded life differently from the paragon nation of the human race . . . And so he had no patience. He hid nothing. He stigmatised the vices and crimes of the Western civilisation with its characteristics of violence, pillage and destruction. Once when he was to speak at Boston on a beau- tiful religious subject particularly dear to him (Ramakrishna), he felt such repulsion at the sight of his audience, the artificial and cruel crowd of men of affairs and of the world, that he refused to yield them the key of his sanctuary, and brusquely changing the subject, he inveighed furiously against a civilisation represented by such foxes and wolves. The scandal was terrific. Hundreds noisily left the hall and the Press was furious. He was especially bitter against false Christianity and religious hypocrisy: 'With all your brag and boasting, where has your Christianity succeeded without the sword? Yours is a religion preached in the name of luxury.

47

It is all hypocrisy that I have heard in this country. All this prosperity, all this from Christ! Those who call upon Christ care nothing but to amass riches! Christ would not find a stone on which to lay his head among you . . . You are not Christians. Return to Christ!' "

Rolland goes on to contrast this reaction with that inspired by England. "He came as an enemy and he was conquered." Vivekananda himself admitted that his ideas about the English had been revolutionized. "No one," he said, "ever landed on English soil with more hatred in his heart for a race than I did for the English . . . There is none among you . . . who loves the English people more than I do now."

A familiar theme—one hears it over and over again. I think of so many eminent men who visited these shores only to return to their native land saddened, disgusted and disillusioned. There is one thing America has to give, and that they are all in agreement about: MONEY. And as I write this there comes to my mind the case of an obscure individual whom I knew in Paris, a painter of Russian birth who during the twenty years that he lived in Paris knew scarcely a day when he was not hungry. He was quite a figure in Montparnasse—every one wondered how he managed to survive so long without money. Finally he met an American who made it possible for him to visit this country which he had always longed to see and which he hoped to make his adopted land. He stayed a year, travelling about, making portraits, received hospitably by rich and poor. For the first time in his whole life he knew what it was to have money in his pocket, to sleep in a clean, comfortable bed, to be warm, to be well nourished—and what is more important, to have his talent recognized. One day, after he had been back a few weeks I ran into him at a bar. I was extremely curious to hear what he might have to say about America. I had heard of his success and I wondered why he had returned.

He began to talk about the cities he had visited, the people he had met, the houses he had put up at, the meals he had been fed, the museums he had visited, the money he had made. "At first it was wonderful," he said. "I thought I was in Paradise. But after six months of it I began to be bored. It was like living with children—but *vicious* children. What good does it do to have money in your pocket if you can't enjoy yourself? What good is fame if nobody understands what you're doing? You know what my life is like here. I'm a man without a country. If there's a war I'll either be put in a concentration camp or asked to fight for the French. I could have escaped that in America. I could have become a citizen and made a good living. But I'd rather take my chances here. Even if there's only a few years left those few years are worth more here than a lifetime in America. There's no real life for an artist in America—only a living death. By the way, have you got a few francs to lend me? I'm broke again. But I'm happy. I've got my old studio back again—I appreciate that lousy place now. Maybe it was good for me to go to America—if only to make me realize how wonderful is this life which I once thought unbearable."

How many letters I received while in Paris from Americans who had returned home—all singing the same song. "If I could only be back there again. I would give my right arm to be able to return. I didn't realize what I was giving up." Et cetera, et cetera. I never received one letter from a repatriated American saying that he was happy to be home again. When this war is over there will be an exodus to Europe such as this country has never seen. We try to pretend now, because France has collapsed, that she was degenerate. There are artists and art critics in this country who, taking advantage of the situation, endeavor with utter shamelessness to convince the American public that we have nothing to learn from Europe, that Europe, France more particularly, is dead. What an abominable lie! France prostrate and defeated is more alive than we have ever been. Art does not die because of a military defeat, or an economic collapse, or a political débâcle. Moribund France produced more art than young and vigorous America, than fanatical Germany or proselytizing Russia. Art is not born of a dead people.

There are evidences of a very great art in Europe as long ago as twenty-five thousand years, and in Egypt as far back as sixty thousand years. Money had nothing to do with the production of these treasures. Money will have nothing to do with the art of the future. Money will pass away. Even now we are able to realize the futility of money. Had we not become the arsenal of the world, and thus staved off the gigantic collapse of our economic system, we might have witnessed the spectacle of the richest nation on earth starving to death in the midst of the accumulated gold of the entire world. The war is only an interruption of the inevitable disaster which impends. We have a few years ahead of us and then the whole structure will come toppling down and engulf us. Putting a few millions back to work making engines of destruction is no solution of the problem. When the destruction brought about by war is complete another sort of destruction will set in. And it will be far more drastic, far more terrible than the destruction which we are now witnessing. The whole planet will be in the throes of revolution. And the fires will rage until the very foundations of this present world crumble. Then we shall see who has life, the life more abundant. Then we shall see whether the ability to make money and the ability to survive are one and the same. Then we shall see the meaning of true wealth.

I had to cover a tremendous stretch of country before I got the inspiration to begin this book. When I think of what I would have seen in Europe, Asia, or Africa, in the space of ten thousand miles, I feel as though I had been cheated. Sometimes I think that the best books on America are the imaginary ones written by those who have never seen the country. Before I get through with my journey I intend to describe some American scenes as I pictured them in my mind's eye when in Paris. Mobile is one of them.

Meanwhile I have good news for you—I'm going to take you to Chicago, to the Mecca Apartments on the South Side. It's a Sunday morning and my cicerone has borrowed a car to take me around. We stop at a flea market on the way. My friend explains to me that he was raised here in the ghetto; he tries to find the spot where his home used to be. It's a vacant lot now. There are acres and acres of vacant lots here on the South Side. It looks like Belgium did after the World War. Worse, if anything. Reminds me of a diseased jawbone, some of it smashed and pulverized, some of it charred and ulcerated. The flea market is more reminiscent of Cracow than of Clignancourt, but the effect is the same. We are at the back door of civilization, amidst the dregs and débris of the disinherited. Thousands, hundreds of thousands, maybe millions of Americans, are still poor enough to rummage through this offal in search of some sorely needed object. Nothing is too dilapidated or rust-bitten or disease-laden to discourage the hungry buyer. You would think the five-and-ten cent store could satisfy the humblest wants, but the five-and-ten cent store is really expensive in the long run, as one soon learns. The congestion is terrific—we have to elbow our way through the throng. It's like the banks of the Ganges except that there is no odor of sanctity about. As we push our way through the crowd my feet are arrested by a strange sight. There in the middle of the street, dressed in full regalia, is an American Indian. He's selling a snake oil. Instantly the thought of the other miserable derelicts stewing around in this filth and vermin is gone. "A *World I Never Made*", wrote James Farrell. Well, there stands the real author of the book—an outcast, a freak, a hawker of snake oil. On that same spot the buffaloes once roamed; now it is covered with broken pots and pans, with worn-out watches, with dismantled chandeliers, with busted shoes which even an Igorote would spurn. Of course if you walk on a few blocks you can see the other side of the picture—the grand façade of Michigan Avenue where it seems as if the whole world were composed of millionaires. At night you can see the great monument to chewing gum lit up by flood-lights and marvel that such a monstrosity of architecture should be singled out for special attention. If you wander down the steps leading to the rear of the building and squint your eyes and sharpen your imagination a bit you can even imagine yourself back in Paris, on the Rue Broca. No Bubu here, of course, but perhaps you will run into one of Al Capone's ex-comrades. It must be pleasant to be stuck up behind the glitter of the bright lights.

We dig further into the South Side, getting out now and then to stretch our legs. Interesting evolution going on here. Rows of old mansions flanked by vacant lots. A dingy hotel sticking up like a Mayan ruin in the midst of yellow fangs and chalk teeth. Once respectable dwelling places given up now to the dark-skinned people we "liberated." No heat, no gas, no plumbing, no water, no nothing —sometimes not even a window-pane. Who owns these houses? Better not inquire too closely. What do they do with them when the darkies move out? Tear them down, of course. Federal housing projects. Model tenement houses. . . . I think of old Genoa, one of the last ports I stopped at on my way back to America. Very old, this section. Nothing much to brag about in the way of conven-

Homes in Chicago's Negro section

iences. But what a difference between the slums of Genoa and the slums of Chicago! Even the Armenian section of Athens is preferable to this. For twenty years the Armenian refugees of Athens have lived like goats in the little quarter which they made their own. There were no old mansions to take over—not even an abandoned factory. There was just a plot of land on which they erected their homes out of whatever came to hand. Men like Henry Ford and Rockefeller contributed unwittingly to the creation of this paradise which was entirely built of remnants and discarded objects. I think of this Armenian quarter because as we were walking through the slums of Chicago my friend called my attention to a flower-pot on the window-sill of a wretched hovel. "You see," he said, "even the poorest among them have their flowers." But in Athens I saw dove-cotes, solariums, verandahs floating without support, rabbits sunning themselves on the roofs, goats kneeling before ikons, turkeys tied to the door-knobs. Everybody had flowers—not just flower-pots. A door might be made of Ford fenders and look inviting. A chair might be made of gasoline tins and be pleasant to sit on. There were bookshops where you could read about Buffalo Bill or Jules Verne or Hermes Trismegistus. There was a spirit here which a thousand years of misery had not squelched. Chicago's South Side, on the other hand, is like a vast, unorganized lunatic asylum. Nothing can flourish here but vice and disease. I wonder what the great Emancipator would say if he could see the glorious freedom in which the black man moves now. We made them free, yes—free as rats in a dark cellar.

Well, here we are—the Mecca Apartments! A great quadrangular cluster of buildings, once in good taste, I suppose—architecturally. After the whites moved out the colored people took over. Before it reached its present condition it went through a sort of Indian Summer. Every other apartment was a dive. The place glowed with prostitution. It must have been a Mecca indeed for the lonely darky in search of work.

It's a queer building now. The locks are dismantled, the doors unhinged, the globes busted. You enter what seems like the corridor of some dismal Catholic institution, or a deaf and dumb asylum, or a Bronx sanatorium for the discreet practice of abortion. You come to a turn and you find yourself in a court surrounded by several tiers of balconies. In the center of the court is an abandoned fountain covered with a huge wire mesh like the old-fashioned cheese covers. You can imagine what a charming spot this was in the days when the ladies of easy virtue held sway here. You can imagine the peals of laughter which once flooded the court. Now there is a strained silence, except for the sound of roller skates, a dry cough, an oath in the dark. A man and woman are leaning over the balcony rail above us. They look down at us without expression. Just looking. *Dreaming?* Hardly. Their bodies are too worn, their souls too stunted, to permit indulgence in that cheapest of all luxuries. They stand there like animals in the field. The man spits. It makes a queer, dull smack as it hits the pavement. Maybe that's his way of signing the Declaration of Independence. Maybe he didn't know he spat. Maybe it was his ghost that spat. I look at the fountain again. It's been dry a long time. And maybe it's covered like a piece of old cheese so that people won't spit in it and bring it back to life. It would be a terrible thing for Chicago if this black fountain of life should suddenly erupt! My friend assures me there's no danger of that. I don't feel so sure about it. Maybe he's right. Maybe the Negro will always be our friend, no matter what we do to him. I remember a conversation with a colored maid in the home of one of my friends. She said, "I do think we have more love for you than you have for us." "You don't hate us ever?" I asked. "Lord no!" she answered, "we just feel sorry for you. You has all the power and the wealth but you ain't happy."

As we were walking back to the car we heard a great voice shouting as if from the roof-tops. We walked another block and still the voice resounded as mighty as before. We were puzzled. We turned round and retraced our steps. The voice grew stronger and stronger. It was the voice of a preacher and he was shouting with the lungs of a bull: "Jesus is the light of the world!" And then other voices joined in. "*Jesus! Jesus! The light of the world!*" We looked about in perplexity. There was nothing in sight but a Jewish synagogue. And from it, from the very walls, it seemed, came this stentorian voice bellowing about the light of the world. Finally we observed some Negroes entering the tabernacle and when we lifted our eyes we saw the amplifiers attached like gargoyles to the cornice of the building. For three blocks, clear as a bell, the voice followed us. It was like a maniac rising up out of No Man's Land and shouting *Peace!* As we stepped into the car I saw a beautiful colored woman hanging out of a window in what looked like a deserted house. What a vista her eyes took in from the fifth floor of that blackened morgue! Even up there she could hear the preacher talking about the light of the world. It was Sunday and she had nothing to do. Downstairs a ragged urchin was putting a number on the door in green chalk—so that the postman would deliver the letters to the right address, no doubt. A few blocks yonder lay the slaughter-house and on a bright day, if the wind were propitious, one could get a whiff from where she was of the blood of the lamb, of thousands of lambs, millions of lambs, in fact. "There were nothing but cribs around here years ago," my friend was saying. Cribs, cribs. I wasn't paying attention. What's he talking about, I thought to myself. I was thinking of the Lamb of God lying in the manger at the Bethlehem Steel Plant. "There, you see?" he said, nudging me and turning his eyes upward towards the Negress on the fifth floor. She was beckoning to us. She had found God, no doubt, up there in Nigger Heaven. If she was thinking of something else I couldn't tell it. She looked positively ecstatic. No heat, no gas, no water; the windows shattered, the mice making merry, the garbage lying in the gutter. She beckoned to us as though to say: "Come! I am the light of the world! I pay no rent, I do no work, I drink nothing but blood."

We got into the car, rode a few blocks and got out to visit another shell crater. The street was deserted except for some chickens grubbing for food between the slats of a crumbling piazza. More vacant lots, more gutted houses; fire escapes clinging to the walls with their iron teeth, like drunken acrobats. A Sunday atmosphere here. Everything serene and peaceful. Like Louvain or Rheims between bombardments. Like Phoebus, Virginia, dreaming of bringing her steeds to water, or like modern Eleusis smothered by a wet sock. Then suddenly I saw it chalked up on the side of a house in letters ten feet high:

GOOD NEWS! GOD IS LOVE!

When I saw these words I got down on my knees in the open sewer which had been conveniently placed there for the purpose and I offered up a short prayer, a silent one, which must have registered as far as Mound City, Illinois, where the colored muskrats have built their igloos. It was time for a good stiff drink of cod liver oil but as the varnish factories were all closed we had to repair to the abattoir and quaff a bucket of blood. Never has blood tasted so wonderful! It was like taking Vitamines A, B, C, D, E in quick succession and then chewing a stick of cold dynamite. Good news! Aye, wonderful news—for Chicago. I ordered the chauffeur to take us immediately to Mundelein so that I could bless the cardinal and all the real estate operations, but we only got as far as the

Bahai Temple. A workman who was shovelling sand opened the door of the temple and showed us around. He kept telling us that we all worshipped the same God, that all religions were alike in essence. In the little pamphlet which he handed us to read I learned that the Forerunner of the Faith, the Founder of the Faith, and the authorized Interpreter and Exemplar of Baha'u'llah's teachings all suffered persecution and martyrdom for daring to make God's love all-inclusive. It's a queer world, even in this enlightened period of civilization. The Bahai temple has been twenty years building and is not finished yet. The architect was Mr. Bourgeois, believe it or not. The interior of the temple, in its unfinished state, makes you think of a stage setting for *Joan of Arc*. The circular meeting place on the ground floor resembles the hollow of a shell and inspires peace and meditation as few places of worship do. The movement has already spread over most of the globe, thanks to its persecutors and detractors. There is no color line, as in Christian churches, and one can believe as he pleases. It is for this reason that the Bahai movement is destined to outlast all the other religious organizations on this continent. The Christian Church in all its freakish ramifications and efflorescences is as dead as a doornail; it will pass away utterly when the political and social systems in which it is now embedded collapse. The new religion will be based on deeds, not beliefs. "Religion is not for empty bellies," said Ramakrishna. Religion is always revolutionary, far more revolutionary than bread-and-butter philosophies. The priest is always in league with the devil, just as the political leader always leads to death. People are trying to get together, it seems to me. Their representatives, in every walk of life, keep them apart by breeding hatred and fear. The exceptions are so rare that when they occur the impulse is to set them apart, make supermen of them, or gods, anything but men and women like ourselves. And in removing them thus to the ethereal realms the revolution of love which they came to preach is nipped in the bud. But the good news is always there, just around the corner, chalked up on the wall of a deserted house: GOD IS LOVE! I am sure that when the citizens of Chicago read these lines they will get up en masse and make a pilgrimage to that house. It is easy to find because it stands in the middle of a vacant lot on the South Side. You climb down a manhole in La Salle Street and let yourself drift with the sewer water. You can't miss it because it's written in white chalk in letters ten feet high. All you need to do when you find it is to shake yourself like a sewer-rat and dust yourself off. God will do the rest. . . .

VIVE LA FRANCE!

THE LITTLE park—between June and Mansfield Streets, curiously enough. It's a melancholy place, even in full sunshine. I have never found a park in America that filled me with anything but sadness or ennui. I would a thousand times rather sit in an abstract park such as Hilaire Hiler gave us in his early canvases. Or a park such as Hans Reichel sometimes sits in when he is doing a water color of his amnesic self. The American park is a circumscribed vacuum filled with cataleptic nincompoops. Like the architecture of the American home, there is never an ounce of personality in the park. It is, as they so rightly call it, "just a bit of breathing space", an oasis amidst the stench of asphalt, chemical fumes and stale gasoline. God, when I think of the Luxembourg, the Zapion, the Prater! For us there are only the natural parks—great tracts of land studded with astounding freaks of nature and peopled with ghosts.

Of all the little man-made parks I think the one in Jacksonville, Florida is perhaps the meanest, drabbest, shabbiest. It belongs in a George Grosz picture. It reeks with tuberculosis, halitosis, varicose veins, paranoia, mendacity, onanism and occultism. All the misfits, the unfits, the has-beens and the would-bes of America seem to drift here eventually. It is the emotional swamp which one has to wade through in order to get to the Everglades. Fifteen years ago, when I first sat in this park, I attributed my feelings and impressions to the fact that I was down and out, that I was hungry and could find no place to sleep. On the return visit I was even more depressed. Nothing had been altered. The benches were littered as of yore with the dregs of humanity—not the seedy sort as in London or New York, not the picturesque sort that dot the quais of Paris, but that pulpy, blemished American variety which issues from the respectable middle class: *clean clots of phlegm*, so to speak. The kind that tries to elevate the mind even when there is no mind left. The flotsam and jetsam which drifts like sewer water in and out of Christian Science churches, Rosicrucian tabernacles, astrology parlors, free clinics, evangelist meetings, charity bureaus, employment agencies, cheap lodging houses and so on. The kind that may be reading the *Bhagavad Gita* on an empty stomach or doing setting up exercises in the clothes closet. The American type par excellence, ever ready to believe what is written in the newspapers, ever on the look-out for a Messiah. Not a speck of human dignity left. The white worm squirming in the vise of respectability!

Sometimes the sight of these human dump heaps touches a button off and I have to run for a taxi in order to get to the type-

Henry Miller in the park at Jacksonville

writer and put down the mad, fiendish irrelevancies whose genesis not even the smartest of critics would suspect to be an American park. It may happen in such instances that I suddenly remember a cow which I had seen ages ago, or it may be a recent cow like the one at Ducktown, Tennessee, the cow with ninety-seven ribs and nothing to chew but a piece of tin foil. Or I may suddenly recall a moment such as the one in Algiers, Louisiana, talking to a railway fireman and his saying—"now it's a strange thing about this town but there ain't a single hotel in it; the people here ain't got no ambition." The words hotel and ambition associated oddly in my mind, and at that instant, while I was wondering what was so strange about these two words, a bus passed going to Venice and then everything seemed astoundingly strange and unreal. Algiers on the Mississippi, a Louisiana Venice, the copperized cow evaporating under a scorching sun, the synagogue music in Jacksonville which because of hunger reduced me to tears, my nocturnal walks back and forth over the Brooklyn Bridge, the medieval castles along the Dordogne, the statues of the queens in the Jardin du Luxembourg, six Russian lessons with an hysterical countess in a dressing booth in the rear of an employment agency, an interview with Dr. Vizetelly, during which I learned that I ought to have a vocabulary of at least seventy-five thousand words though Shakespeare had only about fifteen thousand. . . . A thousand and one such grotesque items could flit through my brain in a few moments.

The cow is tremendously obsessive—and I will never know why. Maybe in the American park I am just a cow chewing a bit of discarded tin foil. Maybe everything I care about has been eroded away and I am just a gaunt idiot whose ribs are cracking under a Southern sun. Maybe I am standing on a dead planet in a scientific film and because everything is strange and new I miss the beauty of it. Maybe my desires are too human, too tangible, too immediate.

One must be patient, one must be able to wait not thousands of years, but millions of years. One must be able to outlive the sun and moon, outlast God or the idea of God, outstrip the cosmos, outwit the molecule, the atom, the electron. One must sit in these parks as in a public toilet, fulfilling one's function—like the spare-ribbed cow on the red hill. Do not think of America as such, America per se, America ad astra: think of skies without atmosphere, of canals without water, of inhabitants without clothes, of words without thought, of life without death, of something going on endlessly and having no name, no rhyme or reason, yet making sense, making grand sense once you lose the obsession of time and space, of destiny, of causality, of logic, of entropy, of annihilation, of Nirvana and of Maya.

You sit in a park with fat palm trees and there are millions of blades of grass and it is warm and the benches are painted green and maybe a dog is piddling against a tree. And all around you are other members of the species, covered with clothes like you, and inside them the same vital organs working like mad day and night. And you say to yourself that they are different, so different that you loathe the sight of them. And then you go off to another planet, by hiring a cheap taxi, and alone with yourself before a noisy little machine you spit out words at random, sputtering firecrackers which, after they have exploded, look like squashed cigarette stubs. You think of a man on the lecture platform, a monster out of the Theosophical world with the body of a vegetable married to a hippogriff, a quiet fiend who has hypnotized himself sufficiently to walk erect from the wings to the center of the platform without giving himself away. He is about to speak for three solid hours without a pause, without taking a sip of water, without blinking an eye. He will hoist himself effortlessly to that fixed dragon which hangs in the sky and keeps the sidereal clock wound up despite all talk of divine entropy or cosmic schizophrenia. For three solid hours he will talk in a voice that comes from beyond the grave, the voice of the medium buried in a silver cone under the floor of a cave. At the end you will be sitting in the park amid dead leaves and silver wrappers, knowing neither more nor less than you knew before, but quietly happy, like a man who has just conjugated an irregular verb down through the harmonies and dissonances of the subjunctive mode.

And then a whistle blows inside you and there comes the thought of food and sex, six minutes of reverie in which you oscillate between Fauster's of Cleveland and the sawdust joint on the rue Le Chapelais (*entre la rue Hélène et la rue des Dames*) just off the Avenue de Clichy. It was at Fauster's that I suddenly realized why I had lost my desire for food. Not that the food was bad, not that the place was smelly, not that the service was slipshod. On the contrary, everything was perfection itself—*American restaurant perfection*. The waitress seemed like an angel who had just stepped out of a perfumed bath; the food had the immaculate appearance of something which had been prepared without having been touched by human hands; the kitchen was invisible and gave out no odors, discreetly hidden away like the urinal in a first-class bordel. There was white linen on the tables, generous-sized napkins, dainty glass cruets for oil and vinegar, still daintier salt and pepper shakers, perhaps even a sprig of flowers. Perhaps an organ was playing—I am not sure any longer. But if not, it should have been. The organ should have played a cavatina whilst the proprietor, fully incorporated, picked his teeth with a silver tooth-pick. There should have been choir boys with soprano voices carrying the trays back and forth. Anyway, it was air-conditioned, heavily carpeted, elegantly jammed, discreetly lit, pompously efficient in every detail. One could not think of the food as being made of such crude, coarse things as parts of animals or vegetables buried in the filthy earth. The food was rather some sort of synthetic nectar smothered with whipped cream, something to swallow with eyes closed and nostrils stopped, a little sermon made expressly for the palate which would permit one to go back to the office and write inspirational letters about sewer pipes and gas masks. In such an atmosphere the tip becomes a gratuity which the waitress accepts with the condescension of a star receiving a compliment from a newspaper reporter. She feels called upon to inform you that conditions, working conditions, are superlatively superlative, that at the least sign of fatigue she is carried to the rest room on a satin-covered stretcher, that if she feels slightly indisposed she is earnestly requested to avail herself of the marble bowling alley at the disposal of the employees. She glides from table to table like a ballerina, her face composed in a smile intended to evoke vague reminiscences of the Mona Lisa. She must not hurry unduly for fear of causing the moisture to start in her arm-pits. She must render personal service with the impersonality of a corpse. Above all she must keep the water glasses choked with ice.

I think it was in Ruston, Louisiana, that I woke up one night thinking about the little restaurant in the rue Le Chapelais. I had had a rotten meal in a café off the concrete strip; I had walked around the town three or four times pretending to look at things like the railway station, the newspaper office, the water tank, etc. Some youngsters were playing tennis on a concrete court under electric lights; their beautiful cars were parked at the curb. Otherwise it might have been midnight, four in the morning or six o'clock the day before. There wasn't a soul to talk to. I had some books but I didn't care to read. I went to bed in sheer disgust and tossed about till almost dawn. Then, after a beautiful dream about a passage in one of Giono's books, I woke up and thought I was still in France, somewhere in the provinces perhaps. I soon realized, however, that I was mistaken. And then I fell back and with eyes wide open I began dreaming of my life in Paris. I began at the very beginning, with that first humble meal on the sidewalk of the Boulevard St. Germain, knowing not a word of French except *oui* and *non*. When I look back on it now it seems as though I packed a thousand years into that brief decade which ended with the war.

I slipped into that period at Clichy when I was rooming with my friend Fred on the Avenue Anatole France. The period of bicycle rides, of evening promenades along the boulevard from Batignolles to Aubervilliers, the period when I became so exalted that I tried to write five books at once. But the image which stood out most prominently was the little restaurant to which I repaired religiously noon and night. It was a cheap restaurant, rather sombre in the daytime, and decidedly smelly. The food was not extraordinary, but reliable, like a friend whom you've known since boyhood. The waitresses were slatternly, not overly polite, and very intent on collecting the tip which was due them. For a franc or two more you could have something really delicious, like roast chicken.

There were two interesting things about the place—the unfailing clientele which never changed and the view of the doorway just opposite which was the entrance to a cosy little *maison publique*. On the corner there were usually two whores and, if it were raining, you could see them standing patiently with their umbrellas up trying to look cheerful and inviting. It was an unostentatious street but one that bore close scrutiny; a man like Carco, had he been a faithful client of the restaurant in question, would certainly have written a novel about it.

Well, there it was—food and sex. Sometimes one predominated, sometimes the other. There was a hunch-backed dwarf, too, whom

65

I must not overlook, a Spaniard with long, greasy locks and a voracious appetite. Every evening I had to pass his table. Every evening I said "*Bon soir, monsieur,*" to which he would reply "*Bon soir, monsieur.*" Never a word more. For over a year we kept up this performance until at last we broke down the barriers and said "*Bon soir, monsieur, comment ça va ce soir?*" I don't remember speaking to any of the other clients. I usually ate alone and in magnificent peace and contentment. Now and then the proprietor, who was from Auxerre, would come over and say a few words to me. He usually spoke about the weather or the increasing cost of food. Now and then he would ask me when I was going to make another trip to Auxerre because I had told him once that I had made a bicycle trip there. If we got on to that subject he would be sure to end the conversation by saying—"It's not like Paris! it's just a quiet little spot." And I would smile and nod my head with the utmost affability, as though I had never heard him say it before. Sometimes, when I was in a mellow mood, after he had finished his little cadenza, I would conduct a long soliloquy in French about the idyllic splendor of Auxerre. Speaking to myself I always commanded an exquisite French; it was a pity he could never have heard these disquisitions, it would have warmed his heart.

It was towards dusk that I came upon the town of Auxerre, which is on the river Yonne if I am not mistaken. There was a bridge, as in all French towns, and we stood there a long while, my wife and I, looking down at the trees which were waving in the water. We were so moved that we couldn't speak; when I looked at her there were tears in her eyes. That was one of the supremely happy days I spent with her in France. We had left Paris a day or two before, by bicycle, and we were filled with dreams. We were trying as much as possible to stick to the narrow tow-paths which border the canals. She had only learned to ride a few days before and she was nervous when she got on the tow-paths. Sometimes we dismounted and strolled along the banks of the canal, time being no object to us. In America we had known nothing but hardships and misery. And now suddenly we were free and all Europe lay before us. We would go to Italy and Austria and Roumania and Poland and Czecho-slovakia and Germany and Russia. We would see everything. Well, it was beginning marvelously. We had had a few little tiffs due to her nervousness but underneath everything was calm and beautiful. We would eat every day, for one thing.

In Auxerre that first evening we ate beside the bank of the river. It was a modest little hostelry and because we were on a holiday we treated ourselves to a good wine. I remember the view of the church from where we sat as the wine trickled down my gullet. I remember the glassy stare of the water, the tall trees swaying against the soft French sky. I remember that I felt a great peace then, a peace such as I had never known in my own country. I looked at my wife and she had become a different person. Even the birds looked different. One would like to hold such moments forever. But part of the deep joy which is in them comes from the knowledge that it is only fleeting. Perhaps to-morrow would come one of those quarrels which annihilate all the beauty of the land-scape and which, because you are in a foreign land, devastate you more than usual.

As the restaurant man in the rue Le Chapelais said—it was certainly not Paris! But in some ways it was far better than Paris. It was more French, more authentic. It created another kind of nostalgia, the nostalgia which later I was to discover in certain French books or through conversation with a whore in bed while quietly smoking a cigarette. What it is no invader will ever destroy. It is something intangible, like the peculiar cast of the French sky. It is the invader who will succumb.

In a way we *were* invaders. With our dirty American dollars we were buying the things we wanted. But with every purchase we were given something gratuitous, something we had not bargained for, and it ate into us and transformed us, until finally we were completely subjugated.

When I left New York on this lugubrious trip about America one of the last things I went in search of was a map of Paris and of France. I knew that in some God-forsaken hole I would suddenly break out into a sweat and want to look up the names of streets and towns and rivers which are already beginning to fade from my memory. In the train, riding from Kansas City to St. Louis, the landscape took on the familiar cast of the Dordogne region. The last hour or so, to be exact. I think it was along the Missouri River. We had come through peaceful, rolling plains dotted with homely farm houses. It was early Spring and the colors of the earth ran from the color of straw to pale green. In the distance were pale, craggy cliffs and escarpments, often the color of ash, fantastically shaped and reminiscent of the castles and châteaux of the Dordogne.

But where was that which goes in hand with the soil, the marriage of heaven and earth, the superstructure which man rears in order to make of natural beauty something profound and lasting? I had just been reading Rolland's book on Vivekananda; I had put it down because I couldn't read any more, my emotions were so powerful. The passage which roused me to such a state of exaltation was the one in which Rolland describes Vivekananda's triumphal return to India from America. No monarch ever received such a reception at the hands of his countrymen: it stands unique in the annals of history. And what had he done, Vivekananda, to merit such a welcome? He had made India known to America; he had spread the light. And in doing so he had opened the eyes of his countrymen to their own weaknesses. All India greeted him with open arms; millions of people prostrated themselves before him, saluting him as a saint and saviour, which he was. It was the moment when India stood nearer to being unified than at any time in her long history. It was a triumph of love, of gratitude, of devotion. I am coming back to him later, to his clean, powerful words spoken like a fearless champion not of India but of the human race. For the moment I must rush on, carry on through the myth of the Dordogne to the tomb of St. Louis which is called a city but which is a foul, stinking corpse rising up from the plain like an advertisement of Albrecht Dürer's "Melancholia". Like its twin-sister, Milwaukee, this great American city creates the impression that architecture itself has gone mad. The true morbidity of the American soul finds its outlet here. Its hideousness is not only appalling but suffocating. The houses seem to have been decorated with rust, blood, tears, sweat, bile, rheum and elephant dung. One can imagine the life which goes on there—something à la Theodore Dreiser at his worst. Nothing can terrify me more than the thought of being doomed to spend the rest of my days in such a place.

I had a wonderful moment or two in St. Louis, thanks to the horror and misery about me. Walking through the old section of the city, where some gigantic piece of reconstruction work is going on, walking through a sort of abattoir upended by an earthquake or a tornado, my disgust grew so great that I passed over into the opposite—into a state of ecstasy. For, in order to preserve my sanity I had to reach out desperately for something which would counterbalance the horror I was moving through. And what should pop into my mind but the remembrance of a magical night in Sarlat. Like Auxerre, Sarlat is also situated in my mind at the very beginning of a glorious trip. My last view of France, on leaving for Greece. I had taken the train from Paris at night and towards dawn got off at Rocamadour. I stayed at Rocamadour a few days, visited the famous Gouffre de Padirac, where I had a most memorable meal suspended between the bottom of the cave and the surface of the earth, and then on an impulse of the moment I took a bus to Sarlat which I had never even heard of before.

It was about four or five in the afternoon. I had just alighted from the bus and was gazing absent-mindedly at the books on display in a book-shop window. The title of one of the books arrested my attention: it was a new book on the prophecies of Nostradamus. The price was more than I thought I could afford at the moment and so I stood there gazing at it intently, almost as though I believed I might read through the cover if I looked hard and long enough. And in that state of fixity I became aware gradually that a man was standing beside me, looking at the same book and talking aloud, talking to *me*, I finally realized.

He was the proprietor of the shop and a good friend of the author of the book who, it appeared, lived in Sarlat. He seemed to be delighted by the fact that I was an American, that I had lived so long in Paris and that I had gone out of my way to visit Sarlat. He said he would be closing the shop in a little while and asked me if I would not join him at the *bistro* across the street. He was obviously very eager to talk to me at length.

I went across the street and sat on the terrace in front of the *bistro*. It was the main street of the town and had no particular charm that I could see; it might have been anywhere in the provinces. I rather liked the *librairien*, however. He was most cordial and enthusiastic and obviously hipped about Americans, as Frenchmen are now and then. I watched him pull the shutters down. He was doing it with zest, like a school boy hurriedly finishing his chores in order to run off and join the gang. He waved his hand at me and shouted: *"Dans un moment!"*

He had hardly sat down when he began to talk full spate—about

70

the war, the war of 1914. He had known some Americans at the front, wonderful fellows, according to him. They were so child-like, so naive, so generous, so full of good spirits. "Not like us," he said. "We're rotten, we're eaten away. France has lost her spirit." He wanted to know what part of America I came from. When I said New York he looked at me as if he could scarcely believe his ears. "Not really?" he exclaimed. "Lucky devil! I have always dreamed of going to New York some day. But now . . ." He shrugged his shoulders in a gesture of despair. Yes, another war was on us. He would indeed be lucky if he got through a second time. Well, how did I like Paris? Where did I live in Paris? Did I know so-and-so or so-and-so? I told him something of my life there in the beginning. "*Tiens!*" he said, "you certainly had guts. You Americans are romantic fellows."

We had another *apéritif* and he began to talk about himself, about his life in Sarlat where he was born and where he would probably die if he was not killed in the war. A curious thing, incidentally, the way Frenchmen always talked about the impending war. They never talked about licking the enemy, they never showed any real hatred for the Germans; they spoke of it as a job which had to be performed, a disagreeable one, which they would do without question because they were citizens of France. But the uppermost thought in their minds, when discussing the subject, was the home-coming, the resumption of normal life, the return to their little niche, whatever it might happen to be. To me their attitude always seemed to reveal the highest form of courage: it was eminently pacifistic. They would fight out of a sense of duty and without hatred. That is why France is strong and why she will rise again and resume her place in the world. France has been conquered but not defeated.

In the midst of an animated conversation we suddenly heard

a band playing and in a moment or two a parade of children filed by us preceded by clowns and mountebanks. There was to be a carnival later, he explained, in honor of some Catholic saint. Wouldn't I do him the honor of having dinner with him? He would like to show me the town after dark—it would be at its very best this evening because of the carnival spirit. I was only too happy to accept the invitation. It was already quite dark and the street lights were rapidly transforming the dull, provincial aspect of the place into something more promising. "I know every house in this town," he said rapidly, as we moved towards a nearby restaurant. "My father was a carpenter and a mason. I used to work for him as a boy. It's a wonderful occupation—far better than being a *librairien*. To do something with your hands—and with love! ah, I regret it now. But I am still a carpenter at heart."

We ate in a modest little restaurant and washed the food down with a *petit vin du pays* which was delicious. After the dinner we strolled back to my hotel in order to get the key—the doors were locked at ten o'clock. The key, like the door itself, was enormous; it was the key to a fortress. We stood in front of the door examining it minutely. He showed me the repairs which his father had made in the door and the big hinge which he himself had fitted to it later. "Come," he said, grasping my arm, "I will show you some of the little streets, the *old* Sarlat which the people of Paris have forgotten about." And with that he began to talk about Charlemagne, about Ronsard and Villon, about the Dukes of Burgundy and the Maid of Orléans. He talked about the past not as a scholar or student of history but as a man remembering something he had lived through. "That book you were looking at this afternoon," he said after a pause, "we will go back to the shop later and get it. I want you to have it as a souvenir of Sarlat. Perhaps you will translate it one day. . . ." And then he began talking about Avignon and Montpelier, of Arles and Nîmes and Orange, of the Provençal tongue, of the great women of France, of the Rosicrucians, of the mysterious portals of Notre Dame, of Paracelsus and of Dante. "My dear friend," he said, stopping short in the shadow of a great doorway out of the Middle Ages, "France is to me the only country in the world. She has experienced everything. But it is in little things that she is great—in tenderness, in patience, in reverence. France does not lust to dominate the world. She is like a woman, rather, who seduces you. She is not even a beautiful woman at first sight. But she knows how to entwine herself in your affections. She reveals herself slowly, circumspectly, always holding back the real charm, the real treasures, until the moment when they will be justly appreciated. She does not fling herself at you like a whore. The soul of France is chaste and pure, like a flower. We are reticent not out of timidity but because we have much to give. France is an inexhaustible treasure vault and we, the people of France, are the humble guardians of that great treasure. We are not generous like you—perhaps because what we possess we have gained through great suffering. Every inch of our soil has been fought over time and again. If we love our soil, as few people in the world do, it is because it has been well watered by the blood of our forefathers. To you it may seem like a small life that we lead but to us it is deep and rich—especially to us who live in the provinces. I have lived in Paris and I adore it, but this is the real life here among the people of the soil. We are bored sometimes, it is true, but that passes. We remain French—that is the important thing."

We had walked back towards the ancient wall of the city into the very heart and bowels of the Middle Ages. At times he had to take my hand and lead me because the narrow, twisting lanes lay in absolute darkness. Once in such a lane he felt his way along the wall with his hand and, having come to the right spot, he lit a match and asked me to rub my hand over the woodwork of a huge portal. By lighting match after match we managed to examine the whole door, a procedure which made that door live in my memory as no other door does. And then it was dark again, a pitch black punctuated by sounds of merriment down below where the innocent festivities were in full swing.

My eyes were brimming with tears. The past was alive again; it lived in every façade, every portal, every cornice, in the very stones under our feet. The children in the white dresses, they were out of the past too. Suddenly I tugged at his sleeve. "Tell me," I said, "do you remember *Le Grand Meaulnes?*"

"The ball?" he said, gripping my arm.

"Yes, the ball! *The children!*"

We said not another word about it. We fell into a deep silence. The book was speaking through us in the silence of the little street, begging us not to break the dream, not to drag the children out of their world of make-believe.

As we descended a broad flight of steps leading to a parapet from which another flight of stairs in the shape of a horse shoe descended I saw nothing but little flames leaping from balustrades and window-sills. The whole square was dancing with tiny flames through which the figures of the merry-makers lurched and reeled as in a shadow play. Again the tears came to my eyes. It was all so gentle in spirit, so unlike the American conception of gayety. And yet the background was sombre, massive, almost sinister in its medieval puissance. It reminded me somehow of the fleur de lys on the heavy escutcheons of the knights errant—that contrast between the heart and the fist, that shock of ancient battle in which the death blow came as an act of grace and deliverance. It reminded me too of the plagues and of the rejoicing which must have followed during the all too brief lulls. It reminded me of the way my butcher in the

74

rue de la Tombe-Issoire handled his meat, the grace and the tenderness of his knife stroke, the almost maternal affection with which he carried a quarter of veal from the chopping block to the marble slab in the window. Yes, France was living again before my eyes, the France of long ago, the France of yesterday, the France of tomorrow. Glorious gentle France! God, with what love and reverence I think of you now. And to think that was my last look. How fortunate I was! And now you are fallen, prostrate under the heel of the conqueror. I can scarcely believe it. It seems that only now, this moment, in living back to that night of absolute enchantment, do I grasp the full enormity of the crime which has been visited upon you. But even if everything is demolished, even if every city of importance is destroyed, levelled to the ground, the France I speak of will live. If the great flame of the spirit be extinguished the little flames are unquenchable; they will burst through the earth in millions of tiny tongues. Another France will be born; another holy day will be added to the calendar. No, what I saw cannot be crushed under the heel of the conqueror. It is a libel against the human spirit to say that France will be no more. France lives. *Vive la France!*

THE SOUL OF ANAESTHESIA

> *"Puissance, justice, histoire: à bas!"*
> —Rimbaud

I WILL call him Bud Clausen because that's not his right name.
I won't say where I met him either, because I wouldn't want any
harm to come to him. He was tortured quite enough by our sadistic
guardians of the peace. No matter what he does, in this life or the
next, I shall always be able to find excuses for him.

I don't want to make a hero of him; I want to portray him
honestly.

Rattner was with me at the time. We had been making a long
journey by train. We had already paid a visit to a famous penal
institution the name of which I prefer to suppress. The warden
there had shown us every courtesy. But there is one detail about the

place which remains fixed in my memory and which serves as a good introduction to the story of Bud Clausen.

In order to enter the portals of this celebrated institution you have to get by a guard who stands above you on a sort of bandstand. You have to go through a grilling before he gives the all clear signal. He had a rifle in his hand, a revolver in his holster, and probably a couple of hand grenades in his trousers pockets. Armed to the teeth. Back of him was the Law, the law which says shoot first and inquire afterwards. He was giving me a thorough going over because I had forgotten to notify the warden over the telephone that I was bringing my friend Rattner along. It was difficult to make him understand how I could have forgotten such an important trifle.

This isn't the place to complain about the punctilio of prison regimes. I know that they have to take every precaution. All I wish to convey is the effect which this individual had upon me. Months have passed since the incident and yet I can't forget his face, his manner, his whole being. He's a man, and I say it calmly and soberly, whom I could kill in cold blood. I could shoot him down in the dark and go quietly about my business, as if I had just brushed a mosquito off my arm.

He was a killer, a man who hunts down human prey—and accepts money for it. He was unclean, unfit to associate with human kind, even with those misfits behind the bars. As long as I live I shall never forget that cruel, ash-gray face, those cold, beady man-hunter's eyes. I hate him and all that he stands for. I hate him with an undying hatred. I would a thousand times rather be the most incorrigible convict than this hireling of those who are trying to maintain law and order. Law and order! Finally, when you see it staring at you through the barrel of a rifle, you know what it means. *A bas puissance, justice, histoire!* If society has to be protected by these inhuman monsters then to hell with society! If at the bottom of law and order there is only a man armed to the teeth, a man without a heart, without a conscience, then law and order are meaningless.

To get back to Clausen. . . . Bud was not a heartless killer. He did his best not to kill, if I am to believe his story. He was weak and vain—like most of us. He had done a bit of thieving first, not anything however to compare with the operations of our illustrious industrial magnates, our bankers, politicians and colonial exploiters. No, Bud was just an ordinary crook, an honest crook, so to speak, with an exaggerated sense of loyalty and honor. Toward the fair sex he was fatuously romantic and chivalrous, far more so than a pugilist or a sex-starved member of the clergy. There were two things he could not countenance—cruelty to children and disrespect for woman. He was adamant there.

He would never shoot a man down except in self-defense, he said, and I believe him. There was a bit of the dandy about him, and of the swashbuckling braggart too, traits which we find among the higher-ups as well. He was a consummate liar, but then what is a diplomat, a politician, a lawyer? The worst thing about him, and I am trying to look at him dispassionately, is that he no longer had any faith in his fellow man. That had been knocked out of him by those who talk about having faith and never show the evidences of it. He had done at least five stretches and was probably wanted by the authorities when our paths met.

He had paid for his crimes in full, that is my belief. If he should commit fresh ones I would blame it on the police, on the lawmakers, on the educators, on the clergy, on all those who believe in punishment, who refuse to help a man when he is down or try to understand him when in impotent rage he turns against the world. It doesn't matter to me what crimes are chalked up

78

against Clausen; our crimes, all of us who are on the outside, who got off scot-free, are greater. If we did not actually force him to become a criminal we most certainly helped him to remain one. And in speaking of Bud Clausen I am speaking for the great majority of men and women who suffered the same fate; I am speaking for all those to come, who will follow in his foot-steps and who have no redress until we on the outside become more enlightened and more humane.

We met on the train. He was a vendor, a "butch", as they call them. He wore a uniform supplied him by the News company and passed back and forth at intervals offering candy, cigarettes, chewing gum, papers, soda water, etc. One would never take him for a criminal. He was soft, gentle, well-spoken—at the worst, a man who had come down in the world, as we say. If he were sitting in the Senate one would remark nothing peculiar about him. He could have passed for a banker, a labor leader, a politician, or a promoter. I would never have given him a thought if it had not been for the few words he let drop just as we were getting off the train. Throughout the long train ride there had been no conversation between us: I had bought nothing from him. Once he had startled me out of a nap by bending over me to lower the shade. I experienced a strange feeling of uneasiness at the moment but instantly dismissed it. He had only wished to protect me from the sun, he said.

As the train pulled in to the station Rattner and I were standing on the platform with our luggage heaped about us. The news vendor was getting off too—it was the end of the line for him. As he brushed by he wished us good luck. Just then the train gave a sudden jerk; he stood for a moment or so balancing himself, holding on to the guard rail which we too were clutching.

"You must be glad to be getting home," I said, by way of acknowledging his good wishes.

"I have no home," he said, looking at me in a strange way. There was a pregnant pause and then, almost without feeling, he told us briefly that he was out of prison only a short while, that he was still unused to being at large. As for the idea of home, of a woman waiting for him, why . . . well, just this . . . he didn't know what it was any more to put his arms around a woman. That was almost too much to hope for. It was a tremendous thing just to be free, to be out in the world, to be able to talk to people. Another moment and he had descended the steps, once again wishing us good luck.

We had an important telephone call to make at the station and in the excitement which followed Clausen dropped out of mind. But as we were going to bed that night Rattner brought up the subject. He was sorry, he said, that we had let the man slip out of our hands. I was relieved to hear him say it; I too felt that we had left something undone.

"Let's look him up the first thing in the morning," said Rattner. "We ought to be able to trace him through the News company. We may be able to do something for him."

At the station next morning we found the man who had hired him. He was a nasty bird and in an irritable mood. He said that the man was quitting. All he was worried about was the uniform—would he get it back or not. He seemed to think that we were the ones who had taken Clausen away from him, that we were employing him.

"You know what he is . . . just a jail-bird. He's no good to anybody, never will be. He'll steal anything he can lay his hands on. But if you want to hire him that's your business. All I want is that uniform. He's not going to get away with that. You can't trust anybody nowadays."

He went on like that, never giving us a chance to speak. Finally we did manage to let him know, though without convincing him,

80

that we had no thought of employing Clausen since we were not in business, but that we wanted to help him in whatever way we could. He seemed baffled by such disinterestedness, then grew even more suspicious than before. Finally he grudgingly gave us the address of the rooming house where Clausen was staying. "Look out he don't play you a dirty trick," he warned as we went out the door. And then, as we were walking off, he shouted: "And tell him I'm coming after that uniform, do you hear?"

We went immediately to the address he had given us. It was a dingy, morbid place and a bit shady looking too—a sort of hide-out. Clausen had left only a few minutes ago, we were told, to buy a hat and get himself a haircut. Were we friends of his, the man wanted to know. We explained that we had met on the train. Yes, we wanted to be his friend. The man nodded as though he understood.

We took a walk and returned in about an hour. Clausen hadn't returned. We sat down and tried to make conversation with the man, but he was thoroughly uncommunicative. Finally I decided to write a note, inviting him out to see us. It was a warm message and I felt certain Clausen wouldn't ignore it. I gave him our telephone number and told him we would call for him if he liked. We were staying a few miles out of town in a tourist cabin.

The day passed without word or sight of him. The next day towards noon there was a telephone message saying that he was on his way out to have lunch with us.

It was rather a cold day and to our surprise Clausen arrived without hat or overcoat, looking as if he pretended it were a lovely Spring day. I noticed his hair-comb immediately—it was parted in the middle. It seemed to alter his whole appearance. I also took in the immaculate starched shirt and the neatly tied tie. He had on a blue serge suit freshly pressed which enhanced the impression he gave of neatness and cleanliness. One might have thought he had been a sailor. One might also have mistaken him for a stock broker or a promoter. His movements were leisurely and deliberate, a little too much so, it seemed to me, to be genuine. Perhaps he was trying to conceal his nervousness; perhaps he was ashamed of revealing his real emotions. So I thought at first. But soon I realized that the mask had become a part of him, that it would require something truly extraordinary to make him drop it. I wasn't sure either that I would care to see him step forth naked; the thought of it made me uneasy.

There was also something in his manner which conveyed to us that he was doing us a favor by coming to visit us. There was nothing any more of the news vendor in him, nor even of the man who had conversed with us for a few brief moments on the platform of the train. He was playing a different role now. He was in character, so to say. He was calm, steady, sanguine, poised. Almost masterful. But his fingers were horribly stained with nicotine. They seemed to belie his whole act. All through the meal I watched his hands. The fingers were like dirty talons; the one hand was crippled.

Asked what had delayed his visit he replied that he had been to see a friend in an army camp some distance away. He had a way of looking one in the eye steadily, while speaking, which was a trifle disconcerting. It was a little too steady. One felt that it had been practiced before a mirror.

After lunch we went back to the cabin to talk at ease. "I suppose you want to hear my story," he said, as he lowered himself into a big easy chair. "Have you another cigarette?"

The way he blurted this out at once gave me the clue to the somewhat patronizing air he had assumed from the outset. It meant that he didn't believe in our desire to help him without thought of return. It also meant that he knew his value, as human interest material, and that he was willing to make a deal. Nobody wanted to help ex-convicts for the pure love of it. Unless they were softies. He had sized us up as newspaper men, he quietly informed us, and he had come prepared to deliver the goods. In fact, there was a book in it for some one, if they had the patience to hear him out. He would have written it himself but he had no talent in that direction. "I knew you were a writer the moment I set eyes on you," he said, turning to me. "As for him," jerking a stained thumb in Rattner's direction, "any one could tell he's an artist. Besides, I saw him sketching in the train."

He was quite surprised when we informed him that we were not newspaper men, that we didn't want to make use of his story, that we had very little money, and that we were doing something which would probably bring very little reward. We told him that our primary purpose in making the trip was to get reacquainted with our own country. We explained that we had been living abroad a number of years. No, we would be interested in hearing anything he cared to tell us about his experiences, but that wasn't the point at all. We wanted him to know that we had a very friendly feeling for him. We didn't know just what we could do for him, but we wanted to help him—if he was in need of help.

He melted visibly on learning this. Yes, he needed help all right. Who didn't? Especially when you had had nothing but the dirty end of it all your life. He had just thrown up his job; there was nothing in it anyway. He had taken it because there was nothing else he could take: nobody wanted to hire a man just out of prison. But he had bigger ideas than just being a "butch". He wanted to get to New York. He had friends there, friends who would see him through. There was one friend in particular, a fellow who ran a music shop on Broadway. They had done a long stretch together somewhere. He was pretty confident his friend would be good for a few hundred right off the bat.

Even if we emptied our pockets it would be impossible to raise enough to pay the bus fare to New York, we explained. It didn't sound very convincing, I'm sure, what with the room strewn with luggage, a car outside, and another 25,000 miles or so to go. I almost felt like a liar in trying to explain our situation.

Despite this unexpected set-back Clausen continued to talk about himself. It was obviously a relief for him to spill it all out, even if nothing came of it. We were *sympathetic* listeners, and that in itself meant a great deal to him.

To rehearse the story of his life is not my purpose. It was not so very unusual: it was in the tradition. In a moment of weakness, in the moment when it seemed that every man's hand was turned against him, he had crossed the line. Living in that other world each day that passed made it more and more difficult to rejoin the herd. Crimes born of necessity soon led to crimes of sheer bravado. While on parole, after serving his first sentence, he committed a purely gratuitous crime—the sort of thing an artist would do just to keep his hand in. Prison of course is the school of crime *par excellence.* Until one has gone through that school one is only an amateur. In prison bonds of friendship are established, often over a trifle, a kind word, a look, a bone. Later, out in the world, one will do anything to prove one's loyalty. Even if one wants with all his heart and soul to go straight, when the critical moment comes, when it is a toss-up between believing in the world or believing in one's friend, one will choose the latter. One has had a taste of the world; one knows enough not to expect justice or mercy from it. But one can never forget an act of kindness shown in a moment of great need. *Blow up a block house?* Why certainly, if that will help your friend out. *But that may mean life imprisonment, or death in the chair!* What of it? One good turn deserves another. You've been humiliated, you've been tortured, you've been reduced to the level of a wild beast. Who cared? Nobody. Nobody on the outside, no, not even God himself, knows what a man suffers on the inside. There's no language to convey it. It's beyond all human comprehension. It's so vast, so wide, so deep that even the angels with all their powers of understanding and all their powers of locomotion could never explore the whole of it. No, when a friend makes a call on you you've got to obey. You have to do for him what God himself wouldn't do. It's a law. Otherwise you'd fall apart, you'd bark in the night like a dog.

As I said, the nature of his transgressions is unimportant. They were not terribly unusual. Nor do I care to dwell on the tortures which were inflicted upon him. They were not so unusual either, considering the times, though they made my hair stand on end. When you know what men are capable of you marvel neither at their sublimity nor their baseness. There are no limits in either direction apparently.

The calm restraint with which Clausen described his crimes and his punishment amazed me more and more. I discarded the thought that his manner was studied or deliberate. I began to believe that his detachment was real. I believe that during the long, silent, solitary stretches of confinement he had so thoroughly reviewed everything that had happened to him, had relived his life so often, had become alternately penitent and crazed so many times, that when released to the outer world the discipline which only a saint or an initiate can stand had to find expression. There was no venom, no malice, no hatred in his utterances. He spoke of his tormentors—and they had obviously been devils masquerading in human flesh—he spoke of them, I say, not with the spirit of forgiveness which you might expect of a holy man, but with an understanding that was exceedingly close to it. Even here I am not sure but what I do him an injustice. Perhaps he *was* ready to forgive—if only he could bring himself to believe that he had been forgiven. He was so close to it. He was like an old tree hanging over the edge of a precipice, with all the gnarled roots exposed, hanging there miraculously through storm and drought and indifference and neglect, as though personifying the empty gesture of hanging on. Hanging in a void really, for surely those old withered roots could not possibly have the strength to eternalize such a gesture of will.

What could not be done with such a leaning tower of strength! Supposing for a moment that punishment has its blessings: where then are the cups to receive them? Who that would punish another is willing to endure the same himself? Who, having accomplished his holy purpose of protecting society, is willing to accept the reward which every victim offers? Blindly we punish and blindly we push the cup away. There are men who study the criminal; there are men who devise more humane methods of treating them; there are men who give their lives to restoring to these men what others have taken from them. They know things which the average citizen never dreams of. They could tell us a thousand better ways of handling the situation than is our wont now. And yet I say that a month in prison is worth ten years of study by a free man. Better the warped judgment of the condemned one than the most enlightened judgment of the on-looker. The condemned one reaches at last to his innocence. But the on-looker is not even aware of his guilt. For one crime which is expiated in prison ten thousand are committed thoughtlessly by those who condemn. There is neither beginning nor end to it. All are involved, even the holiest of the holy. Crime begins with God. It will end with man, when he finds God again. Crime is everywhere, in all the fibres and roots of our being. Every minute of the day adds fresh crimes to the calendar, both those which are detected and punished, and those which are not. The criminal hunts down the criminal. The judge condemns the judger. The innocent torture the innocent. Everywhere, in every family, every tribe, every great community, crimes, crimes, crimes. War is clean by comparison. The hangman is a gentle dove by comparison. Attila, Tamerlane, Genghis Khan—reckless automatons by comparison. Your father, your darling mother, your sweet sister: do you know the foul crimes they harbor in their breasts? Can you hold the mirror to iniquity when it is close at hand? Have you looked into the labyrinth of your own despicable heart? Have you sometimes envied the thug for his forthrightness? The study of crime begins with the knowledge of oneself. All that you despise, all that you loathe, all that you reject, all that you condemn and seek to convert by punishment springs from you. The source of it is God whom you place outside, above and beyond. Crime is identification, first with God, then with your own image. Crime is all that lies outside the pack and which is envied, coveted, lusted after. Crime flashes a million brilliant knife blades every minute of the day, and in the night too when waking gives way to dream. Crime is such a tough, such an immense tarpaulin, stretching from infinity to infinity. Where are the monsters who know not crime? What realms do they inhabit? What prevents them from snuffing out the universe?

In one prison Clausen fell in love with a woman, who was also an inmate. They were never able to speak to one another, never able to touch finger-tips even. Now and then a note was smuggled through. For five years it went on. The woman had killed her children with an axe—that was her crime. She was a beautiful woman, with a soul. It was not she who slew the children, but the sharp blade of the axe. Now and then their eyes met, at a distance. Night and day, month in month out, year in and year out their eyes kept

87

meeting despite all barriers. Their eyes grew tongues, lips, ears; they mirrored every thought, every impulse. What a wild, hopeless, tormenting agony love can be under such circumstances! Love disembodied, roaming the world at will, reaching everywhere, free, free as the insane. Two murderers loving one another to death with their eyes. Isn't that just the most exquisite torture imaginable? Who invented that? Was he there to witness it? Are there blue-prints of it? Yes, somewhere . . . somewhere in the void, under the great tarpaulin stretching from infinity to infinity, somewhere there is an exact blue-print of insatiable love. And somewhere, hanging upside down, is the inventor of insatiable love, the angelic monster for whom crime is an unknown word. There was this which Clausen knew, and there was dynamite. Ah, dynamite! A cosy, calculable word. Nothing ambiguous or ambivalent about it. Dynamite! A word that even the devil himself respects. A word you can do things with. A word that detonates. And when it does, whoopee! Christ himself can be blown to smithereens. Yes, prison love is a logarithmic surd. But dynamite! Dynamite is simple. Dynamite is something you take in your hands and do things with. Dynamite contains every destructible happiness not to be found in the hearts of men. It is not only destruction, but what is destroyed too. Dynamite is the solace of desperation. When you blow up a wing of the prison dynamite tells you to have sharp cleavers handy, to chop right and left, chop, chop, chop. What a beautiful bloody day that was when they set the dynamite off at the north end of the prison! Arms and legs everywhere, sometimes ears and noses, heads with roots dangling, trunks pierced with skewers. St. Bartholomew's Eve à la Frankenstein. *Yes, friend, you asked for it. Here is my hand, pledged in blood. We did it!* At the height of pandemonium a man with a machine gun sits in a cage suspended from the ceiling and moving like a trolley spatters bullets into the cells. This is the world on the inside at the height of frenzy. In some other place some one is asking in a weary voice if the griddle cakes are hot, the coffee still warm. In the dark, and quite unwittingly perhaps, some one steps on a beetle, one of those exoskeletonized little creatures of God, and squashes the life out of it. In an amphitheatre, under a spotlight, a man with extraordinarily clean hands begins to explore the entrails of a warm human body in order to find the tainted meat he wants to cut away. One life is saved in order that a thousand be extinguished. People who are sick of reality are being fed and cared for at the expense of the State. The most healthy, the most intelligent, the most promising ones are rounded up, given a number, and sent to the open slaughter house on sixty-nine fronts. Children die of hunger in their mothers' arms, because it's too big a problem to save them even though they are innocent. This is the world on the outside. Inside or out it's pandemonium, and from the roof of the world bullets rain down in place of manna. This is how the world is, so where does Bud Clausen come in, or you or me or anybody? The gate is always locked, and even if you succeed in crashing it in a high-powered car you will be caught and brought back. And then the devils masquerading in human flesh will go to work on you with the inventiveness which only fiends can muster. What is the most steadfast condition of life? Cruelty to one another. In the middle of the night, when you think you will surely die of suffering, the real torture begins. All you've endured is only a prelude to the agony you are about to experience. Man torturing man is a fiend beyond description. You turn a corner in the dark and there he is. You congeal into a bundle of inanimate fear. You become the very soul of anaesthesia. But there is no escaping him. It is your turn now. . . .

Love again. Let's hear how the warden sings. All courtesy, you remember. At your service, sir, there is nothing to conceal. Everything conducted along humanitarian lines, even the cuisine. . . . *But how about sex?* Sex? That is something we try not to think about. A prisoner has no sex. He is God's own private eunuch. Then everything goes blissfully and peacefully, does it? Like the Twenty-third Psalm? No, not quite. The absence of sex produces more sex; no babies are born because there are no mothers to bring them forth. Inside the walls even the female hyena is taboo. If you're in for a long stretch the simplest thing to do is to let your imagination run wild. If you're in for life you may as well surrender to King Onan immediately; nobody is ever going to open the door of your cell and serve you a naked woman on a platter. You can fall in love with your own kind and forget that woman exists, or you can fall in love with a table or a shoe. Other hungers are recognized, but not sexual hunger. You may not need food or air or recreation, but you will certainly need sex—and you will never be able to get it. If your deportment is good, now and then you may be able to look at a woman, but always fully clothed and always at a distance. She may say things that will set you on fire for a month, but nobody will bring you a fire extinguisher. You are regarded as an animal and yet not an animal. You would be much better off if you were a monkey in the zoo. What does it matter now that you still have a name and a calling, that you are a citizen of this country or that? You are not a man and you are not an animal; neither are you an angel or a ghost. You are not even a Philadelphia capon. What a relief it would be if they came to you in the night with a sharp knife, as they did unto Abelard. Yes, that would be an act of mercy. But there is no such thing as mercy here. There is nothing here but the monotonous excitement of torture.

Torture. That is man's middle name. Man-torture-man. In the middle of all emptiness, where even the beat of eternity is faint,

there is this in-between thing called torture. This is the corner-
stone of man's world, the rock on which the tomb of the womb of
the world is built. This is the world, its end and meaning, its beginning, its evolution, its goal and spawn. *Torture.* So this is the
world! And until they put you behind the bars you may not realize
how simple it is, that it could all be summed up in one word. There
is only one word to remember, as you pass in and out of life, and
that word, as every great soul has said, is LOVE. But in the prison
of life love takes on every form of mockery. *Are you suffering, little
man?*

> *Am I suffering?* Oh Jesus, who asks me that?
> I mean, do you suffer more than other men?
> Who is it dares to ask me that? *Who are you?*
> Just how do you suffer, little man?
> Christ! O Christ! *How* do I suffer?
> Yes, *how?* Just how, can you tell us?

SILENCE

He is thinking if there is any way by which he can explain just
how and what it is he suffers. He is wondering if there is any one in
the whole wide world with a heart big enough to comprehend what
it is he wants to tell. There are so many little things to say first, and
will any one have the patience to listen to the end? Suffering is no
one thing: it is composed of invisible atoms infinite in number,
each one a universe in the great macrocosm of pain. He could begin
anywhere, with anything, with a silly word even, a word such as
flapdoodle, and he could erect a cathedral of staggering dimensions
which would not occupy so much as a pocket in the crevice of the
tiniest atom. To say nothing of the surrounding terrain, of the
circumambient aura, of things like coast lines, volcanic craters,

fathomless lagoons, pearl studs and tons of chicken feathers. The musician has an instrument to work with, the surgeon has his implements, the architect his plans, the general his pawns, the idiot his idiocy, but the one who is suffering has everything in the universe except relief. He can run out to the periphery a trillion times but the circle never straightens out. He knows every diameter but no egress. Every exit is closed, whether it be an inch away or a billion light years distant. You crash a gate made of arms and legs only to get a butt blow behind the ear. You pick up and run on bloody, sawed-off stumps, only to fall into an endless ravine. You sit in the very center of emptiness, whimpering inaudibly, and the stars blink at you. You fall into a coma, and just when you think you've found your way back to the womb they come after you with pick and shovel, with acetylene torches. Even if you found the place of death they would find a way to blow you out of it. You know time in all its curves and infidelities. You have lived longer than it takes to grow all the countless separate parts of a thousand new universes. You have watched them grow and fall apart again. And you are still intact, like a piece of music which goes on being played forever. The instruments wear out, and the players too, but the notes are eternal, and you are made of nothing but invisible notes which even the faintest zephyr can shake a tune out of.

And this is only the melodious element of it, which has to do with time and sallies and forays incommensurable. There is also form, phantasmal form, which includes all evolution, all metamorphosis, all the sprouts of germination, of abortion, of diffraction and deformation, of death and rebirth, of seed, caul, matrix and after-birth. There is mood and atmosphere, foreground and background, the aquatic depths and the astral recesses: there are seasons, climates, temperatures; there are categories and departments, logic within logic, certitudes firm as ice, and then fog-banks,

92

ooze and drift, slime and wrack, or just ozone pouring from the neck of a stopperless bottle.

And as though and as if these were not enough, there are the wild noumena, the pleistocene memories, the placental fugues and subterfuges. Memories that hang by a hair, and in dying give birth to dandruff; faces that burn in luminol, shedding hysterical light on cellular problems; names running back to lethal sources, reverberating like spun harps; words embedded in lymph and cyst, which no form of dynamite can blast away; tears that fall on warm fruit and make waterfalls in far-off Africa; birds that settle between the eyes only to singe their wings and fall like broken crutches; vapors that rise from the arteries and congeal into phosphorescent webs of mica; and devils who laugh like antelopes, bounding in and out of broken teeth or frazzled dreams; and monsters of the underwaters, who suck like the undertow or bleat like pregnant baboons; and hammerclaviers fitted with cloying geraniums, announcing stench and smoke and delirium; and kings like Ebenezer Sock, born blanched with terror, who prey on euphemy; and more of his ilk, and more, and then nothing but cube on cube, pillar upon pillar, tomb upon tomb, as far as the mind can reach and just a little beyond. And as though and as if there were at last a limit there is none, believe me, none, none. A little beyond looms the face of the beloved. Ever larger, ever fuller, ever clearer it grows: a moon-glow that saturates an empty sky. Slowly, slow as claustral fever, the nebulae arrive. Little medallions constellate the panic that clouds the orifices of fright. Intaglio depths gleam from the precipitous walls of new world hearts. Through the laughing mouth oceans leap into being and pain still-born is cried down again. The marvels of emptiness parade their defilement, the embryonic unsheath their splendor. Echolalia mounts her throne. The web stretches tighter, the ravisher is ravished. A slat gives way, an axe falls; little children drop like flowers on the burnished hearth beneath the open door. It is the morning of the day after the night before on the threshold of unsubjugated repetition. It fits like a silver-studded bracelet on a warm wrist.

"THE SHADOWS"

It was in Paris that I first began to dream of visiting New Iberia—
in the Café de Versailles, Montparnasse, to be exact. It was Abe
Rattner, the painter, who put the bug in my head. All evening he
had been relating his experiences as a camouflage artist in the
world war. Suddenly, by some strange transition, he began talking
about his friend Weeks Hall who he said lived in a strange part of
the world, in this place called New Iberia, near Avery Island. His
description of his friend, of the house he lived in and the country
roundabout, was so vivid, so out of the world, as we say, that then
and there I resolved to go to Louisiana one day and see with my
own eyes the wonders he was describing.

I left Paris three months before the war broke out, to spend a Sabbatical year in Greece. Little did I dream then that I would encounter Abe Rattner in New York or plan with him this tour of America which I am now embarked upon. A singular coincidence, too, that he should have been able to accompany me on this trip only as far as New Iberia! Looking back upon it all, it almost seems as though everything had been planned and arranged by some unseen power.

We arrived at "The Shadows" towards dusk on a day in January. Our host was waiting for us at a gas station on the highway, in front of the house. He had been waiting to intercept us in order, as he explained, to have us enter the grounds from the rear. I saw at once that he was a character, a rich, amiable personality, such as my friend Rattner had so faithfully portrayed. Everything had to be done in a prescribed way, not because he was domineering or tyrannical, but because he wanted his guests to derive the utmost from every situation or event.

"The Shadows", as the house is called, is not at all in the traditional Louisiana style of architecture. Technically it would be defined as of the Roman Doric order, but to speak in architectural language of a house which is as organically alive, sensuous, and mellow as a great tree is to kill its charm. For me, perhaps because of the rich pinkish brick which gives to the whole atmosphere of the place a warm, radiant glow, "The Shadows" at once summoned to my mind the image of Corinth which I also had the good fortune to come upon towards the close of day. The wonderful masonry columns, so sturdy and yet so graceful, so full of dignity and simplicity, were also reminiscent of Corinth. Corinth has always been synonymous for me with opulence, a roseate, insidious opulence, fragrant with the heavy bloom of Summer.

All through the South I had been made aware again and again

Weeks Hall's home, "The Shadows" at New Iberia, Louisiana

of the magnificence of a recent past. The days of the great plantations bequeathed to the brief and bleak pattern of our American life a color and warmth suggestive, in certain ways, of that lurid, violent epoch in Europe known as the Renaissance. In America, as Weeks Hall puts it, the great houses followed the great crops: in Virginia tobacco, in South Carolina rice, in Mississippi cotton, in Louisiana sugar. Supporting it all, a living foundation, like a great column of blood, was the labor of the slaves. The very bricks of which the walls of the famous houses are made were shaped by the hands of the Negroes. Following the bayous the landscape is dotted with the cabined shacks of those who gave their sweat and blood to help create a world of extravagant splendor. The pretensions which were born of this munificence, and which still endure amidst the soulless ruins of the great pillared houses, are rotting away, but the cabins remain. The Negro is anchored to the soil; his way of life has changed hardly at all since the great débâcle. He is the real owner of the land, despite all titular changes of possession. No matter what the whites say, the South could not exist without the easy, casual servitude of the blacks. The blacks are the weak and flexible backbone of this decapitated region of America.

It had been a wonderful ride up from New Orleans, past towns and villages with strange French names, such as Paradis and Des Allemands, at first following the dangerous winding road that runs beside the levee, then later the meandering Bayou Black and finally the Bayou Teche. It was early in January and hot as blazes though a few days previously, coming into New Orleans, the cold was so mean and penetrating that our teeth were chattering. New Iberia is in the very heart of the Acadian country, just a few miles from St. Martinsville where the memories of Evangeline color the atmosphere.

January in Louisiana! Already the first signs of Spring were manifesting themselves in the cabin door-yards: the paper-white narcissus and the German iris whose pale gray-green spikes are topped by a sort of disdainful white plume. In the transparent black waters of the bayous the indestructible cypress, symbol of silence and death, stands knee-deep. The sky is everywhere, dominating everything. How different the sky as one travels from region to region! What tremendous changes between Charleston, Asheville, Biloxi, Pensacola, Aiken, Vicksburg, St. Martinsville! Always the live oak, the cypress, the chinaball tree; always the swamp, the clearing, the jungle; cotton, rice, sugar cane; thickets of bamboo, banana trees, gum trees, magnolias, cucumber trees, swamp myrtle, sassafras. A wild profusion of flowers: camellias, azaleas, roses of all kinds, salvias, the giant spider lily, the aspidistra, jasmine, Michaelmas daisies; snakes, screech-owls, raccoons; moons of frightening dimensions, lurid, pregnant, heavy as mercury. And like a leit-motif to the immensity of sky are the tangled masses of Spanish moss, that peculiar spawn of the South which is allied to the pineapple family. An epiphyte, rather than a parasite, it lives an independent existence, sustaining itself on air and moisture; it flourishes just as triumphantly on a dead tree or a telegraph wire as on the live oak. "None but the Chinese," says Weeks Hall, "can ever hope to paint this moss. It has a baffling secret of line and mass which has never been remotely approached. It is as difficult to do as a veronica. The live oaks tolerate it—they do not seem to be at one with it. But to the Louisiana cypress it seems to want to act as a bodyguard. A strange phenomenon." It is also a profitable one, as the mattress and upholstery industry of Louisiana would indicate.

There are people from the North and the Mid-West who actually shudder when they first come upon the giant bewhiskered live oaks; they sense something dismal and forbidding in them. But when one sees them in majestic, stately rows, as on the great estates around

Beaufort, S. C., or at Biloxi—at Biloxi they come to apotheosis!—one must bow down before them in humble adoration for they are, if not the monarchs of the tree world, certainly the sages or the magi.

It was in the shade of one of these great trees that the three of us stood admiring the back of the house. I say the three of us because our host—and that is one of the things I like about Weeks Hall—can stop and examine the place he lives in any hour of the day or night. He can talk for hours about any detail of the house or gardens; he speaks almost as if it were his own creation, though the house and the trees which surround it came into existence over a century ago. It is all that remains of estates which once comprised several thousand acres, including Weeks Island, a Spanish royal grant made to David Weeks by Baron Carondelet in 1792. The entrance to the property, now reduced to three acres, is on Main Street, which is a continuation of Highway 90. Driving past it in a car one would never in the world suspect what lies hidden behind the dense hedge of bamboo which encircles the grounds.

As we stood there talking, Theophile came up to inform our friend that some women were at the front gate demanding permission to visit the grounds. "Tell them I'm out," said our host. "The tourists!" he said wryly, turning to Rattner. "They pour through here like ants; they overrun the place. Thousands and thousands of them—it's like the plague." And then he began to relate one anecdote after another about the women who insist on inspecting the rooms, which is forbidden. "They would follow me into the bathroom," he said, "if I permitted them. It's almost impossible to have any privacy when you live in a place like this." Most of them were from the Middle West, I gathered. They were the type one sees in Paris, Rome, Florence, Egypt, Shanghai—harmless souls who have a mania for seeing the world and gathering information about anything and everything. A curious thing about these show places, and I have visited a number of them, is that the owners, despite the martyrdom inflicted upon them by the steady hordes of visitors, almost never feel at liberty to exclude the public. They all seem to possess a sense of guilt about living alone in such ancient splendor. Some of course can not afford to spurn the modest revenue which this traffic brings, but for the most part there exists a feeling of obligation towards the public, whether conscious or unconscious.

Later, in looking over the register, I came across many interesting names, that of Paul Claudel surprising me not a little. "Claudel, ah yes! He said a wonderful thing about the camellia—how in Japan, when the blossom falls, they speak of it as a beheading." He went on to talk about the camellia, of which he has some marvelous varieties, including the largest Lady Hume's Blush in America. Its rarity, I was informed, is almost legendary; a plant of this size, in fact, is comparable to a black pearl. He dwelt at length on the tones and colors, the Lady Hume's Blush, he insisted, being of the palest pink ivory, whereas the Madame Strekaloff was of a peach-blossom pink streaked with rose, a rose with reddish stripes. He spoke of the tight little blossoms which might have been born under the glass domes of wax flowers. "The new varieties are lush but never sensuous; they have a beauty which forbids. They are coldly unaffected by praise and admiration. Pink cabbages, that's what they are!" And so on and so forth. It seemed to me that the man had given his life to the study of camellias, to say nothing of his wealth. But the more I listened to him the more I realized that he had an almost encyclopaedic knowledge about a great diversity of things. A superabundant vitality also, which permits him, when he feels inclined to talk, to continue like a fount from morning till night. He had always been a great talker, I learned, even before the injury to his arm limited his painting. That first evening, after the dishes had been cleared away, I watched him in fascination as he paced up and down the room, lighting one cigarette after another—he smokes almost a hundred a day—and telling us of his travels, his dreams, his weaknesses and vices, his passions, his prejudices, his ambitions, his observations, his studies, his frustrations. At three in the morning, when we finally begged leave to retire, he was wide awake, making himself a fresh cup of black coffee which he shares with his dog, and preparing to take a stroll about the garden and meditate on things past and future. One of the weaknesses, shall I call it, which sometimes comes upon him in the wee hours of the morning is the desire to telephone some one in California or Oregon or Boston. The anecdotes about these early morning enthusiasms of his are related from one end of the country to the other. Telephoning is not the only one of his imperative impulses; the others are even more spectacular, more weird, such as impersonating a non-existent idiot twin brother . . .

When the guests retire he communes with the dog. There is an unholy sort of bond between them, something quite out of the ordinary. I have forgotten the dog's name—Spot or Queenie, some common name like that. She is an English setter, a bitch, and rather seedy now and smelly, though it would break her master's heart if he should hear me say a thing like that. Weeks Hall's contention about this Alice or Elsie is this—that she does not know that she is a dog. According to him, she does not like other dogs, doesn't even recognize them, so to speak. He contends that she has the most beautiful manners—the manners of a lady. Perhaps. I am no judge of dogs. But of one thing I am in agreement with him—she has absolutely human eyes. That her coat is like falling water, that her ears remind you of Mrs. Browning's portrait, that she makes things handsome with her casual languor—such subtleties are beyond me. But when you look into her eyes, no matter how much or how little you know about dogs, you must confess that this puzzling creature is no ordinary bitch. She looks at you with the soulful eyes of some departed human who has been condemned to crawl about on all fours in the body of this most companionable setter. Weeks Hall would have it that she is sad because of her inability to speak, but the feeling she gave me was that she was sad because nobody except her master had the intelligence to recognize her as a human being and not just a dog. I could never look her in the eyes for more than a few moments at a time. The expression, which I have caught now and then on the face of a writer or painter suddenly interrupted in the midst of an inspiration, was that of a wanderer between two worlds. It was the sort of look which makes one desire to withdraw discreetly, lest the separation between body and soul become irreparable.

The next morning, after breakfast, as I was about to open a door which had blown shut, I saw to my astonishment the signatures in pencil on the back of the door of hundreds of celebrities, written in every scrawl imaginable. Of course we had to add our own to the collection. I signed mine under that of a Hungarian named Bloor Schleppey, a fascinating name which unleashed a story about the door that is worth recounting. The present names, it seems, are all of recent origin. Originally there was an even more scintillating array of names, but about the time of Bloor Schleppey, perhaps because the name had such an uncommon effect upon our host, the latter, after a debauch lasting several days, was so disgusted with the condition of the house that he ordered the servants to clean it from top to bottom. "I want it to be immaculate when I wake up," were his orders. They tried to tell him that it was impossible to put a house of such proportions in order in such a short space of time. There were only two of them. "Well, then, hire a gang," said our host. And they did. And when he awoke from his slumber the house was indeed spic and span, as he had commanded it to be. Certain things, to be sure, had disappeared, what with the zeal and frenzy of the house-cleaners. The real coup came when he observed, in the course of his inspection, that the door with the names had been washed down and the names obliterated. That was a blow. At first he stormed and cussed, but when he had quieted down suddenly an inspiration came to him. He would unhinge the door, crate it, and send it on a round robin to be re-signed by his distinguished visitors. What a journey! The idea was so fascinating that presently he began to think it was too good a treat to offer a mere door—he would go himself from place to place, carrying the door along, and begging like a monk for a fresh signature. Some of the visitors had come from China, some from Africa, some from India. Better to supervise it personally than entrust it to the post or express agencies. Nobody, as far as he knew, had ever travelled around the world with a door. It would be quite a feat, a sensation, in fact. To find Bloor Schleppey, that would be something. God only knew where he had disappeared. The others he thought of as relatively fixed, like certain stars. But Bloor Schleppey—he hadn't the faintest idea where Bloor Schleppey had departed to. And then, as he was planning his itinerary—a delight which lasted for weeks— who should arrive, unheralded, in the dead of night, accompanied by three great Danes on a leash, but Bloor Schleppey himself! Well, to make the story short, the door was put back on its hinges, Bloor Schleppey inscribed his signature again, and the idea of a world tour with a door on his back gradually faded away, like all whimsical ideas. A strange thing about the people identified with this door, which I feel compelled to add in conclusion, is this— that many of them, as if in answer to a silent summons, have returned to sign their names again. It may also be, of course, that

103

some of them were summoned back by an early morning telephone call—who can say?

In the course of a century or more curious events must naturally have occurred in a remote and idyllic domain of this sort. At night, lying in the center of a huge four-poster bed staring at the brass ornament in the center of the tester, the stillness of the house seemed the stillness not of an empty house but of one in which a great family was sleeping the profound and peaceful sleep of the dead. Awakened from a light sleep by the buzz of a mosquito I would get to thinking about the statues in the garden, about that fluid, silent communion which went on like music between these guardians of the Four Seasons. Sometimes I would get up and go out on the broad balcony overlooking the garden, stand there half-naked puffing a cigarette, hypnotized by the warmth, the silence, the fragrance which enveloped me. So many strange, startling phrases were dropped in the course of a day—they would come back to me at night and plague me. Little remarks, such as the one he dropped about the pool, for instance. "A dozen square feet of pool mean more to them than all the soil: it is a transparent mystery." The pool! It brought back memories of the dead fountain which graces the entrance to the now abandoned Mississippi Lunatic Asylum. I know that water is soothing to the insane, just as music is. A little pool in an enclosed and enchanted garden, such as this one, is an inexhaustible source of wonder and magic. One evening, standing thus in a dream, I remembered that there was a typewritten description of the place framed and posted near the pool. I descended the outer staircase and with the aid of a match I read the thing through. I re-read the paragraph about the garden, as though it contained some magic incantation. Here it is:

"A rectangular formal garden to the east of the house is enclosed by a clipped bamboo hedge and is bordered by walks of hand-shaped brick, at the four corners of which are marble statues of the Four Seasons which were once in the gardens of the old Hester plantation. The center of the grass rectangle has a clump of old Camellia trees planted when the house was built. The signed marble sundial is inscribed with the French adage—'Abundance is the Daughter of Economy and Work', and is dated 1827."

A heavy mist had descended. I walked cautiously in my bare feet for the old bricks were slippery with moss. As I got to the far corner of the rectangle the light of the moon broke full and clear on the serene face of the goddess there enshrined. I leaned over impulsively and kissed the marble lips. It was a strange sensation. I went to each of them in turn and kissed their cold, chaste lips. Then I strolled back to the trellised garden house which lies on the banks of the Bayou Teche. The scene before my eyes was that of a Chinese painting. Sky and water had become one: the whole world was floating in a nebular mist. It was indescribably beautiful and bewitching. I could scarcely believe that I was in America. In a moment or so a river boat loomed up, her colored lights scattering the dense mist into a frayed kaleidoscope of ribboned light. The deep fog horn sounded and was echoed by the hooting of invisible owls. To the left the draw-bridge slowly raised its broken span, the soft edges illumined by fulgurant lights of red and green. Slowly, like a white bird, the river boat glided past my vision, and in her wake the mist closed in, bearing down the sky, a fistful of frightened stars, the heavy wet limbs of the moss-covered trees, the density of night, and watery, smothered sounds. I went back to bed and lay there not just wide awake but super-conscious, alive in every tip and pore of my being. The portrait of an ancestor stared at me from the wall—a Manchu portrait, with the dress folded and pressed in the frame. I could hear Weeks Hall's booming voice saying to me: "I should like to do a garden which would not be a seed-catalogue by daylight, but strange, sculptural blossoms by

105

night, things hanging in trees and moving like metronomes, transparent plastics in geometrical shapes, silhouettes lit by lights and changing with the changing hours. A garden is a show—why not make one enormous garden, one big, changing show?" I lay there wondering about those several thousand letters and documents which he had exhumed from the garret and stored in the Archives at Baton Rouge. What a story they would make! And the garret itself—that enormous room on the third floor with the forty trunks! Forty trunks, with the hair still intact on the bear-skin hides. Containing enormous hat boxes for the tall hats of the fifties, a stereoscope of mahogany and pictures for it taken in the sixties, fencing foils, shotgun cases, an old telescope, early side-saddles, dog baskets, linen dancing cloths with rings to fit over the carpets in the drawing room, banjos, guitars, zithers. Doll trunks too, and a doll house replica of the great house itself. All smelling dry and lightly fragrant. The smell of age, not of dust.

A strange place, the attic, with twelve huge closets and the ceiling slanting throughout the length of the house. Strange house. To get to any room you had to walk through every other room of the house. Nine doors leading outside—more than one finds in most public buildings. The both staircases originally built on the outside—a somewhat mad idea. No central hall. A row of three identical double wooden doors placed in the dead center of the grave façade on the ground floor.

And the strange Mr. Persac, the itinerant painter who left a brace of microscopically done wash drawings in black enamel gilt frames on the walls of the reception room where we held our nightly pow-wows. Up and down the country, especially the Teche region, he wandered, just a few years before the War between the States. Making pictures of the great houses and living on the fat of the land. An honest painter who, when the task got beyond his powers, would cut out a figure from a magazine and paste it on the picture. Thus in one of his masterpieces the child standing by the garden gate has disappeared—but the balloon which she held in her hand is still visible. I adore the work of these travelling artists. How infinitely more agreeable and enriching than the life of the present day artist! How much more genuine and congenial their work than the pretentious efforts of our contemporaries! Think of the simple lunch that was served them in the old plantation days. I cull a menu at random from one of Lyle Saxon's books on old Louisiana: "a slice of bread and butter spread with marmalade or guava jelly, accompanied by a slab of jujube paste and washed down with lemonade or orange-flower syrup or tamarind juice." Think of his joy if he had the good fortune to be invited to a ball. I give a description of one culled from the same book:

"... Gorgeous costumes of real lace ... jewels, plumes. The staircase was garlanded in roses for full three flights. Vases on mantels and brackets filled with fragrant flowers ... and gentlemen sampling Scotch or Irish whiskey ... About midnight supper was announced and the hostess led the way to the dining room. On the menu, the cold meats, salads, salamis, galantines quaking in jellied seclusion, and an infinite variety of *à las*, were served from side tables, leaving the huge expanse of carved oak besilvered, belinened and belaced, for flowers trailing from the tall silver *épergne* in the center to the corsage bouquet at each place; fruits, cakes in pyramids or layers or only solid deliciousness, iced and ornamented; custards, pies, jellies, creams, Charlotte Russes or home-concocted sponge cake spread with raspberry jam encircling a veritable Mont Blanc of whipped cream dotted with red cherry stars; towers of nougat or caramel, sherbets and ice creams served in little baskets woven of candied orange peel and topped with sugared rose leaves or violets ... Various wines in cut glass decanters, each with its name carved in the silver grapeleaf suspended from its neck; iced champagne deftly poured by the waiters into gold-traced or Bohemian glasses ... Illuminating the whole were wax candles in crystal chandeliers, and on the table, in silver candelabra . . . More dancing followed supper and at dawn when the guests were leaving a plate of hot gumbo, a cup of strong black coffee and enchanting memories sustained them on the long drive to their abodes." *

Well, Monsieur Persac or Persat, whichever it was, I felicitate you for having had the good fortune to be born in such times! I hope you are chewing the cud of these rich and pleasant memories in the Bardo beyond. When morning comes I shall go down to the reception room and look again at the balloon which is suspended above the gate. If I am in good fettle I will look around for a little child capable of holding such a beautiful balloon and I will paste her back in the picture as I know you would wish me to do. May you rest in peace!

I suppose there is no region in America like the old South for good conversation. Here men talk rather than argue and dispute. Here there are more eccentric, bizarre characters, I imagine, than in any other part of the United States. The South breeds character, not sterile intellectualism. With certain individuals the fact that they are shut off from the world tends to bring about a forced bloom; they radiate power and magnetism, their talk is scintillating and stimulating. They live a rich, quiet life of their own, in harmony with their environment and free of the petty ambitions and rivalries of the man of the world. Usually they did not settle down without a struggle, for most of them possess talents and energies unsuspected by the curious invader. The real Southerner, in my opinion, is more gifted by nature, more far-seeing, more dynamic, more inventive and without a doubt more filled with the zest for life than the man of the North or West. When he elects to retire from the world it is not because of defeatism but because, as with the French and the Chinese, his very love of life instills him with a wisdom

* Courtesy of Miss Louise Butler.

which expresses itself in renunciation. The most difficult adjustment an expatriate has to make, on returning to his native land, is in this realm of conversation. The impression one has, at first, is that there *is* no conversation. We do not talk—we bludgeon one another with facts and theories gleaned from cursory readings of newspapers, magazines and digests. Talk is personal and if of any value must be creative. I had to come to the South before I heard such talk. I had to meet men whose names are unknown, men living in almost inaccessible spots, before I could enjoy what I call a real conversation.

I shall never forget one particular evening, after our friend Rattner had left, when I accompanied Weeks Hall to the home of an old friend of his. The man had given up his house and built himself a little wooden shack in the rear of what was once his home. Not a superfluous object in the place, but everything neat and tidy, as if it were occupied by a sailor. The man's life had been his education. He was a hunter who had temporarily decided to run a truck. I got the impression, after studying him quietly, that he had known great sorrow. He was very mellow, very sure of himself, and obviously reconciled with his lot. His hobby was books. He read widely, as his fancy dictated, seeking neither to improve his knowledge nor merely to kill time. Rather, so I gathered from his remarks, it was a vicarious way of dreaming, of lifting himself out of the world. The conversation originated, I remember, about the poisonous snakes of Louisiana, those with the cat's eye pupils. From that to sassafras and the habits of the Choctaw Indians, then to the various kinds of bamboo—edible and otherwise—and from that to the coral pink moss which is said to be very rare, very beautiful, and grows only on one side of the tree, always the same side too. And then, abruptly switching the conversation, suspecting too that I would receive an interesting response, I asked him point blank

109

if he had read anything about Tibet. "Have I read about Tibet?" he said, pausing to exchange a smile of mutual understanding with his friend. "Why, I've read everything on that subject that I could lay hands on." At this point Weeks Hall got so excited that he had to excuse himself to relieve his bladder. In fact we all got excited and went out to the yard to relieve ourselves.

It's always amazing to me, even though I am prepared for it, to learn that some one is interested in Tibet. I can also say that I have never met any one who *is* deeply interested in the wonders and mysteries of this land with whom I have not established a strong link. Tibet seems to be the countersign for a world-wide community who have this much in common at least—they know that there is something more to life than is summed up in the empirical knowledge of the high priests of logic and science. On the island of Hydra in the Aegean Sea I remember having had a similar experience. Curious, too, how when this subject comes up —it is the same if you should happen to mention Rudolf Steiner's name or Blavatsky's or the Count Saint Germain—a schism immediately takes place and soon there are left in the room only those who are marked, as it were, by the passion for the secret and the obscure. Were a stranger suddenly to enter into the presence of such a gathering he would likely as not find the language employed quite unintelligible. I have had the experience more than once of being understood by some one who scarcely knew English and of not being understood at all by my English-speaking friends. And I have seen a man like Briffault, the author of *Europa*, in whose presence I happened to raise the subject one evening, go into a tantrum at the very mention of the word mysticism.

The conversation left us in an exalted mood. On our way back to "The Shadows" Weeks Hall remarked that he never suspected his friend could be so eloquent. "He's been living alone so long," he said, "that he's grown taciturn. Your visit had an extraordinary effect upon him." I smiled, knowing well that I had nothing to do with it. The experience was simply another proof, to my mind, of the fact that men can always be deeply aroused either by hatred or by touching upon the sense of mystery.

As I was about to go to my room Weeks called me from the studio, the only room he had not yet shown me. "Are you very tired?" he asked. "No, not too tired," I answered. "I've been wanting to show you something," he went on, "I think this is the moment for it." He ushered me into a room that appeared to be hermetically sealed, a room without windows or ventilation of any kind, illuminated only by artificial light. He moved his easel into the center of the room, placed a blank canvas on it, and from what looked like a magic lantern he shot a beam of light on it which threw the projection on the walls. By maneuvering the easel, by expanding and diminishing the frame of the canvas, the colored photograph was made to assume the most astonishing variety of forms and tones. It was like a private séance with Dr. Caligari himself. An ordinary landscape, or a harmless still life, when subjected to these whimsical manipulations, could express the most diversified, the most incongruous and incredible patterns and themes. The walls became a riot of changing color patterns, a sort of colored organ recital, which alternately soothed and stimulated the senses.

"Why should any one paint," he said, "when they can perform these miracles? Perhaps painting isn't all it should be in my life—I don't know. But these things give me pleasure. I can do in five minutes here what it would take me ten years to do in paint. You see, I stopped painting deliberately. It wasn't this arm at all—I smashed that up afterwards, to make sure, as it were—just as people go deaf or blind or insane when they can't stand it any more. I'm not a bad painter, take my word for it. I can still paint with my bad arm—if I really want to. I could have my paintings exhibited, and could probably sell them too, now and then, to museums and private collectors. It's not such a difficult thing, if you have a little talent. In fact, it's too easy, and also too futile. Pictures in an exhibition hall are like wares on a bargain counter. Pictures, if they are to be displayed, should be shown one at a time, at the right time, under the proper conditions. Pictures have no place to-day in the home—the houses are not right. I have the idea that I will never paint again with conviction unless the painting is for some purpose, and the easel picture is for no purpose except to collect a bunch of vapid compliments. It's like an artificial bait with which to catch a tarpon. In itself the easel picture is nil: it doesn't feed one. Just a bait for complacency . . . Listen, I think I said something there—remember that, will you?

"Of course," he went on, "a fellow like Rattner is different. He just had to paint—he was born to it. But for one like him there are a thousand who might just as well be carpentering or driving a truck. The difference, I suppose, is between procreation and creation—a difference of nine months. In the case of the creator it means a life's work—unceasing labor, study, observation—not just to make *a* picture, or even a hundred pictures, but to understand the relation between painting, between all arts, I might say, and living. To put your whole life into a canvas, into every canvas you do. It's the highest form of consecration, and our good friend Abe has it. Whether he's happy or not, I don't know. I don't suppose happiness means as much to an artist as to ordinary folk. . . ."

He lit a fresh cigarette. Paced nervously back and forth. He wanted to say something . . . he wanted to say a lot of things . . . *everything*, if I would only be patient and not run away. He began again, haltingly, clumsily, feeling his way like a man groping through a dark and winding passage.

"Look, this arm!" and he held it out for me to look at intently. "Smashed. Smashed for good. A terrible thing. One moment you have an arm there, the next moment it's a pulpy mess. I suppose the truth is that it was only good for the derrick-use which other arms are good for. This arm was perhaps too slick, too clever; it made me paint like a gambler deals and shuffles the cards. Perhaps my mind is too slick and too brittle. Not disciplined enough. And I know I won't improve it by my mania for research. That's just a pretext to forestall the day when I must really begin to paint. I know all that—but what are you going to do? Here I am living alone in a big house, a place which overwhelms me. The house is too much for me. I want to live in one room somewhere, without all these cares and responsibilities which I seem to have assumed from my forbears. How am I going to do it? Shutting myself up in this room is no solution. Even if I can't see them or hear them I know there are people outside clamoring to get in. And perhaps I *ought* to see them, talk to them, listen to them, worry about what they're worrying about. How should I know? After all they're not all fools. Maybe if I were the man I'd like to be I wouldn't have to set foot outside this door—the world would come to me. Maybe I'd paint under the worst conditions—perhaps right out there in the garden with all the sightseers crowding around me and asking me a thousand and one irrelevant questions. Who knows but that, if I were deadly in earnest, they would let me alone, leave me in peace, without saying a word to them? Somehow people always recognize value. Take Swedenborg, for example. He never locked his door. People came and when they saw him they went away quietly, reverently, unwilling to disturb him though they had travelled, some of them, thousands of miles to ask him for help and guidance." With his good hand he took hold of the smashed arm and gazed at it, as though it belonged to some other person. "Can one change one's own nature—that's the question? Well, eventually this arm may act as the pole does for the tight-rope walker. *The balance*— if we don't have it within we've got to find it without. I'm glad you came here . . . you've done me a world of good. God, when I was listening to you all talk about Paris I realized all I had missed these years. You won't find anything much in New Orleans, except the past. We've got *one* painter—that's Dr. Souchon. I want you to meet him. . . . I guess it's pretty late. You want to go to bed, don't you? I could talk all night, of course. I don't need much sleep. And since you all came here I can't sleep at all. I have a thousand questions to ask. I want to make up for all the time I've lost."

I had difficulty myself in going to sleep. It seemed cruel to leave a man stranded like that on a peak of exaltation. Rattner had prepared me for his exuberance and vitality, but not for his inexhaustible hunger. This hunger of his touched me deeply. He was a man who knew no stint. He gave just as recklessly and abundantly as he demanded. He was an artist to the finger-tips, no doubt about that. And his problems were no ordinary ones. He had probed too deeply. Fame and success would mean nothing to a man like that. He was in search of something which eluded all definition. Already, in certain domains, he had amassed the knowledge of a savant. And what was more, he saw the relatedness of all things. Naturally he could not be content in executing a masterful painting. He wanted to revolutionize things. He wanted to bring painting back to its original estate—painting for painting's sake. In a sense it might be said of him that he had already completed his great work. He had transformed the house and grounds, through his passion for creation, into one of the most distinctive pieces of art which America can boast of. He was living and breathing in his own masterpiece, not knowing it, not realizing the extent and sufficiency of it. By his enthusiasm and generosity he had inspired other painters to do their work—had given birth to them, one might say. And still he was restless, longing to express himself surely and completely. I admired him and pitied him, both. I felt his presence all through the house, flooding it like some powerful magic fluid. He had created that which in turn would recreate him. That hermetically sealed studio—what was it in fact if not a symbolic expression of his own locked-in self? The studio could never contain him, any more than the house itself; he had outgrown the place, overflowed the bounds. He was a self-convicted prisoner inhabiting the aura of his own creation. Some day he would awaken, free himself of the snares and delusions which had gathered in the wake of creation. Some day he would look around and realize that he was free; then he would be able to decide calmly and quietly whether to remain or to go. I hoped that he would remain, that as the last link in the ancestral chain he would close the circle and by realizing the significance of his act expand the circle and circumference of his life to infinite dimensions.

When I took leave of him a day or two later I had the impression, from the look he gave me, that he had come to this conclusion himself. I left knowing that I would always find him at a moment's notice anywhere any time.

"No need to telephone me in the middle of the night, Weeks. As long as you remain centered I am at your side eternally. No need to say good-bye or good luck! Just continue being what you are. May peace be with you!"

DR. SOUCHON: SURGEON-PAINTER

ONE OF THE things which impresses me about America, as I travel about, is that the men of promise, the men of joyous wisdom, the men who inspire hope in this most dismal period of our history, are either boys hardly out of their teens or else boys of seventy or over.

In France the old men, especially if of peasant stock, are a joy and an inspiration to behold. They are like great trees which no storm can dislodge; they radiate peace, serenity and wisdom. In America the old men are as a rule a sorry sight, particularly the successful ones who have prolonged their existence far beyond the natural term by means of artificial respiration, so to speak. They are horrible living examples of the embalmer's art, walking cadavers manipulated by a retinue of handsomely paid hirelings who are a disgrace to their profession.

The exceptions to the rule—and the contrast is abysmal—are the artists, and by artists I mean the creators, regardless of their field of operation. Most of them began to develop, to reveal their individuality, after passing the age of forty-five, the age which most industrial corporations in this country have fixed as the dead line. It must be admitted in passing, of course, that the average worker who has functioned from adolescence as a robot is about ready for the scrap-heap at that age. And what is true of the ordinary robot is largely true of the master robot, the so-called captain of industry. Only his wealth permits him to nourish and sustain the feeble, flickering flame. So far as true vitality goes, beyond forty-five we are a nation of derelicts.

But there is a class of hardy men, old-fashioned enough to have remained rugged individuals, openly contemptuous of the trend, passionately devoted to their work, impossible to bribe or seduce, working long hours, often without reward or fame, who are motivated by a common impulse—the joy of doing as they please. At some point along the way they separated from the others. The men I speak of can be detected at a glance: their countenance registers something far more vital, far more effective, than the lust for power. They do not seek to dominate, but to realize themselves. They operate from a center which is at rest. They evolve, they grow, they give nourishment just by being what they are.

This subject, the relationship between wisdom and vitality, interests me because, contrary to the general opinion, I have never been able to look upon America as young and vital but rather as prematurely old, as a fruit which rotted before it had a chance to ripen. The word which gives the key to the national vice is waste. And people who are wasteful are not wise, neither can they remain young and vigorous. In order to transmute energy to higher and more subtle levels one must first conserve it. The prodigal is soon spent, a victim of the very forces he has so foolishly and recklessly toyed with. Even machines have to be handled skilfully in order to obtain from them the maximum results. Unless, as is the case in America, we produce them in such quantities that we can afford to scrap them before they have grown old and worthless. But when it comes to scrapping human beings it is another story. Human beings can not be turned out like machines. There is a curious correlation between fecundity and the scrap-heap. The desire to procreate seems to die when the period of usefulness is fixed at the early age of forty-five.

Few are those who can escape the tread-mill. Merely to survive, in spite of the set-up, confers no distinction. Animals and insects survive when higher types are threatened with extinction. To live beyond the pale, to work for the pleasure of working, to grow old gracefully while retaining one's faculties, one's enthusiasms, one's self-respect, one has to establish other values than those endorsed by the mob. It takes an artist to make this breach in the wall. An artist is primarily one who has faith in himself. He does not respond to the normal stimuli: he is neither a drudge nor a parasite. He lives to express himself and in so doing enriches the world.

The man I am thinking of at the moment, Dr. Marion Souchon of New Orleans, is not altogether typical. He is, in fact, a curious anomaly and for that reason all the more interesting to me. A man of seventy now, a successful and distinguished surgeon, he began painting seriously at the age of sixty. Nor did he abandon his practice in doing so. Fifty years ago, when he began to study medicine, following in his father's footsteps, he inaugurated for himself a

Spartan regimen which he has adhered to ever since. A regimen, I must say, which enables him to do the work of three or four men and yet leaves him full of vitality and optimism. It is his custom to rise at five, to breakfast lightly and go to the operating room, then to his office where he performs the administrative duties of an officer in an insurance company, answer his mail, receive patients, visit the hospitals and so on. By lunch time he has already done a hard day's work. For the past ten years now he has contrived to find a little time each day to do his painting, to see the work of other painters, to converse with them, to study his métier as would a young man of twenty just embarking on his career. He does not leave his office to go to a studio—he paints in his office. In the corner of a small room lined with books and statuary stands an object which looks like a covered musical instrument. The moment he is left alone he goes to this object, opens it, and sets to work; all his painting paraphernalia is contained in this mysterious-looking black musical box. When the light fails he continues by artificial light. Sometimes he has an hour to spend this way, sometimes four or five. He can turn at a moment's notice from the easel to the performance of a delicate surgical operation. No mean accomplishment, and for the artist a procedure, to say the least, rather unorthodox.

When I asked him if he had not thought of making painting his sole pursuit, especially now that he had only a few years before him, he said that he had rejected the idea because "I must have one other occupation in order to vary the great pleasure of working and of never tiring." Later, after I had visited him a number of times, I made bold to restate the question. It didn't seem possible to me that a man who was as passionate about painting as he and who, moreover, was obviously trying to crowd the work of twenty years into four or five, could not have some sort of problem over this dual or multiple life. If he had been a bad painter, or a bad surgeon, if he had been a master at one and a dabbler at the other, I would not have bothered to pursue the subject. But he is acknowledgedly one of the great surgeons of the day, and as for his painting there is no question, especially in the opinion of other estimable artists, that he is a serious artist whose work is growing more important day by day, improving with a celerity that is astonishing. Finally he confessed to me that he was beginning to realize that "this thing called paint is a soul-stirring, brain-twisting, time-absorbing, all-exacting something which monopolizes one's whole being and eventually transcends all other interests." "Yes," he added reflectively, "I must admit that it has disturbed the pattern of my life, has started me afresh on a new journey."

That was what I wanted to hear. Had he not admitted this I should have held quite a different opinion of him. As to his reasons for continuing his other life, that I feel is none of my business.

"If you had your life to live over again," I asked him, "would it be quite different from the one we know? Would you, let us say, have given art the first place instead of medicine?"

"I would do exactly the same thing over again," he replied without a moment's hesitation. "Surgery was my destiny. My father was a surgeon of note, and a wonderful example of his profession. Surgery is science and art combined, and for that reason it satisfied, for the time being, the urge for art."

I was curious to know if his preoccupation with paint had sharpened his interest in the metaphysical aspects of life.

"I will answer you in this way," he said. "Since life in all its human aspects has been my life work, painting has only been an enlargement of that sphere. Whatever success I may have had as a physician I attribute to my knowledge of human nature. I have treated people's minds as much as their bodies. Painting, you see, is very much akin to the practice of medicine. Though they both treat with the physical, by far the greater influence and power is psychic. The word picture to the patient is much the same as color, line and form to the painter; it is almost incredible how much a mere word or dot or line can mould and influence the life of an individual. Is it not so?"

There was another discovery which I made in the course of our discussion that confirmed my intuitions, and that was that from childhood he had had the desire to paint and draw. In his twenties he amused himself by doing water colors. After a lapse of almost thirty years he took to sculpturing figures in clay and wood. Examples of this latter diversion were scattered about his tiny office, all of them historical figures whom he had become enamored of in the course of his wide reading. It was another illustration of his passion and thoroughness. In preparation for a great tour of the world he had begun to read history and biography. Owing to circumstances beyond his control the trip was aborted, but the books which lined the walls and which he had read with ardor and diligence testified to that habitual passion with which he flings himself into everything.

Such men, I thought to myself, when I left his office that evening, are the nearest approach in the lay world to the sages and saints. Like the latter they practise concentration, meditation and devotion. They are absolutely single-minded in their consecration to a task; their work, which is pure and uncompromising, is the prayerful offering which they make each day to the Creator. It is only in the realm or medium in which they operate that they differ from the great religious figures.

The meeting with Dr. Souchon I owe to Weeks Hall of New Iberia. He has been the sponsor and champion, and in a subtle way his guide and mentor, from the very beginning of the doctor's artistic career. The meeting took place fifteen minutes after my friend Rattner and myself had arrived in New Orleans. Our luggage was in the car standing at the curb; we had not even begun to look for a room when the opportunity presented itself. It was in the late afternoon when we arrived at his office in the Whitney Building. He had undoubtedly already put in a big day's work. One would never have thought so from the way in which he received us. His very presence was electrifying. With that clear mind and conscience of the man who has performed his duties to the utmost he put himself completely at our service, alert and attentive to our least wishes.

The way in which he greeted my friend Rattner was for me a memorable event, a tribute to Dr. Souchon's greatness of soul. "I've been waiting to see you for twenty years!" he exclaimed as he drew Rattner to him in a cordial embrace. "I've followed your work ever since I first learned of you. I know all your pictures by heart—I've lived with them for years. What a painter you are! God, if I had had your talent, your eye, where would I not be now?" He went on at this rate, deluging Rattner with compliments, all of them humbly and profoundly sincere. "You've got to tell me things," he said. "I have hundreds of questions to put to you. How long are you going to stay in New Orleans? Will you look at my work? Will you tell me if I am on the right track?" And so on, one burst of enthusiasm after another, like a young boy in the presence of a great and loving master.

Rattner, who is the personification of modesty and who, in this country at least, is more used to hearing his work denigrated and ridiculed, was confused and embarrassed. I don't suppose that he had ever received such frank, warm, unstinted praise, especially from a fellow artist. Nor, as is usually the case with artists, did Dr. Souchon follow up his glowing words of tribute by dwelling on the things he disliked in Rattner's painting. On the contrary, he took advantage of the occasion to profit as much as possible from the latter's sure knowledge and wide experience. He was the personification of humility and deference, the mark, I repeat, of a truly great soul. Though proud of his own work, he has no illusions about his worth. In fact, considering the bold assurance with which he tackles every problem he confronts, I was rather surprised that, in displaying his canvases, he should have exhibited the timidity and perplexity which he did. But in art as in medicine, apparently, he retains the faculty of preserving an open mind. His ego, which is by no means eclipsed, is completely subordinated to the task it must serve. He proceeds directly to his goal, like a monomaniac on roller skates. He inquires as to the laws which govern things. He is the first to acknowledge his limitations. When I asked him during a pause whom he admired most among the great historical figures of the world, he answered readily—"Moses." *Why?* "Because the Ten Commandments are the basis of the laws of the civilized world, and also the foundation of all religions."

At the first sitting we saw perhaps a dozen representative canvases, sufficient to establish in my own mind the fact that, Rattner apart and excepting that great wizard John Marin, here was the most joyous, vital, interesting painter in America. The evolution from the early pictures, conventional, murky, faltering, was lightning-like. Those who may have seen his work a few years ago at the Julien Levy Gallery in New York cannot possibly conceive of the strides he has made since then, particularly in the realm of color. Had Dr. Souchon been content to remain an amateur, as George Biddle erroneously distinguished him at that time, he would always have pleased and enchanted the dilettantes who frequent the art galleries. The passing craze for American primitives is but a reflection of the snobbish, light-hearted attitude of those Americans who "go in for painting", who seek to be titivated and amused but never shocked or disturbed by paint. Dr. Souchon is not a primitive and never was, except that like our "popular masters of reality" he reveals a sincerity, a passion, a daring, as well as a candor and simplicity, which only the unaccepted ones seem capable of exhibiting. As with their work also, there runs through Dr. Souchon's canvases a strong vein of humor and fantasy, enhanced by a total disregard for political and sociological theories. Like them again he paints largely from remembrance, from a wealth of rich experiences, visions, dreams, which upon being released after years of confinement in the attic of his being, assume the qualities which only the genuine products of the imagination possess. If he is an instinctivist he is certainly not a barbarian or a gorilla. When he is most natural and uninhibited he is most sensitive and profound. In those canvases which reveal the least influences Dr. Souchon comes nearest to situating himself in the great tradition of European art. Though he confesses to admiring Cézanne most, among the modern painters, his work in my humble opinion bears no resemblance whatever to the spirit of that untiring gray genius. Those who have obviously influenced him are such as Van Gogh, Toulouse-Lautrec, Rouault, Matisse, Seurat, Gauguin, and I should add, in the domain of color, Abe Rattner. Had he not been born a Creole, had he never been to France, had he never concerned himself with the history of other epochs, Dr. Souchon would still have been a suave, cultured individual alive and sensitive to all the civilizing influences of our day. His vitality and enthusiasm are due to his boundless curiosity. He remains young, fresh, gay, insouciant because he looks to the future, not the past. And because each day he accomplishes that which he sets out to do. He starts each day with a clean slate. It is not singular therefore that he has never met with failure of any kind. Even his paint-

"The Roof," a painting by Dr. Marion Souchon

ing brought about immediate recognition, though there was every possibility of incurring ridicule and contempt.

Never shall I forget a gesture which he made at the dinner table one evening when this subject of "success" was broached. Some one had endeavored to elicit from him a more explicit formulation of his phenomenal success. By way of answer he raised his two hands to his lips and kissing them reverently he said: *"Je dois tout à celles-ci."* Though it was really not an answer the gesture revealed the humility and impersonality so characteristic of the artist who works with his hands. At the moment he was thinking of his deft surgeon's skill, acquired through long and arduous apprenticeship. But that ability to use his hands and fingers with extraordinary finesse was also indicative of an even more interesting mental attitude, namely, the conviction which seized him as a young man that to make his way in the world he must rely upon his own powers, upon the strength and skill, in short, of his own two hands.

There was another incident in connection with this dinner which pleased me beyond words. When the waiter came round with the menus Dr. Souchon turned to us and said: "Put those things away, please—don't look at them. Just tell me what you would like to eat; you can have anything you want." I don't recall anybody ever having said a thing like that to me before. It had a regal ring and even if I had ordered something abominable I am sure it would have tasted delicious coming after that exhortation. I made a resolve then and there that if the day should ever come when I could afford to forget the price of food I would be just as indulgent with myself as he had been with us. I've always had the desire to step into a taxi and say to the driver: "Just drive around a bit, I don't know where I want to go yet." Must give one a beautiful feeling of ease and assurance.

Of course the New Orleans people are extremely hospitable.

125

The meals I had there at private homes are memorable. It is the most congenial city in America that I know of and it is due in large part, I believe, to the fact that here at last on this bleak continent the sensual pleasures assume the importance which they deserve. It is the only city in America where, after a lingering meal accompanied by good wine and good talk, one can stroll at random through the French Quarter and feel like a civilized human being.

After the dinner I speak of Dr. Souchon left us in the hands of his good friend Charles Gresham who conducts an interesting little art gallery on Royal Street. In showing us through the Quarter Gresham acted like a man who was seeing it himself for the first time in many a year. His love for this miniature world of the past reminded me forcibly of my own conducted tours through the streets of Paris in the period before I became fed up with such adventures. He seemed to know every inch of the way by heart, as only a man would who walks the streets night after night probing deeper and deeper into the secret layers of the past. Pausing a moment or two at a crossing, to permit him to finish a story he was relating, I suddenly lost interest in what he was saying because of the vivid remembrance of an almost identical setting one evening when I was guiding an American through the heart of the Latin Quarter. I say guiding him, but as a matter of fact the man was guiding me. It was his first visit to Paris—he was on his way to Manila at the time—and he had just this one evening to spend in Paris. It was the strangest tour of the city I ever made. The man had told me at dinner that he was writing a play on the French Revolution and that in the course of his researches he had studied the map so thoroughly that he was convinced he could lead me through the streets like a veritable Parisian. As a matter of fact he knew the city, it soon turned out, better than the ordinary Parisian. But it was a dead city which he was wandering through. He hardly seemed to notice the actual, living Paris which greeted his eyes at every turn. His observations were accompanied by dates and figures which belonged to the musty pages of books. I must confess, never did Paris seem so lifeless and uninteresting as through the eyes of this historical zealot. When we got to the rear of Notre Dame, a spot which at night usually silences even the most garrulous idiot, and when to my dismay he was still raving about the dead puppets of the French Revolution, I informed him that I was too tired to continue farther and we parted there in a cool and nonchalant manner. It may be that a man can write a thrilling historical drama without even visiting the locale of his selection, but a man who can be impervious to the drama of the living street, who walks through the present seeing only the past, has about as much attraction for me as a guide book to Vienna would have if I were living in Sierra Leone.

At the next session in Dr. Souchon's office my appreciation of his work increased. Again we saw a dozen or more canvases, ranging over a period of five or six years. The talk with Gresham seemed to have freshened my vision. That stroll through the French Quarter the night before had brought to life the Louisiana whose splendor is still smouldering. Standing in Jackson Park, whose ambiance is unique in America, I suddenly realized why the place held such a fascination for me. That row of apartment houses which flanks the park—the first apartments in America, I was told—why, they were strangely reminiscent of those little hotels which enclose the spot I love most in Paris—the Place des Vosges. Near the one is the famous French Market; near the other is the Bastille. Both breathe an air of quiet and seclusion, and both are but a stone's throw away from the pullulating life of the common people. Nothing could be more aristocratic than the atmosphere of the Place des Vosges, situated in the very heart of the Faubourg St. Antoine. Jackson

Park has very much the same flavor. It hardly seems to belong to America.

It is the same with Dr. Souchon's paintings as with the whole atmosphere of Louisiana—it is American and it is not American. Many of his pictures might have been the work of a contemporary French artist. Not in subject matter, but in feeling and approach. There is something wise and gay in all of them, something which at times comes close to the great Nature spirit of the Chinese painters. Something which revives in one the thought that "we are near awakening when we dream that we dream." How utterly remote, these imaginings of his, from the pallid, sterile stylizations of a Grant Wood or the convulsive, Neanderthal efforts of a Thomas Benton! What a slick, barren, imitative world of art American painting is! Except for the primitives, except for that wizard John Marin whose presence among us is a miraculous phenomenon, what is there of value or meaning to single out amidst the muck of canvases which we manufacture like candle-sticks? Where is the vision, the individuality, the courage and daring which the "effete" Europeans display? Where is our Picasso, our Van Gogh, our Cézanne, our Matisse or Braque—or even a simple, honest Utrillo? Could we ever give birth to a Rouault, or a Paul Klee, to say nothing of those giants out of the past from Italy, Spain, Holland, Belgium, Germany, France and so on? To such questions one always receives the same response—*we are still a young country!* For how many centuries to come are we going to lean back on that crutch? Think of what the Buddha accomplished in a lifetime. Think of what the Arabs accomplished in a few decades after the appearance of Mahomet. Think of the unparalleled cluster of geniuses born to Greece in the space of a century. In no instance did the genius of a people wait until the political and economic life had been arranged in Utopian fashion. The condition of the masses, in any period we choose to select, has always been deplorable. In fact, I think I am safe in saying that the greatest periods of art have coincided with the periods of greatest misery and suffering on the part of the common people. If one quarter of the American people are to-day living on a level of subsistence far below the norm, there remain nevertheless a hundred million who enjoy comforts and advantages unknown to men in any period of the past. What is to hinder them from revealing their talents? Or is it that our talents lie in other directions? Is it that the great goal of American manhood is to become the successful business man? Or just a "success", regardless of what form or shape, what purpose or significance, success manifests itself in and through? There is no doubt in my mind that art comes last in the things of life which preoccupy us. The young man who shows signs of becoming an artist is looked upon as a crackpot, or else as a lazy, worthless encumbrance. He has to follow his inspiration at the cost of starvation, humiliation and ridicule. He can earn a living at his calling only by producing the kind of art which he despises. If he is a painter the surest way for him to survive is to make stupid portraits of even more stupid people, or sell his services to the advertising monarchs who, in my opinion, have done more to ruin art than any other single factor I know of. Take the murals which adorn the walls of our public buildings—most of them belong in the realm of commercial art. Some of them, in technique and conception, are even below the aesthetic level of the Arrow collar artist. The great concern has been to please the public, a public whose taste has been vitiated by Maxfield Parrish chromos and posters conceived with only one idea, "to put it over".

Had Dr. Marion Souchon brought forth these paintings of his at twenty-five or thirty, had he been dependent on his art for a living, he would most likely have been starved and kicked around like a soft football. The critics would have laughed at his work and advised him to go to an academy and learn how to draw; the dealers would have told him to wait another ten years. Part of his success —no fault of his, mind you!—is attributable to the fact that he could be exploited as a freak and a sensation. That is the way in which the American primitives are handled to-day—a sort of burlesque performance in paint for the hoi polloi. Yet there are canvases by these same freaks and monsters which no American artist has yet rivalled in quality, conception and execution. The same is true of the work of the insane in our lunatic asylums: many of these canvases are unapproachable by our academic masters.

In one of our Federal penitentiaries the Irish priest who showed me about the chapel pointed out the stained glass windows done by one of the convicts—as if it were a huge joke. What he admired were the cigar box illustrations of the Bible executed by convicts who "knew how to paint," as he put it. When I told him bluntly that I did not share his viewpoint, when I began to talk reverently and enthusiastically about the humble but sincere efforts of the man who had done the windows, he confessed that he knew nothing about art. All he understood was that the one man knew how to draw and the other didn't. "Is that what makes a man an artist, knowing how to draw arms and legs, knowing how to make a human face and put a hat properly on a man's head—is that it?" I asked him. He scratched his head in perplexity. Evidently the question had never entered his head before. "What is the fellow doing now?" I inquired, meaning the one who had done the windows. "*Him?* Oh, we're teaching him to copy pictures from magazines." "How is he getting on?" "He doesn't take any interest in it," said the priest. "He doesn't seem to care to learn."

Idiot! I thought to myself. Even in prison they try to ruin the artist. The only thing in the whole penitentiary which interested me was these stained glass windows. It was the one manifestation of the human spirit free of cruelty, ignorance and perversion. And they had taken this free spirit, a devout, humble man, a man who loved his work, and they were trying to transform him into an educated jackass. Progress and enlightenment! Making a good convict into a potential Guggenheim prize winner! Pfui!

"I hate to think what the artist without means has to go through!" said Dr. Souchon. "There is no worse hell that I can think of." Like every other big city in America New Orleans is full of starving or half-starved artists. The quarter which they inhabit is being steadily demolished and pulverized by the big guns of the vandals and barbarians from the industrial world. We rail about the vandalism of the Huns, our erstwhile enemy, the Germans, and yet in our own midst, in the last architectural refuge of America, the garden spot of a world which we wrecked with our own hands, the insidious work of destruction continues. At the rate we are going, in another hundred years or so there will be scarcely a trace or evidence on this continent of the only culture we have been able to produce—the rich slave culture of the South. New Orleans worships the past, but it watches impassively as the barbarians of the future bury the past cynically and ruthlessly. When the beautiful French Quarter is no more, when every link with the past is destroyed, there will be the clean, sterile office buildings, the hideous monuments and public buildings, the oil wells, the smokestacks, the air ports, the jails, the lunatic asylums, the charity hospitals, the bread lines, the gray shacks of the colored people, the bright tin lizzies, the stream-lined trains, the tinned food products, the drug stores, the Neon-lit shop windows to inspire the artist to paint. *Or*, what is more likely, persuade him to commit suicide. Few men will have the guts to wait until they are sixty before picking up the brush. Fewer still will

131

have the chance to become a surgeon. When a noted dentist has the audacity to say that for the working man teeth—one's own teeth —are an economic luxury, what are we coming to? Soon the physicians and surgeons will be saying: "Why try to preserve life when there is nothing to live for?" Soon, out of sheer human kindness, they will be banding together to form a euthanasia society to do away with all those who are unfit for the terrors of modern life. The battlefield, together with the industrial field, will provide them with all the patients they can handle. The artist, like the Indian, may become the ward of the government; he may be allowed to putter around in desultory fashion simply because, as with the Indian, we have not the heart to kill him outright. Or perhaps only after he has performed "useful service" to society will he be permitted to practice his art. It seems to me we are coming to some such impasse. Only the work of dead men seems to have any appeal for us, or any value. The wealthy can always be induced to support another museum; the academies can always be counted upon to provide us with watch-dogs and hyenas; the critics can always be bought who will kill what is fresh and vital; the educators can always be rallied who will misinform the young as to the meaning of art; the vandals can always be instigated to destroy what is powerful and disturbing. The poor can think of nothing but food and rent problems; the rich can amuse themselves by collecting safe investments furnished them by the ghouls who traffic in the sweat and blood of artists; the middle classes pay admission to gape and criticize, vain about their half-baked knowledge of art and too timid to champion the men whom in their hearts they fear, knowing that the real enemy is not the man above, whom they must toady to, but the rebel who exposes in word or paint the rottenness of the edifice which they, the spineless middle class, are obliged to support. The only artists at present who are being handsomely rewarded for their toil are the

132

mountebanks; these include not only the imported variety but the native sons who are skilled in raising a cloud of dust when real issues are at stake.

The man who wants to paint not what he sees but what he feels has no place in our midst. He belongs in jail or in the lunatic asylum. Unless, as in the case of Dr. Souchon, he can prove his sanity and integrity by thirty or forty years of service to humanity in the role of surgeon.

Such is the state of art in America to-day. How long will it endure? Perhaps the war is a blessing in disguise. Perhaps, after we have gone through another blood bath, we will give heed to the men who seek to arrange life in other terms than greed, rivalry, hatred, death and destruction. Perhaps. . . . *Qui vivra verra*, as the French say.

ARKANSAS AND THE GREAT PYRAMID

ARKANSAS is a great State. It *must* be, otherwise De Soto, who discovered about everything there was to be discovered in the Southwest, would have passed it by, ignored it. Ninety years before the Pilgrims landed at Plymouth the Spaniards, who were also white men, it seems, penetrated this land. After De Soto's death a hundred years passed before white men again set foot in the territory which was to be admitted to the Union as a State only as late as 1836. There were about 60,000 people then in the whole State. To-day its population numbers 2,000,000. Arkansas fought on the side of the Confederacy, another point in its favor! In Little Rock one can still see the Old State Capitol, built in 1836, one of the most exquisite pieces of architecture in America. To appreciate it fully one has to see the monstrosity in Des Moines. Will Rogers, that great American figure whose stature is now beginning to rival that of Mark Twain or Abe Lincoln, thought well enough of Arkansas to pick a wife from the town which bears his name. There are all sorts of facts and figures about Arkansas to lend it distinction. I will pass over such as the following—that the largest watermelons in the world, some of them weighing 160 pounds, are grown at Hope; that the only diamond mine in the United States is to be found near Murfreesboro in the south-west corner of the State; that the world's largest peach orchard (17,000 acres, with one and a half million trees) is also to be found here; that Mississippi county is the largest cotton producing county in the world; that 99% of the inhabitants of this State are of pure pioneer American stock, most of them having migrated from the Appalachian mountains; that in a log cabin, now a museum, about two miles south of Mt. Gaylor, Albert Pike once taught school. I glide over these interesting items to dwell at some length on two men, now dead, whom many Americans have possibly never heard of: Brigadier-General Albert Pike, one time Sovereign Grand Commander of the Ancient and Accepted Scottish Rite of Freemasonry of the Southern Jurisdiction, U.S.A. and "Coin" (William Hope) Harvey, builder of the Pyramid which was never built at Monte Ne, Arkansas.

It was at Judge McHaney's home in Little Rock that I first heard of "Coin" Harvey, the sobriquet "Coin" having been given him because of his association with William Jennings Bryan when the latter was advocating "free silver." Harvey by all accounts was one of those eccentric, independent, free-thinking men who have the courage of their convictions—a type now fast becoming extinct in America. He had made quite a fortune, it appears, through the sale

135

of a book (a little greenback book, illustrated, 224 pages, price 25¢) which he had written and entitled *The Book* (sic). The book had to do with the effect of usury "on the organism of governments since the birth of this civilization down to the present time and the destructive effect of a financial system based on usury (Usury always in capital letters!) in the United States, and in the world." In the early 1930's Harvey called a convention in order to organize a New Political Party, having lost all faith in either of the two old political parties. In a sheet called "The Bugle Call", which sold for 25¢ a year, there is an interesting report of The Impromptu National Committee which suffered a still-birth, if I am not mistaken. Harvey was of the opinion that the spot selected for the meeting of the National Convention of his new party should be centrally located *west* of the Mississippi River. Rather significant, it seems to me, and indicative of the ever-increasing schism between the East and the West in these United States. As to the credentials of the delegates to the Convention, Harvey had a rather original idea. "An application to join any fraternity, any organization, or perform duties under the Civil Service rules requires an examination," he explained in "The Bugle Call". "There will be no time for the examination of those applying to enter the Convention as delegates; and yet, it is practical to substitute in lieu of an examination a signed statement showing that the applicant is informed and has knowledge of those things which a personal examination would cover." So Harvey had the brilliant idea that the said delegates, in lieu of an examination, should read his book, *The Book*, and thus make themselves eligible. "It is the only book to our knowledge," he sets forth, "containing this historical data (about Usury and the rise and fall of civilizations); if the applicant has read *The Book* it is convincing proof that he is in possession of a knowledge that in this respect entitles him to admission in the Convention."

136

Needless to say, the Convention was a flop. But I don't in the least think that "Coin" Harvey was a flop even though his name is already forgotten and the great idea of The Pyramid smothered between the musty pages of a 25¢ booklet called "The Pyramid Booklet". As a result of a chance meeting in Rogers with an obliging Arkansas gentleman, I managed after some digging to acquire one of the three or four existent copies of this extraordinary document. I shall draw liberally on the text of this booklet to explain Harvey's project which, I must add, was partially realized, though the Pyramid itself was never erected.

I visited the site of the project early one morning of a balmy Spring day. The feeling I carried away with me was that Harvey was by no means a fool, a crack-pot, or an idle dreamer. With it there came the somewhat saddening thought that perhaps a hundred years from now the purpose and significance of this aborted undertaking will assume its true importance.

What was the purpose of the Pyramid? I quote his own words: "The purpose of the Pyramid is to attract the attention of the people of the world to the fact that civilizations have come and gone attended with untold suffering to hundreds of millions of people, and that this one is now in danger—on the verge of going. This signal warning that the Pyramid heralds to the world, it is hoped, will set the people thinking and arouse them to an unselfish consciousness of the steps to be taken to save and perfect this civilization. If this is not done, quickly, before utter confusion sets in, time will, in the unlettered language of oblivion and savagery, write an epitaph on the tomb of this civilization."

"When the Pyramid is completed," he adds, "the intention is to erect a broadcasting station and to get and keep in touch with the world, having always in view the thought of arousing the practical, thinking people of the world to the making of a perfect civilization."

137

Harvey had originally intended to finance the Pyramid himself, but after sinking $10,000.00 into the fund he became financially embarrassed and called for volunteer contributions. Sums ranging from one dollar to fifty dollars were received from all parts of the world, totalling, at the time he wrote the booklet, about $1,000.00. The cost of the Pyramid when completed and sealed up was estimated to be about $75,000.00.

The thing which impressed Harvey and which spurred him on was the fact that, as he puts it, "there is no other undiscovered country to which to flee! Truth and Falsehood, Good and Evil, God and Satan are now face to face in all the world in a deadly conflict. It is the same crisis that came to other civilizations that went down! Individual selfishness crystallized into the laws of nations has destroyed democracies and republics and is the mother of monarchies and despotism. Selfishness uncontrolled is a consuming fire that eats like a cancer at the vitals of governments, bringing with it corruption, prejudices, vanity, a runted, ill fed, and an anaemic race. How are we to meet this crisis? How are the people of the world to meet this crisis?"

The Pyramid was to have been 130 feet high, resting on a base 40 feet square. To the north of it was to be a concrete foyer or terrace capable of seating about a thousand people. At its base, in a lake of cold, clear water, a concrete island equipped with cement furniture was actually built. An expert from the Portland Cement Association gave it as his opinion that, when a water proof finish had been applied to the surface, "the Pyramid would last a million years and longer—indefinitely."

Monte Ne, the site of the project, is situated at the edge of a valley at the end of a spur. Harvey, realizing that the Ozarks by the process of erosion had already been lowered from 14,000 to 1,400 feet, took the precaution of choosing his site at a point where the distance to the top of the mountain was only about 240 feet. "If," he writes, "by process of erosion the valley is filled in and the mountains about it lowered in the long time to come, the Pyramid, at the height of 130 feet, will be visible sticking out of the ground. Geologically, it is figured a certainty that there is no danger from earthquake or volcanic action in these mountains. So the Pyramid is safe to endure for all time."

On top of the shaft in the most enduring metal known there was to be placed a plate containing the following inscription: "When this can be read, go below and find a record of and the cause of the death of a former Civilization."

Similar plates were to have been placed on the exterior wall of the two vaults and the room, except that "go below" would be changed to "go within". In the large room at the base of the shaft and in the two vaults there were to be placed copies of "a book giving the rise and growth of this civilization, dangers threatening its overthrow, and a symposium of opinions as to the cause of its threatened impending death. It will be a leather bound book of probably 300 pages or more printed on paper on which a paper expert in New York City will pass, and each page of the book will be covered with transparent paper that is now made for such purpose, through which one can readily read, thus preserving the ink from fading. When the Pyramid is completed, except for the closing of the entrance to the room and two vaults, it will be given a year to dry. And during that year (sic) the book will be written and three volumes printed and prepared to go therein."

The booklet goes on to explain how these books will be placed in air-tight containers, and how the proceeds from the sale of the book will be used to improve the grounds and provide for the expense of a caretaker. Other volumes were also to be sealed up in the Pyramid—books on industry, science, inventions, discoveries, etc. The Bible, too, and encyclopaedias and histories. Also pictures of people and animals at different stages of our civilization. In the large room were to be placed "small articles now used by us in domestic and industrial life, from the size of a needle and safety pin up to a victrola."

A sagacious piece of foresight was the provision for a key book to the English language "which will aid in its translation, no matter what language is spoken at the time the Pyramid is opened." I like particularly this which then follows:

"It is presumed that a new civilization rising from the ashes of this one will rise slowly, as this one has, making discoveries gradually as prompted by human reason, knowing no more of what we have discovered than we know now, of the stages of advancement of pre-historic civilizations, and that it must arrive at a period when steel and dynamite have been discovered by them, before they can break into the Pyramid. Which presupposes an intelligence for appreciation of what they find in the Pyramid. As the room and each vault will contain information of the existence of the other two compartments, if by explosion of dynamite the contents of the first one entered destroys in part its contents. they will use more care in entering the other two.

"The record of ancient civilizations which we have unearthed do not tell the merits and demerits of those civilizations, the struggles of those people and why they fell. The Pyramid to be erected here will contain all such records. Upon opening the Pyramid and reading the documents contained therein, mankind thousands of years hence will learn of the railroads, the telegraph, the radio, the phonograph, the telephone, the linotype, the flying machine and of the circulation of the blood through the human body, all discoveries of the last 400 years. Of the 5,000 years that this civilization has been groping forward it is only in the last 500 years that the Earth was

140

discovered to be round. A globular map of the world will be seen by those who enter the Pyramid.

"Wonderful discoveries have been made by this civilization in a knowledge of the universe and in the sciences as applied to the human anatomy and industries, but comparatively few in statesmanship and none in the study of civilization as a science. Upon the mastery of this latter depends the perfection of a civilization. Nothing less than this in the mental and soul structure embraces this all important divine knowledge.

"This purpose of the Pyramid is as stated and the person of no one will be entombed therein. There will be nothing about it that partakes of self or vanity and no one's name will appear on the outside of it. The only inscription will be what appears on the metal plates."

There was, however, one ironic concession to human vanity which Harvey evidently thought wise to make, harassed as he was by lack of funds. It follows closely upon the foregoing:

"The names *and addresses* (sic) of all contributors to the Pyramid Fund will be written on parchment paper and placed in a glass container with the air taken out and placed on the pedestal in the center of the large room. Their names will also be in the book before mentioned that goes to the public. This assistance will be appreciated and it will hasten the finishing and closing of the Pyramid."

In conclusion there is appended a statement by the treasurer, the First National Bank, Rogers, Arkansas:—"We believe historically and archaeologically it is an undertaking of worldwide importance and we gladly give our cooperation to its construction. We are personally acquainted with Mr. Harvey. He is a valued depositor of this bank and is a gentleman of esteemed reputation for honor and reliability." Et cetera, et cetera.

This little statement ought also to have been written on the finest parchment, put under a glass bell, sealed and entombed with the other documents, it seems to me. One is constrained to wonder if, with that miraculous key to the English language, the men of future millennia, having again arrived at the knowledge of the making of steel and dynamite, would also be able to unravel the meaning of the word "gentleman". I can well imagine them racking their brains for a clue to this extinct animal. I feel positive that, with all the photographs and pictures of men, machines, costumes, animals, birds, inventions, and what not which he thought to leave a touching record of, there never entered Harvey's mind the thought that the appellation "gentleman" would be a term completely devoid of significance to the men of the future. I doubt very much that the people opening the Pyramid one day in the distant future would have the least conception of the type of man Mr. Harvey represented. It would be extremely interesting, could we do it, to read the learned thesis of a savant analyzing the contents of this peculiar repository of a civilization supposed to have existed 250,000 years ago. We who have followed the cavortings of our learned 'ologists in all fields of research may indeed be skeptical of the readings of those to come in that hazy, undefinable period which only Portland Cement might hope to witness. Portland Cement, indeed! My first years out of school were spent in the asphyxiating atmosphere of a cement company. All I remember now of that life is the term f.o.b. That meant that I had to get off the high perch on which I sat filling in inquiry blanks and run downstairs two flights to get the freight rate to Pensacola, Nagasaki, Singapore or Oskaloosa. I never saw a sack of cement during the three years I worked with the cement company. I saw pictures of the plants on the walls of the vice-president's office when on rare occasions I was obliged and permitted to enter that sanctum. I

142

used to wonder what cement was made of. And, judging from the letters we received now and then from irate customers, not all Portland cements were of the same high quality. Some apparently wouldn't outlast a good rain. However, that's neither here nor there. What I should like to say, before leaving the subject of the Pyramid, is this—that in my humble opinion young couples about to set forth on their honeymoon, after having properly passed the required Wassermann test, might do well, instead of taking a ticket for Niagara Falls, to go to Monte Ne. If possible, they ought to provide themselves beforehand with a copy of *The Book*. And while staying at Rogers, which is the logical place to stay when visiting Monte Ne, they should put up at the Harris Hotel—it is one of the best and the most reasonable hotels in the whole United States. I recommend it without reservation.

In dealing with Albert Pike we have a man equally concerned with the aspirations and welfare of humanity at large but of quite a different temperament and outlook. I had never heard of Pike until I got to Kansas City where I was visiting a painter whom I knew in Paris. Among other things my friend was a Mason. He used to talk to me about Freemasonry and other interesting subjects during our evening walks from the Café du Dôme to the rue Froideveaux opposite the cemetery of Montparnasse, where he lived, and where for a period he put me up when I was without food or shelter. He was rather a queer chap in those days, I thought. Many things he talked about then I couldn't make head or tail of. In fact, I used to ridicule him in a sly way behind his back, which I regretted later and which, to be truthful, I was trying to make amends for by going a thousand miles out of my way to say hello to him in Kansas City. Of course I never said a word about my change of heart. I allowed my actions to speak for themselves. The reward which I unexpectedly received, on parting from him, was the loan of a book which I was terribly eager to read and which I never thought he would part with for an instant, particularly since I knew that he had always regarded me as a rather irresponsible individual. The book, which is entitled *The Phoenix*, is described as an illustrated review of Occultism and Philosophy. The author is Manly Hall. It is the 1931–32 edition. At any rate, long before I had reached Little Rock, where I was received with great cordiality and hospitality by another high Mason, I had devoured the contents of the book. I had also forgotten, when racing breathlessly through the pages of this awkwardly sized book—more like an atlas in appearance than an occult review—that Albert Pike's home had been in Little Rock. I had hardly got my bearings when I ran straight into the Consistory and a few hours later I was listening to Judge McHaney discourse about the extraordinary accomplishments of this distinguished citizen of the world, Albert Pike. It was fortunate, indeed, that I had not waited to learn about the man from the lips of the guide who conducted me through the Consistory. The mind of this sad individual—a Mason too, I suppose, in his humble way —was cluttered with the bric-à-brac of forlorn statistics which may have interested the Chinese Bishop, whom he seemed inordinately proud to have escorted through the gloomy building, but which left me not only cold but depressed. Particularly the Swedish painting which because it was Swedish had given him the notion that it was more distinguished than the other chromos which adorned the walls. When we came to the auditorium he patiently went from one switchboard to another backstage, throwing on all the degrees and variety of light which were employed on occasion to make the hideous, ginger-bread scenery take on the semblance of poetry and mystery. It was a lugubrious tour, punctuated by dry figures anent the number of people who could be served at one time in the refectory, the number of days and nights required to prepare for an advance from the third degree to the thirty-second degree, and so forth. I liked best of all the wardrobe room where in neatly arranged lockers there was concealed a most astonishing variety of costumes, the most unique among them being that of "the poor man". There was something Asiatic about the more resplendent ones. Something almost Tibetan, were it not for the obtrusive taste of the local fire department. There were the York rites, I gathered, for the Jews and "others" (what others? I wonder), and the Scottish rites which had been inaugurated by Pike. Catching sight of the masks I was immediately intrigued. But when I started to question him he realized at once that I was not a Mason and quickly put them out of sight, as though he had been guilty of an indiscretion. I was wondering vaguely what the devil all this non-sense, this hocus pocus, had to do with the genius of Albert Pike. It was useless to formulate the query aloud for the guide was evidently very much at home in this ridiculous atmosphere of mummery and flummery. He was lying in wait to point out the "millionaires' club room", a little joke of his about the billiard room where the poor members sought distraction for a few brief hours during the endless tedium of their days.

On returning to my cabin that evening I dug up the Manly Hall book and reread his lucid, inspired essay on the great American Freemason. On opening the book my eye fell at once upon this paragraph:

"The Freemasonry of Albert Pike is too vast and grand a thing to be grasped by those who have not spread the pinions of their inspiration and soared upward into the rational sphere. Albert Pike was a real Masonic initiate. He felt the dignity and profundity of the work. He knew the high calling to which master builders are dedicated. Piercing the veil of futurity with his prophetic eyes, he dreamed with Plato and Bacon of a world ruled by wisdom and the return of the golden age."

Hall asserts that what Pike endeavored to make clear to the world is that Freemasonry is not *a* religion but *the* religion. "Freemasonry," says Hall, "does not align itself with any individual institution of faith that seemingly exists largely for the purpose of confuting some other cult. Freemasonry serves and nurtures man's natural impulse to worship and venerate God in the universe and Good in the world. It interferes with the creed of no man for it is above creeds. Calling its members from vain wrangling over jot and tittle, it invites them to unite in harmonious adoration of the universal Creator. It calls men from theory to practice, from vain speculation to the application of those great moral and ethical truths by which the perfection of human nature is wrought."

It was said of Pike that he was a giant in body, in brain, in heart and in soul. He ran the whole gamut of earthly honors. Throughout the thirty-two years of his office, as Sovereign Grand Commander, he was visited and consulted by important persons from all over the world. "Who knows," says one of his admirers, "but that Albert Pike was a reincarnation of Plato, walking these nineteenth century streets of ours?" He was called Albertus Magnus, the Homer of America, the Master Builder, the Real Master of the Veils, the Oracle of Freemasonry, and the Zoroaster of modern Asia. He was a Greek and Latin scholar who taught himself many languages and a great number of dialects, among them the Sanskrit, Hebrew, Old Samaritan, Chaldean, Persian, and American Indian. Sanskrit he taught himself after he was seventy years of age. "His unpublished manuscripts in the library of the Supreme Council represent," says Manly Hall, "the most important known collection of research work into Craft symbolism."

I should like to quote Pike's own lofty words, the better to summarize his character and vision. They are from the essay on "Masonic Symbolism".

"But those who framed its Degrees adopted the most sacred and significant symbols of a very remote antiquity, used many centuries before the Temple of the King Solomon was built, to express to those who understood them, while concealing from the profane, the most recondite and mysterious doctrines in regard to God, the universe and man. And those who framed the Degrees and adopted these symbols, used them as expressions of the same sacred and holy doctrine, and interpreted them quite otherwise than they are now interpreted in our Lodges. I have, at least, arrived at this conviction after patient study and reflection during many years. I entertain no doubt, and am ready to give the reasons for my faith, that the principal symbols of Freemasonry, all that are really ancient, concur to teach the fundamental principles of a great and widespread religious philosophy, and hieroglyphically express certain profound ideas as to the existence, manifestations and action of the Deity, the harmony of the Universe, the Creative Word and Divine Wisdom, and the unity of the divine and human, spiritual, intellectual and material, in man and nature, that have re-appeared in all religions, and have been expounded by great schools of philosophy in all the ages. The ancient symbols of Freemasonry teach, I think, the profound religious truths and doctrines that in reality ARE Freemasonry. I am so far from being one of those who think that it teaches no religious creed or doctrine, as that I firmly believe that it consists in the religious philosophy that it teaches; and that he only is a true Freemason who correctly interprets for himself the Symbols."

As Manly Hall points out, "Pike herein commits himself in no uncertain manner to the fundamental premise of metaphysics and occultism: namely, that under the outer symbols and dogmas of religion there exists an esoteric key to the secrets of Nature and the purpose of human existence."

As I read on I came at last to the message (and the answer to my unvoiced query in the Consistory) which Pike left to the Brethren of the Craft. It is a message which should appeal to artists, particularly the artist in words who, though he seldom realizes it, is closer to the initiates than the chosen representatives of God.

"So religions decay into idle forms and the mummery of meaningless words. The Symbols remain, like the sea shells washed up from the depths, motionless and dead upon the sandy beaches of the ocean; and the Symbols are as voiceless and lifeless as the shells. Shall it always be so with Masonry, likewise? Or shall its ancient Symbols, inherited by it from the primitive faiths and most ancient initiations, be rescued from the enthralment of commonplace and trivial misinterpretation, be restored to their ancient high estate and again become the Holy Oracles of philosophical and religious Truth, their revelation of Divine Wisdom to our thoughtful ancestors; and thus make true and real the immense superiority of Freemasonry over all the modern and ephemeral associations that ape its forms and caricature its Symbolism?"

It seems almost incredible that in such a remote place as the Ozarks, in a century given over to crass materialism, there should have emerged a figure such as Albert Pike, self-educated, self-made, who combined in one magnificent, radiant personality the eminent qualities of poet, jurist, military leader, scholar, sage, Cabalist,

148

Hermetist and grand old man of Masonry. In the photos of him one sees a resemblance to Whitman, that other great patriarchal figure of the 19th century. In both there were traces of strong sensuality. Pike, it is said, was a gourmand. "Six feet two inches tall, he had the proportions of a Hercules and the grace of an Apollo. A face and head massive and leonine, recalling in every feature some sculptor's dream of a Grecian god." So one contemporary writes of him. Another describes him thus: "His broad expansive forehead, his serene countenance, and his powerful frame awoke thoughts in me of some being of a far-off time. The conventional dress of an American citizen did not seem suited to such a splendid personality. The costume of an ancient Greek would have been more in keeping with such a face and figure—such a habit as Plato wore when he discoursed upon divine philosophy to his students among the groves of the Academy at Athens, beneath the brilliant sun of Greece."

Remarkable that from a region looked upon by other Americans (unjustly, it is true) as being peopled with primitive, backward souls, there should step forth this truly royal figure of a man who could discourse with wisdom and grace on the teachings of Pythagoras, Plato, Hermes Trismegistus, Paracelsus, Confucius, Zoroaster, Eliphas Levi, Nicolas Flamel, Raymond Lulle and such like.

Extraordinary that in a milieu seemingly hostile to the study and pursuit of the arcane, this man, in *Morals and Dogma*, should have been able to summarize in a paragraph what eminent scholars elsewhere have failed to do in thick tomes. "One is filled with admiration," he writes, "on penetrating into the Sanctuary of the Kabalah, at seeing a doctrine so logical, so simple, and at the same time so absolute. The necessary union of ideas and signs, the consecration of the most fundamental realities by the primitive characters; the Trinity of Words, Letters and Numbers; a philosophy simple as

149

the alphabet, profound and infinite as the Word; theorems more complete and luminous than those of Pythagoras; a theology summed up by counting on one's fingers; an Infinite which can be held in the hollow of an infant's hand; ten ciphers and twenty-two letters, a triangle, a square, and a circle—these are all the elements of Kabalah. These are the elementary principles of the written Word, reflection of that spoken Word that created the world!"

LETTER TO LAFAYETTE

I DON'T suppose I'd ever have used an automobile if it hadn't been for Dudley and Flo of Kenosha. Dudley is one of the geniuses I promised to talk about earlier in this book. Dudley and Lafe, because if it hadn't been for Lafe, Dudley might have died in the womb and *The Letter to Lafayette* never been written.

Dudley says it starts with the rowing machine: "I dream an empire," etc. But for me it starts in the deep South, just prior to the arrival of Salvador Dali and his Caligari cabinet. No, it starts even a little before that—with *Generation*, a still-birth that ushered in a great friendship. It was like this, to be specific. . . . About

151

four in the morning a friend of mine received a telephone call from Kenosha, or maybe it was from Des Moines. A young man named Dudley (not to be confused with Joe Dudley, the drummer) and another young man named Lafayette Young, both of good parentage, sound in wind and limb, somewhat exalted and somewhat befuddled, telephoned to ask if Henry Miller was in town and could they meet him. About a month later they arrived in a broken-down Ford with a little black trunk, phonograph records and other necessities. To make it brief we became friends immediately. They had with them their embryo, *Generation.* I think it was late winter at the time, or early spring. Behind *Generation* was a then non-existent book to be called *Letter to Lafayette,* Lafayette being none other than little Lafe, Lafe Young of Des Moines. In a few weeks *Generation* had been killed. But the *Letter to Lafayette* survived the ordeal. In fact, it began to sprout like a liverwort. By summer we found ourselves thrown together under the same roof on a great Southern estate. That is, Dudley, little Flo, his wife, and myself. Lafe was off in limbo, but promising to arrive any day. Then one night, towards three in the morning, a visitor arrived unexpectedly and we all fled precipitately. That's another story, one that I may have to write posthumously, so to speak, because it involves libel and slander.

Our next meeting took place in Kenosha, at the home of Dudley and Flo. Lafe was then in Des Moines, sucking his big toe. To my great delight Dudley had begun the *Letter to Lafayette.* He was writing it with a stub of a pencil in a microscopic scrawl in a big ledger. It was no longer a dream but a fat, stubborn actuality. I had just seen the rowing machine upstairs in the attic where the contents of the mysterious black trunk had been spilled about. "I have another vehicle," said Dudley—"an abandoned car rescued from the auto cemetery: *my empire.* I stand still and go everywhere. No wheels, no motor, no lights, no traction. I wander through jungles, rivers, swamps, deserts—in search of the Mayas. We are trying to find our father, our name, our address."

When I heard this last sentence I jumped. I knew at once he had found the clue. A few months ago he was confused, obfuscated, struggling to wean himself of the piano man, that obsessive, paranoiac image which he had been describing in hundreds of drawings and which he talked about so magnificently that I almost became obsessed by the piano man myself.

"It's like a grand sickness," said Dudley, speaking of the Letter which he had at last begun. "I want to wash up my own life and literature too. The book opens with a nightmare, an evacuation, a *complete waste of images*."

There again was a phrase which captivated me. Imagine a young man in Kenosha, who had never written a line, declaring that he was opening up with "a complete waste of images"!

As I said, Lafe was still in Des Moines, sitting in the lavatory which he had turned into a workshop. Lafe is a masterful letter writer, a practised hand, as it were. "It'll all be blue," he writes. "I demit. I abdicate. I renounce." Or else "I've got faith—*in death*." The words are strewn over the pages like leaves tossed about by a storm. There's always a green wind, green boughs, the rustle of spring, the beat of the tom-tom, the click of the adding machine, the snores of the demented. "It's all washing up," he writes, and then goes on to speak of Stavrogin or Sade or Villon or Rimbaud, or the little straw men beneath the ice whom he glimpsed while walking through the inferno with Dante and Virgil. "What's a letter?" says Lafe. "A few hundred words, a ream of paper, a barrel of pork, a spew here, there or in any public place. I don't need you. I abdicate. I demit." Et cetera. He's like a man building a bonfire under the seat of your pants. He has nothing to

153

do but live out the life of the grand duke in a madhouse located in a city inhabited by ghosts, indulging every whim and caprice which enters his bean while realizing in action the behavior of characters whom he admires in the books he devours like a tapeworm. In a short while Lafe will pack his bag and go to Mexico, there to write a book on Norman Douglas or Henry Miller, of which he will publish just two copies, one for his subject and one for his family —just to prove that he is not altogether worthless.

"Dear Lafayette," the book begins—in the studio the morning after. *What studio?* Don't ask me! Flo is down with fever. She becomes prophetic. She annihilates in all directions. There are soliloquies in the grand manner. "I begin here," says Dudley, "at the lowest point of my life. I work backwards and forwards—a counterpoint. Yes, an infinite jam session. I will go on writing it eternally. It will never finish. It is the book of life going on forever. *It's process*, that's what it is." (You can imagine how thrilling this will be to the listeners of "Information Please!")

Back of everything is the piano man whom he met in a dive in Chicago one evening. I saw the drawings he made of him and they haunted me. He makes soap carvings of him too—always "the solitary ego." He carves him little suits to wear, a little chair, a little toilet, a little mistress—all for the little man, his ego. The piano man has become for Dudley the symbol of the final artist in the world. "He's smothered in the womb," he says. "He's drugged, hypnotic and hypnotized, obsessed. *He's also all evolution.*" (That "also" is another magnificent idiosyncrasy.) He goes on sublimating about the solitary ego, the forgotten man who is part ape, part Negro, the piano man playing in the womb under water amidst the vestigial wrack of the evolutionary wheel. At times he's a skeleton— or just an aristocrat with fluorescent lighting. Sometimes he's a

154

nervous system. Or again he's God, the God of Dudley's conceptual world. In the end, when there is nothing left but sand and a green wind blowing over all, he becomes an octopus strumming a pearl shell. The great thing, as Dudley puts it, is that he makes the dream a process. As the final artist he becomes the dream realized. . . . As Lafe would say—"Jesus, this is *it!*" Meanwhile, as the form unrolls, as the oracular melts into the prophetic, as the images waste away, some one seems to be sleeping upstairs, some one as profoundly asleep as that cataleptic figure in the foreground of Marc Chagall's famous picture. A man, or maybe a woman, on the road to Verona, passing a night in Gary off the highway with a sandwich in his pocket and a revolver to his lips. The man is writing a letter to some one he may never see again, a man without an address, a man whose father no pulmotor could restore to life again even though the fire department had been called out. A man, let us be brief and succinct, who has just been released from the nut house. It becomes necessary, therefore, to define, to redefine, everything: life, art, human relations, the habits of birds and dogs, the species and genera of plant life, water animals, the marine tides, the oceanic currents, the earth's bulge, the meteor drifts, and so on. Even perspective comes in for its share, and swamp grass and fire damp and rust and mould. "I'm no writer," he keeps repeating. "I'm just talking. A lost soul. I'm communicating with the one man I know. I'm talking blind." The talk swings backwards and forwards, from the studio where Cassandra lies prophesying, to the hole in the woods which he had dug to die in after stealing all the books from the public library at Chickamauga. There is the tailor-made suit, also, an item of rare and unpredictable consequences: the Daniel Boone period when everything had to be unique and purposive. There are nostalgic tonsorial pictures on the lawn when little Flo plies the shears and Samson is bereft of his locks. It goes on in two-four time, a steady, diminishing procrastination which comes to a lather under a sycamore tree.

There are passages which emerge clearly, like stained glass, when Nellie, for instance, Nellie of Arkadelphia, gets ready to play bridge with the rich widows of a certain city. Or when the American Legion parade passes a certain bank and Lafe and Dudley really meet for the first time. Or when Lafe arrives in Kenosha on a stream-lined train in a blue denim suit, big boots, horn-rimmed specs, long hair and a goatee. When he puts his walking stick down and walks around with an intense stare. *What do you think of it?* (Anything) And Lafe says: "It's great. It's *inexplicably* great!" Or another occasion, when Lawrence Vail brings in a pigeon bleeding from the rectum and Lafe, filled with sympathy, takes it, looks at it reverently, and then in his inexplicable way, as he wrings the pigeon's neck, says the one inexplicable word: *Haemorrhoids!*

As I see it, this *Letter to Lafayette* will be the flood and the ark both. The meteorological conditions are just right. Somebody has to pull the switch which will open the celestial flood-gates. I think Dudley is the man. If not, some other man of genius will do it. The young men of America are growing desperate; they know they haven't a chance any more. It's not simply that the war is drawing closer each day, it's that war or no war things have to come to a violent end.

A man born in Kenosha, Oshkosh, White Water, Blue Earth or Tuscaloosa is entitled to the same privileges as a man born in Moscow, Paris, Vienna or Budapest. But the American white man (not to speak of the Indian, the Negro, the Mexican) hasn't a ghost of a chance. If he has any talent he's doomed to have it crushed one way or another. The American way is to seduce a man by bribery and make a prostitute of him. Or else to ignore

156

him, starve him into submission and make a hack of him. It isn't the oceans which cut us off from the world—it's the American way of looking at things. Nothing comes to fruition here except utilitarian projects. You can ride for thousands of miles and be utterly unaware of the existence of the world of art. You will learn all about beer, condensed milk, rubber goods, canned food, inflated mattresses, etc., but you will never see or hear anything concerning the masterpieces of art. To me it seems nothing less than miraculous that the young men of America ever hear of such names as Picasso, Céline, Giono and such like. He has to fight like the devil to see their work, and how can he, when he comes face to face with the work of the European masters, how can he know or understand what produced it? What relation has it to him? If he is a sensitive being, by the time he comes in contact with the mature work of the Europeans, he is already half-crazed. Most of the young men of talent whom I have met in this country give one the impression of being somewhat demented. Why shouldn't they? They are living amidst spiritual gorillas, living with food and drink maniacs, success-mongers, gadget innovators, publicity hounds. God, if I were a young man today, if I were faced with a world such as we have created, I would blow my brains out. Or perhaps, like Socrates, I would walk into the market place and spill my seed on the ground. I would certainly never think to write a book or paint a picture or compose a piece of music. For whom? Who beside a handful of desperate souls can recognize a work of art? What can you do with yourself if your life is dedicated to beauty? Do you want to face the prospect of spending the rest of your life in a strait-jacket?

Go West, young man! they used to say. Today we have to say: Shoot yourself, young man, there is no hope for you! I know some who stuck it out and got to the top—meaning Hollywood—

157

which is like saying the top of a circus tent. Only the other day I was talking to one of them, a chap who when he was hungry killed a calf in the field with a hammer and dragged it home to eat in secret. I was walking along the beach at Santa Monica as he was telling me the story. We had just passed the mansion of an ex-movie star who had fitted up her dog kennels with parquet flooring so that her dear little Pekinese would not get its paws muddy or itchy. Across the way was the home of a wealthy widow who had grown so stout that she couldn't walk up and down the stairs any longer, so she had an elevator put in to ride back and forth from the bed to the table. Meanwhile another young writer was informing me in a letter how his publisher had given him a job as a handy man about the house, how he worked fourteen hours a day typing, keeping the books, mailing packages, hauling ashes, driving the car, etc., etc. His publisher, who is as wealthy as Croesus, hails the young writer as a genius. He says it's good for the young man to do some honest to God work.

What I like about Dudley and some of the others is that they know enough not to want to do a stroke of honest work. They would rather beg, borrow and steal. Six months in harness and they learn their lesson. Dudley could be an art director if he wanted to. Lafe could be the head of an insurance company if he chose to be. They choose not to be. Sink or swim is their motto. They look at their fathers and grandfathers, all brilliant successes in the world of American flapdoodle. They prefer to be shit-heels, if they have to be. Fine! I salute them. They know what they want.

"Dear Lafayette: I am sitting here with the corpse of my youth. . . ." I don't remember how it begins any more, but that's a good enough beginning. Begin with the guano, the little black box filled with the relics of the past. Begin in the vacant lot just outside Gary. Begin with the stench of chemicals, of blasted hopes, of mildewed promises. Begin with the oil wells jutting up from the sea. Begin with the defense program and a fleet of cement boats. Begin with Liberty Bonds and death to the Filipinos. Begin anywhere in the desert of black misery, oppression and humdrum. Start the dynamo going. Put the piano man on his piano stool and give him a reefer. Put the 58,946 crippled and killed this year back on the asphalt pavement and collect the insurance money. Call the Western Union and sing Happy Birthday to You. Buy six Packards and an old Studebaker. Get your spark plugs cleaned. Dial 9675 and tune in on Bing Crosby or Dorothy Lamour. Have your straw hat bleached and your white pants pressed. If you're Kosher see that you have a Jewish funeral service—it costs no more than any other service. Be sure to buy a slab of gum, it will sweeten the breath. Do anything, be anything, say anything that comes into your head, because it's all cuckoo and nobody will know the difference. There are now 9,567 magazines on the counters throughout the length and breadth of the land. One more voice, even if it's screechy and hysterical, will not be noticed. The best-sellers are still selling best. Christmas will come earlier this year because of the war. Next year you will have a platinum leg, unless the government commandeers the platinum supply for aeroplane wings. Sing your song and dance your dance—time is short. We are going over the top in 1943 or sooner, if the "dirty Communists" will permit us. Buy bundles for Britain, it will help to keep another Hindu alive. When you practice the bayonet drill remember always to aim for the soft parts, never for the bone or cartilage or gristle. If you're a dive bomber be sure that your parachute is in order. If you're bored, drop in to your neighborhood cinema and see the bombing of Chungking—it's quite beautiful despite the noise and smoke. Of course, you want to make sure that you drop your bombs on the right people, on the

Japs not the Chinks, on the Huns not the Tommies, et cetera. When people scream in pain and terror stuff your ears: *it's only the enemy screaming, remember that.* This year will be a good year for business men in America. Comforting thought. Wages will increase to the bursting point. There will be 349 new novels written and 6,008 new paintings, all by sworn successes, and each one better than the preceding one. A few new lunatic asylums will also be opened during the course of the year. So get in your rowing machine, Dudley, and row like hell. This is a banner year in every respect.

The last message I had from Dudley was about a bicycle trip he was going to make, because the *Letter to Lafayette* was driving him crazy. Little Flo was going to stay behind and open a ward for neurotics. If it hadn't been for Dudley I would never have bought a car, that's what I started to say. Driving back and forth from one place to another I got attached to Dudley's 1926 Ford. Especially after the record-breaking trip to meet the great Salvador Dali and his belongings, all of which we brought home intact except the bird cage and the musical ink well. Nights when we had nothing to do except to take a stroll to the end of the road and back I talked it all over with Dudley. I mean about the universe and how the cogs mesh. I realized that Dudley was an artist to the fingertips. I realized it more when I compared him with the great Salvador Dali. Dali was always working. When he had finished work he was nothing, not even a dish-rag that you could squeeze a drop of water from. Dudley seemed unable to work—*then*. He was gestating. When he talked he broke out in a sweat. Some people thought he was just a neurotic. Dali hardly noticed him. Dali noticed nothing. It didn't make any difference to him, so he said, where he was; he could work just as well at the North Pole. Dudley was impressionable. Everything filled him with wonder and curiosity. Sometimes, in order not to let the stagnation soak in too deeply, we went to Fredericksburg and ate an Italian meal. Nothing ever happened. We just ate and talked. We talked about everything. We felt elated. We had solved nothing. At noon the next day it would be 110 degrees in the shade, as usual. We would have to sit in our drawers and drink Coca-colas while Dali worked. We would look at the lawn, at the dragon flies, at the big trees, at the Negroes working, at the flies droning. We had Count Basie for breakfast, lunch and dinner. Towards dusk we had a gin fizz or a Scotch and soda. More talk. More languor and idleness. The universe again. We took it apart like a Swiss watch. Dali had by now covered at least three square inches of canvas. He seemed to be glued to his stool. When he joined us at table he thought it his duty to amuse us. Dudley found it difficult to laugh at Dali's antics. He didn't want to be crazy in that way. We had a better time going over to Shep's shack and visiting him and Sophie, his spouse. There were eight or nine kids in the family and they were always hungry and thirsty. Sometimes we brought the phonograph over and the kids would sing and dance. There were no paranoiac images on hand, just Shep and his family. Coming away Dudley would talk a blue streak. He always had "a complete waste of images" to garnish his talk. He would make us drunk listening to him. When we got tired he went downstairs to the cellar, where he had made himself a studio, and he would draw the piano man again in sixty different attitudes. He was like a miner going down into the pit. He was digging for ore. Now and then he struck a piece and probably hid it away in the big coat which he had made to last the next ten years. He kept everything of value in his coat pockets. When he had nothing else to do, when he got tired of wasting time, he sharpened all his pencils, of which he had a most astounding variety. Sometimes he'd walk over to the car and raise the hood, just to see if all the vital parts were still intact. Some-

161

times he'd go out with a pick and shovel and mend the road a bit. Dali must have thought him nuts. But he wasn't nuts. He was gestating. If we got real bored we would sit down opposite each other and imitate Lafe coming into a small town and asking for a postage stamp. Dudley knew every crack and crevice in Lafe's psyche. He could even diminish his height by six or seven inches and impersonate Lafe asking for a clean, up-to-date timetable. Or if that got too repetitious he could take out his back teeth and make a noise like Dali chewing mashed potatoes in Spanish. Or he could stretch himself full length on the lawn and cover himself with leaves as he did when he committed suicide once in St. Petersburg, Florida. He could do anything but fly—not because he lacked wings but because he didn't want to fly. He wanted to burrow in the earth, deeper and deeper. He wanted to become a mole and give birth to magnesium or chloride of lime some day. All the time, of course, he was searching for his father, who had once been a football star. And so, little by little, it came time to put it all down and so he began—"Dear Lafayette . . ." I know that it will be the best letter one man ever wrote another, even better than Nijinsky's letter to Diaghilev. And as he says, it will go on forever, because a letter like this one isn't written in a week, a month or a year, it's infinite, infinitely painful, infinitely instructive. Lafayette may never live to read the last line. Nobody will. The book will go on writing itself with an automatic pistol. It will kill off everything in sight. It will make a clean slate of these ghastly, ghost-ridden places so that those to come may have free range, free fodder, free play, free fantasia. It will do away once and for all with Murder, Death & Blight, Inc. It will free the slaves. Good luck, Dudley, and to you too, little Lafe! Let us all sit down now and write another Letter to Lafayette. Amen!

162

WITH EDGAR VARÈSE IN THE GOBI DESERT

THE WORLD AWAKE. HUMANITY ON THE MARCH. NOTH-
ING CAN STOP IT. A CONSCIOUS HUMANITY, NEITHER
EXPLOITABLE NOR PITIABLE. MARCHING! GOING! THEY
MARCH! MILLIONS OF FEET ENDLESSLY TRAMPING,
TREADING, POUNDING, STRIDING. **Rhythms** CHANGE.
QUICK, **slow,** STACCATO, DRAGGING, TREADING, POUND-
ING, STRIDING. **Go.** THE FINAL CRESCENDO GIVING THE
IMPRESSION THAT CONFIDENTLY, PITILESSLY, THE GO-
ING WILL NEVER STOP. . . . PROJECTING ITSELF INTO
SPACE. . . .

Voices in the sky, as though magic, invisible hands were turning on and off the knobs of fantastic radios, filling all space, criss-crossing, over-lapping, penetrating each other, splitting up, superimposing, repulsing each other, colliding, crashing. Phrases, slogans, utterances, chants, proclamations: China, Russia, Spain, the Fascist states and the opposing democracies, all breaking their paralyzing crusts. . . .

What sort of proclamation can this be? An anarchist running amok? A Sandwich Islander on the war-path?

No, my friends, these are the words of Edgar Varèse, a composer. He is giving the theme of his coming opus. He has more to say about it. . . .

"What should be avoided: tones of propaganda, as well as any journalistic speculation on timely events and doctrines. I want the epic impact of our epoch, stripped of its mannerisms and snob-berisms. I suggest using here and there snatches of phrases from American, French, Russian, Chinese, Spanish, German revolutions: shooting stars, also words recurring like pounding hammer blows. I should like an exultant, even prophetic tone—incantatory, the writing, however, bare, stripped for action, as it were. Also some phrases out of folk-lore—for the sake of their human, near-the-earth quality. I want to encompass everything that is human, from the most primitive to the farthest reaches of science."

I foresee the reactions which the above will produce. "He's mad," they will say. Or, "What is he—a nut?" And—"Who the hell is this Edgar Varèse?"

Millions of benighted Americans are able to-day to glibly reel off such names as Picasso, Strawinski, Joyce, Freud, Einstein, Blavat-

164

sky, Dali, Ouspenski, Krishnamurti, Nijinsky, Blenheim, Mannerheim, Messerschmitt, et cetera. Everybody knows who Shirley
Temple is, of course. Many even know the name Raimu. Ramakrishna—probably not one out of a hundred thousand ever heard
of that name, nor are they apt to as long as they live—unless this
book happens to become a best-seller, which I doubt.

What am I driving at? Just this—that there is something cock-
eyed in this best of all democratic worlds about the manner in
which vital information is disseminated. A man like André Breton,
who is the father of Surrealism, walks about the streets of Manhattan practically unknown and unrecognized. Millions of Americans are now acquainted with the word Surrealism, thanks to the
Bonwit Teller episode. Surrealism, if you should happen to ask any
one off-hand, means Salvador Dali. This is the golden age of information. If you want to know about the dead you listen in to the
"Invitation to Learning" program. If you want to be misinformed
about world events buy a newspaper—or listen to President Roosevelt on one of those occasions when he gives his little fireside chat.
If you can't absorb it all at once, this plethora of information and
misinformation, why buy a Digest—any one will do.

For real information about Edgar Varèse, and in lyric style, I
refer you to Paul Rosenfeld's article in the last issue of "Twice a
Year," an anthology put out twice a year by Dorothy Norman at
509 Madison Avenue, New York. There you will find Alfred
Stieglitz guarding the fort. It's "An American Place," by the way,
so there's no need to be alarmed.

Rosenfeld has written so amply and understandingly about
Varèse's music that anything I might choose to say would most
certainly sound redundant. What interests me about Varèse is the
fact that he seems unable to get a hearing. He is about in the same
position that John Marin would be in to-day, after fifty years of

work, had it not been for the loyalty and devotion of his great friend Alfred Stieglitz. The situation with regard to Varèse is all the more incomprehensible because his music is definitely the music of the future. And the future is already here, since Varèse himself is here and has made his music known to a few. Certainly it is not music that will make an instant appeal to the mob.

Some men, and Varèse is one of them, are like dynamite. That alone, I suppose, is sufficient to explain why they are handled with such caution and shyness. As yet we have had no censorship of music, though I remember Huneker writing somewhere that it was surprising we hadn't censored certain masterpieces. As for Varèse, I honestly believe that if he were given a clear field he would not only be censored but stoned. Why? For the very simple reason that his music is *different*. Aesthetically we are probably the most conservative people in the world. We have to have the blind staggers before we get a release. Then we break one another's heads with glee and impunity. We have been educated to such a fine —or dull—point that we are incapable of enjoying something new, something different, until we are first told what it's all about. We don't trust our five senses; we rely on our critics and educators, all of whom are failures in the realm of creation.

In short, the blind lead the blind. It's the democratic way. And so the future, which is always imminent, gets aborted and frustrated, shoved around the corner, stifled, mangled, annihilated sometimes, creating the familiar illusion of an Einsteinian world which is neither fish nor fowl, a world of finite curves that lead to the grave or to the poor-house or the insane asylum or the concentration camp or the warm, protective folds of the Democratic-Republican party. And so madmen arise who try to restore law and order with the axe. When millions of lives have been lost, when finally we get to them and pole-axe them, we breathe a little more com-

Edgar Varèse

fortably in our padded cells. Under such conditions it's refreshing, to be sure, to listen to Mozart being mesmerized by a great hypnotist like Toscanini. If you are well off and can afford to spend ten or twenty-five or fifty dollars a day tò hire some patient soul to listen to your troubles you can be readjusted to the crazy scheme of things and spare yourself the humiliation of becoming a Christian Scientist. You can have your ego trimmed or removed, as you wish, just like a wart or bunion. Then you can enjoy Mozart even more than before—as well as the warblings of Tetrazzini or the lullabies of Bing Crosby. Music is a beautiful opiate, if you don't take it too seriously.

THE WORLD AWAKE!

Just to repeat that to yourself five times a day is enough to make an anarchist of you. How would you awaken the world—if you were a muscian? With a sonata for rusty can openers? Have you ever thought about it? Or would you rather remain asleep?

A CONSCIOUS HUMANITY!

Have you ever tried to imagine what that would mean? Be honest. Have you ever paused one minute of your life to think what it would mean for humanity to become fully conscious, to be *neither exploitable nor pitiable*? Nothing could possibly hinder the advance of a conscious humanity. Nothing will.

How to become conscious? It's very dangerous, you know. It doesn't necessarily mean that you will have two automobiles and own your own home with a pipe organ in it. It means that you will suffer still more—that's the first thing to realize. But you won't be dead, you won't be indifferent, you won't be insensitive, you won't be alarmed and panicky, you won't be jittery, you won't throw rotten eggs because you don't understand. You will want to under-

167

stand everything, even the disagreeable things. You will want to accept more and more—even what seems hostile, evil, threatening. Yes, you will become more and more like God. You won't have to answer an advertisement in the newspaper in order to find out how to talk with God. God will be with you all the time. And if I know what I'm talking about, you will listen more and talk less.

ARRIVALS ARE DEPARTURES

How long you stay in Mr. Jordan's company depends on *you*. Some souls evolve quickly; others progress at a snail's pace. "There is only going," as Varèse says. That's the law of the universe. If you don't accommodate your rhythm to the universal rhythm you relapse, regress, become a vegetable, an amoeba or a Satan incarnate.

No one asks you to throw Mozart out the window. Keep Mozart. Cherish him. Keep Moses too, and Buddha and Laotse and Christ. Keep them in your heart. But make room for the others, the coming ones, the ones who are already scratching on the window-panes.

Nothing is deader than the status quo, whether it be called Democracy, Fascism, Communism, Buddhism, or Nihilism. If you have a dream of the future, know that it will be realized one day. Dreams come true. Dreams are the very substance of reality. Reality is not protected or defended by laws, proclamations, ukases, cannons and armadas. Reality is that which is sprouting all the time out of death and disintegration. You can't do anything to it; you can't add or subtract, you can only become more and more aware. Those who are partly aware are the creators; those who are fully aware are the gods and they move among us silent and unknown. The function of the artist, who is only one type of creator, is to wake us up. The artists stimulate our imagination. ("Imagination is the last word," says Varèse.) They open up for us portions of reality, unlatch the doors which we habitually keep shut. They disturb us, some more than others. Some, like Varèse, remind me of those Russians who are trained to go forth single-handed and meet the invading tanks. They seem so puny and defenseless, but when they hit the mark they cause inestimable havoc. We have good reason to fear them, those of us who are asleep. They bring the light that kills as well as illumines. There are lone figures armed only with ideas, sometimes with just one idea, who blast away whole epochs in which we are enwrapped like mummies. Some are powerful enough to resurrect the dead. Some steal on us unawares and put a spell over us which it takes centuries to throw off. Some put a curse on us, for our stupidity and inertia, and then it seems as if God himself were unable to lift it.

Back of every creation, supporting it like an arch, is faith. Enthusiasm is nothing: it comes and goes. But if one *believes*, then miracles occur. Faith has nothing to do with profits; if anything, it has to do with prophets. Men who know and believe can foresee the future. They don't want to put something over—they want to put something *under* us. They want to give solid support to our dreams. The world isn't kept running because it's a paying proposition. (God doesn't make a cent on the deal.) The world goes on because a few men in every generation believe in it utterly, accept it unquestioningly; they underwrite it with their lives. In the struggle which they have to make themselves understood they create music; taking the discordant elements of life, they weave a pattern of harmony and significance. If it weren't for this constant struggle on the part of a few creative types to expand the sense of reality in man the world *would* literally die out. We are not kept alive by legislators and militarists, that's fairly obvious. We are kept alive by men of faith, men of vision. They are like vital germs in the endless process of becoming. Make room, then, for the life-giving ones!

"This revolutionary age we are living in," says a contemporary,* "does not mark only the transition between two small cultural cycles, between the Piscean and the Aquarian Ages so-called. It represents a much greater beginning, the opening of gates that will be the threshold of an era which may encompass hundreds of thousands of years; possibly still vaster periods. . . ."

In talking of "musical space" the same author has this to say:

"Western classical music has given practically all of its attention to the frame-work of music, what it calls musical form. It has forgotten to study the laws of Sonal Energy, to intuit music in terms of actual sound-entities, in terms of energy which is life. It has thus evolved mostly splendid abstract frames in which no painting is to be seen. Therefore the Oriental musicians often say that our music is a music of holes. Our notes are edges of intervals, of empty abysses. The melodies jump from edge to edge. It neither flies nor glides. It has hardly any contact with the living earth. It is a music of mummies, of preserved and stuffed animals which look alive enough perhaps, yet are dead and motionless. *The inner space is empty.* The tone entities are dead, because they are empty of sonal energy, of sonal blood. They are but bones and skin. We call them 'pure' tones. They are so pure they will never move to do any harm! —the true religious ideal of manhood: the singer of the Sistine Chapel, men without creative power. This is the symbol of classical European music, of pure music. . . .

"But now with the sense of atonalism so-called, with the increasing realization that, as Edgar Varèse said: 'Music must *sound*': that it is nothing if not the actual tone experience of some living human being—we are slowly and hesitatingly coming, in spite of the European reactionary movement called neo-classicism, to a new sense of music based on the feeling of tone-fulness, the sense

* *Art as Release of Power* by Dane Rudhyar.

170

of what a Russian called 'Pansonority' and what we had named a few years before *Tonepleromas*, which another modernist, Henry Cowell, tried to produce by means of his so-called 'tone-clusters'."

The whole emphasis, in this disquisition on musical space, is laid on tone. "Every tone actually heard is a complex entity made up of various elements ordered in various ways, presenting a certain typical relationship to each other. Every tone, in other words, is a molecule of music, and as such can be dissociated into component sonal atoms and electrons, which ultimately may be shown to be but waves of the all-pervading *sonal energy* irradiating throughout the universe, like the recently discovered cosmic rays which Dr. Millikan calls interestingly enough 'the *birth-cries* of the simple elements: helium, oxygen, silicon, iron.' "

But is it music? That's the inevitable question which comes up whenever you mention the name Varèse. Varèse himself eludes the question thusly—I quote from a recent article of his called "Organized Sound for the Sound Film."

"As the term 'music' seems gradually to have shrunk to mean much less than it should, I prefer to use the expression 'organized sound,' and avoid the monotonous question: 'But is it music?' 'Organized sound' seems better to take in the dual aspect of music as an art-science, with all the recent laboratory discoveries which permit us to hope for the unconditional liberation of music, as well as covering, without dispute, my own music in progress and its requirements."

But is it music? Say what you like, people go nuts not being able to name it and categorize it. Always fear, always panic, in face of the new. Do we not hear the same cry with regard to the other arts? But is it *literature?* But is it *sculpture?* But is it *painting?* Evidently it is and it isn't. Certainly it's not plumbing, nor railway engineering, nor hockey, nor tiddlywinks. If you catalogue all the things which a new work of art or a new art form is *not* you finally get pretty close to something which is either music, painting, sculpture or literature, as the case may be. When Judge Woolsey gave his memorable decision on Joyce's *Ulysses* there was quite a stir. But we are inclined to forget that in defending the book the venerable old codger stressed the fact that its appeal was limited to a very small minority, that on the whole it was a difficult book to understand, and that consequently what harm its obscene passages might cause would be limited to a negligible number of our good citizens. This is a timid, cautious way of letting down the bars when confronted with a work of controversial merit—not a very enlightened one, I should say. Instead of asking—"How much damage will the work in question bring about?" why not ask—"How much good? How much joy?" Taboos, though unadmitted, are potent. What is it that people fear? *What they don't understand.* The civilized man is not a whit different from the savage in this respect. The new always carries with it the sense of violation, of sacrilege. What is dead is sacred; what is new, that is, *different*, is evil, dangerous, or subversive.

I remember vividly the first time I heard Varèse's music—on a magnificent recording machine. I was stunned. It was as though I had been given a knock-out blow. When I recovered I listened again. This time I recognized emotions which I had experienced in the first instance but which, because of the novelty, because of the continuous, uninterrupted succession of novelties, I had been unable to identify. My emotions had piled up to a crescendo whose impact came as a self-delivered sock in the jaw. Later, talking to Varèse about his new work, asked if I would care to contribute some phrases for the chorus—"magical phrases," said Varèse—all that I had previously heard came back to me with redoubled force and significance. "I want something of the feeling of the Gobi Desert," said Varèse.

The Gobi Desert! My head began to spin. He couldn't have used an image more accurate than this to describe the ultimate effect which his organized sound music produced in my mind. The curious thing about Varèse's music is that after listening to it you are silenced. It is not sensational, as people imagine, but awe-inspiring. It is shattering, yes, if you insist that music be soothing and nothing more. It is cacophonous, yes, if you think that melody is all. It is nerve-racking, yes, if you can't bear the thought of dissonance not being ultimately resolved. But what has been the result of the sedulous avoidance of these disturbing, perhaps disagreeable, elements? Does our music reflect peace, harmony, inspiration? What new music have we to boast of other than Boogie-Woogie? What are our conductors giving us year after year? Only fresh corpses. Over these beautifully embalmed sonatas, toccatas, symphonies and operas the public dances the jitterbug. Night and day without let the radio drowns us in a hog-wash of the most nauseating, sentimental ditties. From the churches comes the melancholy dirge of the dead Christ, a music which is no more sacred than a rotten turnip.

Varèse wants to bring about a veritable cosmic disturbance. If he could control the ether waves and blast everything off the map with one turn of the dial I think he would die in ecstasy. When he talks about his new work and what he is trying to achieve, when he mentions the earth and its inert, drugged inhabitants, you can see him trying to get hold of it by the tail and swing it around his head. He wants to set it spinning like a top. He wants to speed up the murdering, the buggering, the swindling, and have done with it once and for all. Are you deaf and dumb and blind? he seems to

173

ask. Sure there is music to-day—but there is no *sound* to it. Sure there is slaughter going on—but it doesn't produce any effect. Sure the headlines are full of tragedy—but where are the tears? Is it a world of rubber goods pounded with rubber mallets? Is it croquet or is it cosmological eye-wash? *Death is one thing and deadness another*.

If we can't hear people screaming in agony how can we hear at all? Every day I pass an institution called the Sonotone on Fifth Avenue, where the public is invited to step in and have its hearing tested. We have become ear-conscious at last. It doesn't mean that our hearing will improve—it means simply that another item has been added to the long list of things to worry about. Anyway, now we know that millions of Americans are deaf or on the way to deafness. How we carry on, statistically crippled, poisoned, mutilated as we are, is nothing less than miraculous. Now we are growing deaf. Soon we will become speechless.

When the bombs begin to drop from the sky even those sonorous Chinese gongs which Varèse keeps on hand will have no effect on the audience. True, there remains the electrical apparatus—one can screw these machines up to a pitch of diabolical intensity. But even then one will have to go some to compete with the noise of the dive bomber. Whoever saw and heard the documentary film called "Kukan" will surely remember for the rest of his life the sound of those Japanese planes when they swarmed over Chungking. And the roar of the flames afterwards, that too is unforgettable. And then silence—a silence unlike anything we have experienced. A city lying stunned and prostrate. What a harrowing silence that makes! Imagine what it will be like, should New York, San Francisco, Los Angeles and other of our big cities suffer the same fate! It won't be music to our ears, that's a cinch. But it will be *sound*. Even the silence will be filled with sound. It will be a sort of inter-spatial chamber music to fill the void of our unfeeling souls.

To-morrow all that we take for granted may wear a new face. New York may come to resemble Petra, the cursed city of Arabia. The corn fields may look like a desert. The inhabitants of our big cities may be obliged to take to the woods and grub for food on all fours, like animals. It is not impossible. It is even quite probable. No part of this planet is immune once the spirit of self-destruction takes hold. The great organism called Society may break down into molecules and atoms; there may not be a vestige of any social form which could be called a body. What we call "society" may become one interrupted dissonance for which no resolving chord will ever be found. That too is possible.

We know only a small fraction of the history of man on this earth. It is a long, tedious, painful record of catastrophic changes involving the disappearance of whole continents sometimes. We tell the story as though man were an innocent victim, a helpless participant in the erratic and unpredictable revolutions of Nature. Perhaps in the past he was. But not any longer. Whatever happens to this earth to-day is of man's doing. Man has demonstrated that he is master of everything—except his own nature. If yesterday he was a child of nature, to-day he is a responsible creature. He has reached a point of consciousness which permits him to lie to himself no longer. Destruction now is deliberate, voluntary, self-induced. We are at the node: we can go forward or relapse. We still have the power of choice. To-morrow we may not. It is because we refuse to make the choice that we are ridden with guilt, all of us, those who are making war and those who are not. *We are all filled with murder.* We loathe one another. We hate what we look like when we look into one another's eyes.

What *is* the magic word for this moment? What am I to offer

175

Varèse for that Gobi Desert stretch of his sonorous score? Peace? Courage? Patience? Faith? None of these words will serve any longer, I fear. We have worn them out mouthing them unmeaningfully. What good are words if the spirit behind them is absent?

All our words are dead. Magic is dead. God is dead. The dead are piling up around us. Soon they will choke the rivers, fill the seas, flood the valleys and the plains. Perhaps only in the desert will man be able to breathe without being asphyxiated by the stench of death. Varèse, you have put me in a dilemma. All I can do is to append a footnote to your new opus. Here goes then. . . .

> Let the chorus represent the survivors. Let the Gobi Desert be the place of refuge. Around the rim of the desert let the skulls pile up in a formidable barricade.
>
> A hush comes over the world. One does not dare to breathe even. Nor to listen. Every one has grown still. There is absolute quiet. Only the heart beats. It beats in a silence supreme. Let a man arise and make as if to open his mouth. Let him fail to make a sound. Let another man arise and let him fail likewise. Now a white stallion descends from the sky. He prances about in dead silence. He whisks his tail.
>
> The silence becomes deeper. The silence becomes almost unbearable.
>
> A dervish springs up and begins to whirl like a top. The sky turns white. The air grows chill. Suddenly a knife flashes and in the sky a gleam of light appears. A blue star coming nearer and nearer—a dazzling, blinding star.
>
> Now a woman arises and shrieks. Another and another. The air is filled with piercing shrieks. Suddenly

a huge bird drops from the sky. It is dead. No one
moves to approach it.

Faintly one hears the sound of cicadas. Then the
notes of a lark, followed by the mocking bird. Some
one laughs—an insane laugh which is heart-breaking.
A woman sobs. Another begins to wail.

From a male a great shout: WE ARE LOST!

A woman's voice: WE ARE SAVED!

Staccato cries: Lost! Saved! Lost! Saved!

SILENCE

A huge gong resounds, drowning everything.

Again, and again, and again.

Then a shattering silence. When it has become almost insupportable a flute is heard—the flute of a
shepherd invisible. The music, which is fugitive, monotonous, repetitive—almost insane—goes on and on
and on. The wind stirs.

The moment the sound of the flute dies out a great
choir of brass gives a mighty blare.

THE MAGICIAN APPEARS

Raising his hands heavenward he begins in a clear,
even voice, neither high nor loud nor shrill: a voice
which carries, which stills the heart. This is what he
says:

"Believe no more! Hope no more! Pray no more!
Open wide your eyes. Stand erect. Cast out all fear.
A new world is about to be born. It is yours. From
this moment all will change. What is magic? The

177

knowledge that you are free. *You are free!* Sing!
Dance! Fly! Life has just begun."

Gong!

followed by black-out.

As we leave the auditorium the familiar racket of the street
assails our ears. This is not the sound made by naked feet clamber-
ing up the golden ladder; it is not even the rattle of the golden
chain which binds the hierarchies of man. It is the death rattle.
Those who have refused to advance and stake out the claims which
are waiting for them are giving up the ghost. This rattle in the
throat, this rale, this horripilating glug-glug of the drowned is the
chamber music of the defeated.

We are now listening to the cadenza. It is made of garbage and
emery wheels. It is perforated with bullet holes which gives the
illusion of cheers. *Music?* Yes, a sort of weird, anachronistic funeral
march. Title: *Mort à Credit.*

I walk through the vacant lot on my right, which happens to
be the Gobi Desert, and as I think of the last million or two being
butchered under a cold moon I say to Varèse: *"Now blow your
horn!"*

What a sound that makes in a world lying cold and dead! *Is it
music?* I don't know. I don't need to know. The last dud has just
been rubbed out. All's quiet now along the Western, the Eastern,
the Southern and the Northern Front. We're in the Gobi at last.
Only the chorus is left. And the elements: helium, oxygen, nitrogen,
sulphur, et cetera. Time rolls away. Space folds up. What is left
of man is pure MAN. As the old fades away Station WNJZ of Auck-
land can be heard playing "It's a long, long way to Tipperary!"
Varèse sneezes. *"Allez-oop!"* he says, and on we go. . . .

178

MY DREAM OF MOBILE

THE OTHER night, having no money to eat with, I decided to go to the public library and look up a chapter in a famous book which I had promised a friend of mine in Washington I would read. The book was *The Travels of Marco Polo*; the chapter was devoted to a description of the city of Kin-sai or Hang-cheu. The man who asked me to read about this splendorous city is a scholar; he has read thousands of books and will probably read thousands more before he dies. He had said to me at lunch one day: "Henry, I've just found the city I'd like to live in. It's Hang-cheu of the 13th century." The conversation took place about a year ago. I had

179

forgotten all about it until the other night when I was hungry. So instead of physical nourishment I decided on a spiritual feast.

I must confess I was disappointed in Marco Polo. He bores me. I remember having tried to read him about thirty years ago and coming to the same conclusion. What did interest me this time, however, was John Masefield's introduction to the book. "When Marco Polo went to the East," writes Masefield, "the whole of Central Asia, so full of splendour and magnificence, so noisy with nations and kings, was like a dream in men's minds." I have read this sentence over several times. It stirs me. I would like to have written that sentence myself. With a few strokes of the pen Masefield evokes a picture which Marco Polo himself, who had seen the splendour and magnificence of the East, fails to do—*for me.*

I would like to quote a few more lines from this splendid foreword of Masefield's. It has a lot to do with my trip through the United States—and with my dream of Mobile.

"It is accounted a romantic thing to wander among strangers and to eat their bread by the camp-fires of the other half of the world. There is romance in doing this, though the romance has been over-estimated by those whose sedentary lives have created in them a false taste for action. Marco Polo wandered among strangers; but it is open to any one (with courage and the power of motion) to do the same. Wandering in itself is merely a form of self-indulgence. If it adds not to the stock of human knowledge, or if it gives not to others the imaginative possession of some part of the world, it is a pernicious habit. The acquisition of knowledge, the accumulation of fact, is noble only in those few who have that alchemy which transmutes such clay to heavenly eternal gold. . . . It is only the wonderful traveller who sees a wonder, and only five travellers in the world's history have seen wonders. The others have seen birds and beasts, rivers and wastes, the earth and the (local) fullness thereof. The five travellers are Herodotus, Gaspar, Melchior, Balthazar and Marco Polo himself. The wonder of Marco Polo is this—that he created Asia for the European mind. . . ."

Marco Polo was seventeen when he departed from Venice with his uncles. Seventeen years later he returned to Venice in rags. Almost immediately thereafter he enlisted in the war against Genoa, was taken prisoner and, during the course of his incarceration, wrote the book which immortalized his journey. Curious, *what?* Consider the state of his mind, locked up in a dungeon as he was, after having lived out a dream of splendour and magnificence. *"When Marco Polo went to the East . . ."* The phrase repeats itself like a refrain. *"Like a dream in men's minds . . ."* Think of Balboa, of Columbus, of Amerigo Vespucius! Men who dreamed, and then realized their dreams. Men filled with wonder, with longing, with ecstasy. Sailing straight for the unknown, finding it, realizing it, and then returning to the strait-jacket. Or dying of fever in the midst of a mirage. Cortez, Ponce de Leon, de Soto! Madmen. Dreamers. Fanatics. In search of the marvelous. In quest of the miracle. Murdering, raping, plundering. The Fountain of Youth. Gold. Gods. Empires. Splendour and magnificence, yes—but also fever, hunger, thirst, poisoned arrows, mirages, death. Sowing hate and fear. Spreading the white man's poison. Spreading the white man's fears and superstitions, his greed, his envy, his malice, his restlessness.

When the Spaniards sailed West . . . Quite another story.

The Gold Rush. The Stampede. The Gadarene Swine. A sequel enacted by their successors, the Americans. Gone the splendour and magnificence. Noisy now with dynamos and factory whistles. The wonders have been extirpated, the quest is ended. The gold has been put back into the earth, deep down where no bomb can ever reach it. We have almost all there is, and it is rotting there, of

181

no use to any one, least of all to those who hoard it and guard it with their lives.

"*When Marco Polo went to the East . . .*" You have only to incant the phrase and the fullness of the earth opens up. The imagination is drowned before the sentence is finished. Asia. Just Asia, and the mind trembles. Who can fill in the picture of Asia? Marco Polo gives us thousands of details, but they are like a drop in the bucket. No matter what man has accomplished since, no matter what miracles he has wrought, the word Asia floods his memory with a splendour and magnificence unequalled. Prophets, scholars, sages, mystics, dreamers, madmen, fanatics, tyrants, emperors, conquerors, all of them greater than Europe has ever known, came out of Asia. Religions, philosophies, temples, palaces, walls, fortresses, paintings, tapestries, jewels, drugs, liquors, incense, clothing, foodstuffs, culinary arts, metals, the great inventions, the great languages, the great books, the great cosmogonies, all came out of Asia. Even the stars came out of Asia. There were gods and demi-gods—thousands and thousands of them. And God-men. Avatars. Precursors. Asia was inspired. Asia is still inspired. If in the thirteenth century Asia was like a dream in men's minds to-day it is even more so. Asia is inexhaustible. There is Mongolia, there is Tibet, there is China, there is India. Our conception of these places, of the people that fill them, of the wisdom they possess, of the spirit that animates them, of their striving, their goals and their fulfillment is almost nil. Our adventurers and explorers lose themselves there, our scholars are confounded there, our evangelists and zealots and bigots are reduced to nullity there, our colonials rot there, our machines look puny and insignificant there, our armies are swallowed up there. Vast, multiform, polyglot, seething with unharnessed energy, now stagnant, now alert, ever menacing, ever mysterious, Asia dwarfs the world. We are like spiders trying to cope with giant cedars. We spin our webs, but the slightest tremor of the slumbering giant which is Asia can destroy the work of centuries. We are giving our guts, hollowing ourselves out, but the Asiatics swim on the breast of a mighty ocean, and they are tireless, endless, inextinguishable. They move with the great earth currents; we struggle vainly against the tide. We sacrifice everything to destruction; they sacrifice everything to life.

Well, *Mobile*. . . . Supposing now that you were me, that you were living in Paris and content to remain there for the rest of your life. Supposing that every night, when you came back to your studio, you stood a few minutes with hat and coat on, a big, fat pencil in your hand, and you wrote down in a big book whatever came into your head. Naturally, if you went to bed with the names of cities jingling in your head, you would dream some fantastic dreams. Sometimes you might find yourself dreaming with eyes wide open, not certain whether you were in bed or standing up at the big table. And sometimes, when you had hoped to close your eyes and give yourself up to the most delicious dream sensations, you found yourself wrestling with a nightmare. Take a classic one such as the following. . . .

Some one you think is you is looking in the mirror. He sees a face he doesn't recognize. It is the face of an idiot. He becomes terrified and soon thereafter finds himself in a concentration camp where he is kicked around like a football. He has forgotten who he was, forgotten his name, his address, even what he looked like. He knows he is crazy. After years of the vilest torture he suddenly finds himself at the exit and, instead of being driven back to the pen with a bayonet, he is pushed out into the world. Yes, by a miracle he is made free again. His emotion is indescribable. But then, as he looks around, he realizes that he hasn't the faintest conception of where he might be. It could be Queensland, Patagonia, Somaliland,

Rhodesia, Siberia, Staten Island, Mozambique—or a corner of an unknown planet. He is lost, more completely lost than ever. A man approaches and he starts to explain his predicament, but before he can form a phrase he finds that he has lost his language too. Fortunately at this point he wakes up. . . .

If you have never experienced that particular form of nightmare try it some time: it will make your hair stand on end, if nothing else.

The dream of Mobile is another thing, and why I couple the two I don't know, but for some obscure reason the one and the other *are* coupled in my mind. The Freudian know-it-alls will probably have the answer. They can unravel everything but their own private dilemmas.

I think what really started me dreaming about Mobile and other places in America which I had never visited was the extraordinary curiosity which my friend Alfred Perlès evinced whenever the name America came up. He used to grab me by the sleeve sometimes and beg me with tears in his eyes to solemnly promise that I would take him with me if I ever returned. Arizona was the place he was particularly nuts about. You could talk all night about the deep South or the Great Lakes or the Mississippi basin and he would sit goggle-eyed, with mouth wide open, the perspiration dripping from his brow, apparently thoroughly absorbed, thoroughly carried away. But when you had finished he would pipe up fresh as a daisy: "*Now tell me about Arizona!*" Sometimes, having talked for half the night, having exhausted myself, having drunk enough to fill a tank, I would answer—"The hell with Arizona, I'm going to bed." "All right," he would say, "go to bed. You can talk in bed. I won't go home till you tell me about Arizona." "But I've told you all I know," I would remonstrate. "That doesn't matter, Joey," he'd answer, "I want to hear it all over again." It was almost like the

Steinbeck duet between Lennie and the other guy. He was a glutton for Arizona. Now he's "somewhere in Scotland", with the Pioneer Corps, but I swear to Christ if he ever runs across an American in that God-forsaken place the first thing he'll say will be: "Tell me about Arizona!"

Naturally when a man has such an unbounded enthusiasm for a place you are familiar with, a place you think you know, you begin to wonder if you do know. America is a vast place, and I doubt if any man knows it thoroughly. It's possible too to live in a place and not know anything about it, because you don't want to know. I remember a friend of mine coming to Paris on a honeymoon, finding it not at all to his liking, and finally coming to me one day to ask if I would give him some typing to do—because he didn't know what to do with himself.

There were certain places, like Mobile again, which I never mentioned in the presence of Perlès. The Mobile I knew was thoroughly imaginary and I wanted to enjoy it all by myself. It gave me a great pleasure, I might say, to secretly resist his prying curiosity. I was like a young wife who delays telling her husband that she has become a mother. I kept Mobile in the womb, under lock and key, and day by day it grew, took on arms and legs, hair, teeth, nails, eye-lashes, just like a real foetus. It would have been a marvelous accouchement, had I been equal to it. Imagine a full-fledged city being born out of a man's loins! Of course it never came off. It began to die in the womb, from lack of nourishment, I suppose, or because I fell in love with other cities—Dômme, Sarlat, Rocamadour, Genoa, and so on.

How did I visualize Mobile? To tell the truth, it's all quite hazy now. Hazy, fuzzy, amorphous, crumbling. To get the feel of it again I have to mention the name of Admiral Farragut. *Admiral Farragut steamed into Mobile Bay.* I must have read that somewhere when a child. It stuck in my crop. I don't know to this day whether it's a fact or not—that Admiral Farragut steamed into Mobile Bay. I took it for granted then, and it was a good thing I did probably. Admiral Farragut has nothing more to do with the picture than that. He fades out *instanter*. What is left of the image is the word Mobile. Mobile is a deceptive word. It sounds quick and yet it suggests immobility—*glassiness*. It is a fluid mirror which reflects sheet lightning as well as somnolent trees and drugged serpents. It is a name which suggests water, music, light and torpor. It also sounds remote, securely pocketed, faintly exotic and, if it has any color, is definitely white. Musically I would designate it as guitarish. Perhaps not even that resonant—perhaps mandolinish. Anyway, pluckable music—accompanied by bursting fruit and thin light columns of smoke. No dancing, except the dancing of mote-beams, the evanescent beat of ascension and evaporation. The skin always dry, despite the excessive humidity. The slap-slap of carpet slippers, and figures silhouetted against half-drawn blinds. Corrugated silhouettes.

I have never once thought of work in connection with the word Mobile. *Not anybody working.* A city surrounded with shells, the empty shells of by-gone fiestas. Bunting everywhere and the friable relics of yesterday's carnival. Gaiety always in retreat, always vanishing, like clouds brushing a mirror. In the center of this glissando Mobile itself, very prim, very proper, Southern and not Southern, listless but upright, slatternly yet respectable, bright but not wicked. Mozart for the mandolin. Not Segovia feathering Bach. Not grace and delicacy so much as anaemia. Fever-coolth. Musk. Fragrant ashes.

In the dream I never pictured myself as entering Mobile by automobile. Like Admiral Farragut, I saw myself steaming into Mobile Bay, generating my own power. I never thought I would pass through places like Panama City, Apalachicola, Port St. Joe, or that I would be within striking distance of Valparaiso and Bagdad, or that by crossing Millers Ferry I would be on the way to the Ponce de Leon Springs. In their dream of gold the Spaniards had preceded me. They must have moved like fevered bedbugs through the swamps and forests of Florida. And when they hit Bon Secours they must have been completely whacky—to give it a French name, I mean. To cruise along the Gulf is intoxicating; all the water routes are exfoliative, if one can put it that way. The Gulf is a great drama of light and vapor. The clouds are pregnant and always in bloom, like oneiric cauliflowers; sometimes they burst like cysts in the sky, shedding a precipitate of mercurium chromide; sometimes they stride across the horizon with thin, wispy legs of smoke. In Pensacola I had a crazy room in a crazy hotel. I thought I was in Perpignan again. Towards dusk I looked out the window and saw the clouds battling; they collided with one another like crippled dirigibles, leaving streamers of tangled wreckage dangling in the sky. It seemed as though I were at a frontier, that two wholly different worlds were fighting for domination. In the room was a monstrous poster that dated back to the days of the sewing machine. I lay back on the bed and before my eyes there passed in review all the screaming, caterwauling monstrosities of the poster art which had assaulted my innocent vision when a child. Suddenly I thought of Dolly Varden—God only knows why!—and then a perfect avalanche of names, all theatrical, all sentimental, assailed me: Elsie Ferguson, Frances Starr, Effie Shannon, Julia Sanderson, Cyril Maude, Julian Eltinge, Marie Cahill, Rose Coghlan, Crystal Herne, Minnie Maddern Fiske, Arnold Daly, Leslie Carter, Anna Held, Blanche Bates, Elsie Janis, Wilton Lackaye, Kyrle Bellew, William Collier, Rose Stahl, Fritzi Scheff, Margaret Anglin, Virginia Harned, Henry Miller, Walker Whiteside, Julie Opp, Ada

187

Rehan, Cecilia Loftus, Julia Marlowe, Irene Franklin, Ben Ami, Bertha Kalich, Lulu Glaser, Olga Nethersole, John Drew, David Warfield, James K. Hackett, William Faversham, Joe Jackson, Weber & Fields, Valeska Suratt, Snuffy the Cabman, Richard Carle, Montgomery & Stone, Eva Tanguay, the great Lafayette, Maxine Elliott, David Belasco, Vesta Victoria, Vesta Tilly, Roy Barnes, Chick Sales, Nazimova, Modjeska, the Duse, Ida Rubenstein, Lenore Ulric, Richard Bennett and his most lovely, beautiful wife whose name I have forgotten, the only actress to whom I ever penned a love letter.

Was it the Talafax Hotel? I can't remember any more. Anyway, it was Pensacola—and again it wasn't Pensacola. It was a frontier and there was an aerial drama going on which subsequently drenched the earth with violent hues. The stage stars were traipsing back and forth over my closed eyelids, some in full length tights, some décolleté, some with flaming red wigs, some with laced corsets, some with pantaloons, some in ecstasy, some morbid, some smoked like hams, some defiant, some piquant, but all of them posturing, gesturing, declaiming, all trying to crowd one another off the stage.

I had never anticipated an appetizing banquet like that when dreaming of sailing down Mobile Bay. It was like being in limbo, a levitation act on the threshold of the dream. A day or two before we had crossed the Suwanee River. In Paris I had dreamed of taking a boat and sailing right into the Okefinokee Swamp, just to trace the river to its source. That was a pipe dream. If I had another hundred years to live, instead of fifty, I might still do it, but time is getting short. There are other places to visit—Easter Island, the Papuan Wonderland, Yap, Johore, the Caroline Islands, Borneo, Patagonia—Tibet, China, India, Persia, Arabia—and Mongolia. The ancestral spirits are calling me; I can't put them off much longer. *"When Henry Miller left for Tibet . . ."* I can see my future biographer writing that a hundred years from now. What ever happened to Henry Miller? He disappeared. He said he was going to Tibet. Did he get there? Nobody knows. . . . That's how it will be. Vanished mysteriously. Exit with two valises and a trunkful of ideas. But I will come back again one day, in another suit of flesh. I may make it snappy, too, and surprise everybody. One remains away just long enough to learn the lesson. Some learn faster than others. I learn very quickly. My home work is all finished. I know that the earth is round, but I know also that that is the least important fact you can mention about it. I know that there are maps of the earth which designate a country called America. That's also relatively unimportant. *Do you dream?* Do you leave your little *locus perdidibus* and mingle with the other inhabitants of the earth? Do you visit the other earths, whatever they be called? Do you have the stellar itch? Do you find the aeroplane too slow, too inhibited? Are you a wanderer who plays on muted strings? Or are you a cocoanut that falls to the ground with a thud? I would like to take an inventory of man's longings and compare it with his accomplishments. I would like to be master of the heavens for just one day and rain down all the dreams, desires, longings peculiar to man. I would like to see them take root, not slowly through the course of historical aeons, *but immediately*. God save America! That's what I say too, because who else is capable of doing the trick? And now before I jump Mobile by way of Pascagoula I give you the greetings of a "hotel de luxe", The Lafayette, in New Orleans:—

"To you who enter this room as a guest, we who manage this hotel give hearty greeting.
"We may never get to know you, but just the same we

189

want you to feel that this is a 'human house', and not a soulless institution.

"This is your Home, be it for a day or night only.

"Human beings own the place.

"Human beings care for you here, make the bed and clean the room, answer your telephone, run your errands. We keep a human being at the desk and a human being carries your valise. They are all made of flesh and blood, as you are; they have their interests, likes and dislikes, ambitions, dreams and disappointments, just as you have.

"Of course you have to pay your price. Everybody has to do that everywhere. But the best part of any business transaction is the flow of human interest that goes with it.

"We are going to take care of you. Whatever rules there are here are made for the purpose of protecting you and insuring your comfort, not to annoy you. A good rule for a hotel, as for anything else, is The Golden Rule—Do as you'd be done by.

"We shall try to put ourselves in your place. We ask ourselves, 'How would I like to be treated if I were stopping at a hotel?'

"And we ask you to put yourself in our place. Before you condemn us, ask yourself, 'What would I do if I were running a hotel?'

"If we fail to measure up to that standard, let us know.

"We assume that every man guest here is a Gentleman, every woman guest a Lady. We believe the average American is courteous, quiet, law abiding, anxious to avoid trouble, considerate of others, and willing to pay as he goes.

"May you be healthy under our roof, and no evil befall you.

"May you find here convenience, a cheerful atmosphere, and your days be full of success, so that your stay in this hotel shall be a happy memory.

"For a little space you lodge with us—and we wish to put these good thoughts upon you—so God keep you, stranger, and bring you your heart's desire. And when you go away, leave for this hotel a bit of grateful feeling."

(What a friend we have in Jesus! I brush the pearly tears from my eyes, spit a good healthy gob, and quietly eviscerate the cockroaches I left behind in the cuspidor of Room 213. Make a mental note to reread Ouspenski's *Tertium Organum*. About face!)

I am back in the fourteenth arrondissement and the cot on which I am lying is steaming into Mobile Bay. The exhaust pipe is open, the tiller is at the till. Below me are the crustaceans of the zinc and tin age, the omnivorous anemones, the melted icebergs, the oyster beds, the hollyhocks and the huge hocks of ham. The Lufthansa is conducting a pilgrimage to Hattiesburg. Admiral Farragut has been dead for almost a century. In Devachan most likely. It is all so familiar, the ricocheting mandolins, the ashen fragrance, the corrugated silhouettes, the glassy stare of the bay. Neither toil nor spin, neither bubble nor trouble. The cannons look down on the moat and the moat speaks not. The town is white as a sepulchre. Yesterday was All Souls Day and the sidewalks are peppered with confetti. Those who are up and about are in white ducks. The heat waves make their ascent slantwise, the sound waves move

191

seismographically. No rataplan, no rat-a-tat, but slap-slap, slap-slap. The ducks are floating up the bay, their bills all gold and iridescence. Absinthe is served on the verandah with scones and bursting paw-paws. The caw, the rook, the oriole gather up the crumbs. As it was in the time of Saul, as were the days for the Colossians and the nights for the Egyptians, so it is now. To the south the Horn, eastward the Bosphorus. East, west, clock, counter-clock, Mobile revolves like a torpid astrolabe. Men who knew the shade of the baobab swing lazily in their hammocks. Haunched and dehaunched the boneless bronzed women of the Equatorial regions amble by. Something Mozartian, something Segovian, stirs the air. Maine contributes her virginity, Arabia her spices. It is a merry-go-round standing stock still, the lions affable, the flamingos poised for flight. Take the milk of aloes, mix clove and brandywine, and you have the spiritual elixir of Mobile. There is no hour when things are different, no day which is not the same. It lies in a pocket, is honey-combed with light, and flutters like a plucked cat-gut. It is mobile, fluid, fixed, but not glued. It gives forth no answers, neither does it question. It is mildly, pleasantly bewildering, like the first lesson in Chinese or the first round with a hypnotist. Events transpire in all declensions at once; they are never conjugated. What is not Gog is Magog—and at nine *punkt* Gabriel always blows his horn. *But is it music?* Who cares? The duck is plucked, the air is moist, the tide's out and the goat's securely tethered. The wind is from the bay, the oysters are from the muck. Nothing is too exciting to drown the pluck-pluck of the mandolins. The slugs move from slat to slat; their little hearts beat fast, their brains fill with swill. By evening it's all moonlight on the bay. The lions are still affably baffled and whatever snorts, spits, fumes and hisses is properly snaffled. *C'est la mort du carrousel, la mort douce des choux-bruxelles.*

DAY IN THE PARK

HOLLYWOOD reminds me vividly of Paris by reason of the fact that there are no children in the street. As a matter of fact, now that I think about it, I don't recall seeing children about anywhere except in the Negro quarters of certain Southern cities. Charleston and Richmond particularly. I remember a boy in Charleston, a colored boy about eight years of age, who impressed me by his impudent swagger. He was a sawed-off, hammered-down runt in long pants with an unlit cigarette hanging from the corner of his mouth. He sauntered into the drug store where I was having a drink, looking for all the world like a miniature edition of Sam

Langford. At first I thought he was a Lilliputian, but no, he was just a kid, no more than seven or eight years old. His head didn't even reach to the top of the bar, despite the mannish hat he was wearing. And though he was looking up at us, he gave the impression of looking down, surveying us as if we were fresh vegetables or something. He walked round the bar to where the soda water jerker was standing and coolly asked for a match. The man pretended to be angry and tried to shoo him off, as though he were a big horse-fly. But the kid stood his ground and looked up at him with humorous defiance. He had one hand in his pocket and with the other hand he was nonchalantly twirling a bunch of keys attached to a piece of twine. As the man behind the bar began to assume a more menacing attitude, the kid calmly turned his back on him and strolled over to the rack where the magazines were stacked up. There was an endless series of magazines called "Comics" on the lower shelf just above his head. He moved down the line, reading the titles slowly—Planet, Heroic, Thrilling, Speed, Smash, Jungle, Exciting, Fight, Wings, Startling, True, Magic, Wonderful, etc., etc.—a seemingly inexhaustible variation on the same theme. Finally he picked one out and leisurely flipped the pages. When he had satisfied himself that he wanted it, he tucked it under his arm and then, as he came slowly back towards the bar, he bent down to pick up a parlor match which he found lying on the floor. As he got to the bar he flipped a coin high in the air; it bounced on the counter and fell behind the bar. He did it like a showman, with punctilious braggadocio, which enraged the clerk no end. Meanwhile he looked us all over once again in that impudent way of his and, striking the parlor match on the marble slab of the bar, he lit his cigarette. He held his hand out for the change without looking at the clerk, like a business man too abstracted to be conscious of such a trivial thing as change. When he felt the pennies in his hand he turned his head slightly and spat on the floor. With that of course the clerk made a pass for him but missed. The kid had made a running slide to the doorway. There he paused a moment, grinned insolently at all and sundry and suddenly thumbed his nose at us. Then he took to his heels like a frightened rabbit.

Later, strolling about the Negro quarter with Rattner, I encountered him again, this time leaning against a lamp post reading the "Comics" magazine which he had just bought. He seemed thoroughly absorbed, removed from the world. His hat was tilted back on his head and he had a tooth-pick in his mouth. He looked like a broker who has just finished a hard day on the floor of the Exchange. I felt like ordering a Scotch and soda for him and placing it within his reach without disturbing him. I wondered what the devil he could be reading that held him so enthralled. He had picked out an issue called "Jungle" with a lurid cover depicting a half-naked girl in the arms of a sex-crazed gorilla. We stopped a few feet away to watch him. He never once looked up; he was absolutely impervious to the world.

What a contrast to Bruce and Jacquelin, whom I met in Albuquerque! Bruce was six and Jacquelin about four, I should say. They were the children of Lowell and Lona Springer at whose auto court I was staying for a few days. Lowell worked at the Standard Station at the western end of the town; his wife, Lona, ran a fountain at the entrance to the court. Simple, natural people who seemed happy just to be alive. It was a delight to talk to them. They were intelligent and sensitive, and gracious as only the common people of the world can be. Lowell, the young husband, I was especially intrigued with. He seemed to me to be about the most good-natured person I had ever encountered. You didn't care whether he had any other qualities or not—his goodness of heart was like a tonic. His extraordinary patience and gentleness with the children won my admiration. No matter how busy he was, and he seemed to be working all hours of the day and night, he always had time to answer their inumerable questions or to mend their toys or to bring them a drink when they clamored for it.

The children used to play all day in the court. After a little time, seeing that I left my door open, they got friendly and began to visit me. Soon they began to make known to me that there was a park nearby, where there were lions and tigers and skups and sand piles. They were too well-behaved to ask me outright to take them there, but they threw broad hints in their childish way. "Do you have to work all day every day?" they would ask. "No," I said, "one day I'll take a day off and then we'll go to see the lions and tigers, yes?" That made them terribly excited. Ten minutes later little Jacquelin put her head in the doorway to ask if I was going to work much longer today. "Let's go in your car," she said. "It's a beautiful car."

I was afraid to take them in the car so I asked Lona if it would be all right to walk them to the park—could they walk that far? "Oh, heavens, yes," she said, "they can outwalk me."

I went back and told the youngsters to make themselves ready. "We're all ready," said Bruce, "we're waiting for you." And with that the two of them got me by the two hands and started leading me out of the court.

The park seemed like a good mile off, and we had a lot of fun pretending to lose our way and find it again. They were running ahead of me most of the time, taking short cuts through the tall grass. "Hurry up! Hurry up!" they would yell. "It'll soon be time to feed the lions."

There was an extraordinary grove of trees set in a patch of golden light, a setting I had never expected to find in Albuquerque. It reminded me of a Derain landscape, so golden and legendary it was. I threw myself on the grass and the kids tumbled about like acrobats. In the distance I could hear the lions roaring. Jacquelin was thirsty and kept tugging at me to lead her to the fountain. Bruce wanted to help feed the lions. I wanted simply to lie there forever in the golden lake of light and watch the new sap green moving like mercury through the transparent leaves of the trees. The children were working over me like industrious gnomes to rouse me from the trance; they were tickling my ear drums with blades of grass and pushing and pulling as if I were a fat behemoth. I pulled them on top of me and began tumbling them about like young cubs.

"I want a drink of water, Henry," begged Jacquelin.

"He's not Henry, he's Mr. Miller," said Bruce.

"Call me Henry," I said. "That's my real name."

"Do you know what my name is?" said Bruce. "It's Bruce Michael Springer."

"And what's your name?" said Jacquelin.

"My name is Henry Valentine Miller."

"Valentine! That's a pretty name," said Bruce. "My father's name is Lowell—and my mother's name is Lona. We used to live in Oklahoma. That was years ago. Then we moved to Arkansas."

"And then to Albuquerque," said little Jacquelin, pulling me by the sleeve to get me to my feet.

"Are there any camels or elephants here?" I asked.

"Elephants? What are elephants?" asked Bruce.

"I want to see the tigers," said Jacquelin.

"Yes, let's see the elephants," said Bruce. "Are they tame?"

We moved towards the playground, the children running ahead and clapping their hands with joy. Jacquelin wanted to be put on the skups. So did Bruce. I seated them and began swinging them gently. "Higher!" screamed Jacquelin. "Higher! Higher!" I ran from one to the other pushing as hard as I could. I was afraid that Jacquelin might lose her grip. "Push harder!" she yelled. "Push *me!*" yelled Bruce.

I thought I would never get them down from the skups. "I almost touched the sky, didn't I?" said Bruce. "I bet my father could touch the sky. My father used to take us here every day. My father . . ." He went on about his father. My father this, my father that.

"And Lona?" I said, "what about Lona?"

"She's my mother," said Bruce.

"She's *my* mother, too," said Jacquelin.

"Yes," said Bruce, "she comes too sometimes. But she's not as strong as my father."

"She gets tired," said Jacquelin.

We were approaching the birds and the animals. "I want some peanuts," said Jacquelin. "Please buy me some peanuts, Henry," she said, coaxingly.

"Have you any money?" I asked.

"No, you've got money, haven't you?" she said.

"My father has lots of money," said Bruce. "He gave me two pennies yesterday."

"Where are they?" I asked.

"I spent them. He gives me money every day—all I want. My father makes lots of money. More than Lona."

"I want peanuts!" said Jacquelin, stamping her foot.

We got some peanuts and some ice cream cones and some jelly beans and some chewing gum. They ate everything at once as if they had been starved.

We were standing in front of the dromedaries. "Give him some of your ice cream," I suggested to Jacquelin. She wouldn't do it.

198

She said it would make them sick. Bruce, I noticed, was hastily finishing his ice cream cone.

"Supposing we get them some beer," I said.

"Yes, yes," said Bruce eagerly, "let's get them some beer." Quite as though that were the customary thing to do. Then he paused to reflect. "Won't they get drunk?" he asked.

"Sure," I said. "They'll get very drunk."

"Then what'll they do?" he asked delightedly.

"They'll stand on their hands maybe or . . ."

"Where are their hands?" he said. "Are those his hands?" and he pointed to the front feet.

"He's got his hands in his pocket now," I said. "He's counting his money."

Jacquelin was tickled at the idea. "Where's his pocket?" she asked. "What does he want money for?" asked Bruce.

"What do *you* want money for?" I answered.

"To buy candy."

"Well, don't you think *he* likes to buy candy too, once in a while?"

"But he can't talk!" said Bruce. "He wouldn't know what to ask for."

"He can too talk!" said Jacquelin.

"You see!" I said, turning to Bruce. "And he can whistle."

"Yes, he *can* whistle," said Jacquelin. "I heard him once."

"Make him whistle now," said Bruce.

"He's tired now," I said.

"Yes, he's very tired," said Jacquelin.

"He can't whistle neither," said Bruce.

"He can too whistle," said Jacquelin.

"He can't!" said Bruce.

"He can!" said Jacquelin. "Can't he, Henry?"

We moved on to where the bears and foxes and pumas and llamas were. I had to stop and read every inscription for Bruce.

"Where's India?" he asked, when I read him about the Bengal tiger.

"India's in Asia," I answered.

"Where's Asia?"

"Asia's across the ocean."

"Very far?"

"Yes, very far."

"How long does it take to get there?"

"Oh, about three months," I said.

"By boat or by aeroplane?" he asked.

"Listen, Bruce," I said, "how long do you think it would take to get to the moon?"

"I don't know," he said. "Maybe two weeks. Why, do people go to the moon sometimes?"

"Not very often," I said.

"And do they come back?"

"Not always."

"What's it like on the moon? Have you ever been there? Is it cold? Do they have animals there like here—and grass and trees?"

"They have everything, Bruce, just like here. Peanuts, too."

"And ice cream?" he said.

"Yes, only it tastes differently."

"How does it taste?"

"It tastes more like chewing gum."

"You mean it doesn't melt?"

"No, it never melts," I said.

"That's funny," he said. "Why doesn't it melt?"

"Because it's rubbery."

"I'd rather have this ice cream," he said. "I like it to melt."

We moved on to where the birds were sequestered. I felt sorry for the eagles and condors cooped up in tiny cages. They sat ruefully on their perches as if they knew their wings were atrophying. There were birds of brilliant plumage which hopped around on the ground like chippies; they came from remote parts of the world and were as exotic as the places they came from. There were peacocks too, incredibly vain and, like society women, seemingly of no use to the world except to display their vulgarity. The ostriches were more interesting—tough bimbos, you might say—with strong individualities and plenty of malice. Just to look at their long, muscular necks made me think of thimbles, broken glass and other inedibles. I missed the kangaroo and the giraffe, such forlorn creatures, and so intimately connected with our intra-uterine life. There were foxes of course, creatures which somehow never impress me as being very foxy, perhaps because I've only seen them in menageries. And at last we came to the monarchs of the jungle pacing restlessly back and forth like monomaniacs. To see the lion and tiger caged up is to me one of the cruelest sights in the world. The lion always looks inexpressibly sad, bewildered rather than infuriated. One has an irresistible desire to open the cage and let him run amok. A caged lion somehow always makes the human race look mean and petty. Every time I see lions and tigers in the zoo I feel that we ought to have a cage for human beings too, one of each kind and each in his proper setting: the priest with his altar, the lawyer with his fat, silly law books, the doctor with his instruments of torture, the politician with his dough bag and his wild promises, the teacher with his dunce cap, the policeman with his club and revolver, the judge with his female robes and gavel, and so on. There ought to be a separate cage for the married couple, so that we could study conjugal bliss with a certain detachment and impartiality. How ridiculous we would look if we were put on exhibition! The human peacock! And no studded fan to hide his pusillanimous figure! The laughing stock of creation, that's what we would be.

It was time to be getting home. I had to tear the children gently away. Again we walked beneath the fresh green leaves of the trees that stood in the golden light. Near by ran the Rio Grande, her bed littered with gleaming boulders. Around the broad plain of Albuquerque a great circle of hills which towards dusk assume a variety of fascinating hues. Yes, a land of enchantment, not so much because of what is visible as because of what is hidden in the arid wastes. Walking with the two children in this boundless space I suddenly thought of that South American writer, the poet who wrote about kidnapping children, and the weird, fantastic journey over the pampas in an atmosphere of lunar splendor. I wondered what it would be like to make the rest of the trip with Bruce and Jacquelin in tow. How different my experiences would be! What delicious conversations too! The more I thought about it, the more obsessive became my desire to borrow them of their parents.

Presently, I noticed that Jacquelin was getting tired. She sat down on a rock and looked about her wistfully. Bruce was running ahead, blazing the trail, as it were. "Do you want me to carry you?" I asked Jacquelin. "Yes, Henry, please carry me, I'm so tired," she said, putting out her arms. I lifted her up and placed her little arms around my neck. The next moment the tears were in my eyes. I was happy and sad at the same time. Above all I felt the desire to sacrifice myself. To live one's life without children is to deny oneself a great realm of emotion. Once I had carried my own child this way. Like Lowell Springer I had indulged her every whim. How can one say No to a child? How can one be anything but a slave to one's own flesh and blood?

It was a long walk back to the house. I had to put her down now and then to catch my breath. She was very coy now, flirtatious almost. She knew she had me at her mercy.

"Can't you walk the rest of the way, Jacquelin?" I asked, testing her out.

"No, Henry, I'm too tired." And she held out her arms again appealingly.

Her little arms! The feel of them against my neck melted me completely. Of course she wasn't nearly as tired as she pretended to be. She was exercising her female charms on me, that was all. When we reached the house and I set her down, she began to frisk about like a colt. We had found a discarded toy in back of the house. The unexpected discovery of something she had completely forgotten revived her magically. An old toy is so much better than a new one. Even to me who had not played with it the thing possessed a secret charm. The memories of happy hours seemed to be embedded in it. The very fact that it was worn and dilapidated caused it to create a feeling of warmth and tenderness. Yes, Jacquelin was terribly happy now. She forgot me completely. She had found an old love.

I watched her with fascination. It seemed so completely honest and just to pass like that from one thing to another without thought or consideration. That is a gift which children possess in common with very wise people. The gift of forgetting. The gift of detachment. I went back to the cabin and sat there dreaming for a full hour. Presently a messenger boy arrived with money for me. That brought me back to life, to the monkey world of human values. Money! The very word sounded insane to me. The broken toy in the refuse pile seemed infinitely more valuable and meaningful to me. Suddenly I realized that Albuquerque was a town with stores and banks and moving picture shows. A town like any other town. The magic had gone out of it. The mountains began to assume a touristic look. It began to rain. It never rains in Albuquerque at this time of the year. But it did just the same. It poured. In the little clearance where the children used to play there was now an enormous puddle. Everything had changed. I began to think of sanitariums and deflated lungs, of the little cups which the aeroplane corporations place conveniently beside your seat. Between the cabins a continuous sheet of rain fell slantwise. The children were silent and out of sight. The outing was over. There was neither joy nor sorrow left —just a feeling of emptiness.

AUTOMOTIVE PASSACAGLIA

I FEEL like doing a little passacaglia now about things automotive. Ever since I decided to sell the car she's been running beautifully. The damned thing behaves like a flirtatious woman.

Back in Albuquerque, where I met that automotive expert Hugh Dutter, everything was going wrong with her. Sometimes I think it was all the fault of the tail wind that swept me along through Oklahoma and the Texas panhandle. Did I mention the episode with the drunk who tried to run me into a ditch? He almost had me convinced that I had lost my generator. I was a bit ashamed, of course, to ask people if my generator were gone, as he said, but every time I had a chance to open up a conversation with a garage man I would work him round to the subject of generators, hoping first of all that he would show me where the damned thing was hidden, and second that he would tell me whether or not a car could function without one. I had just a vague idea that the generator had something to do with the battery. Perhaps it hasn't, but that's my notion of it still.

The thing I enjoy about visiting garage men is that one contradicts the other. It's very much as in medicine, or the field of criticism in literature. Just when you believe you have the answer you find that you're mistaken. A little man will tinker with your machinery for an hour and blushingly ask you for a dime, and whether he's done the correct thing or not the car runs, whereas the big service stations will lay her up in dry dock for a few days, break her down into molecules and atoms, and then like as not she'll run a few miles and collapse.

There's one thing I'd like to advise any one thinking of making a trans-continental journey: see that you have a jack, a monkey wrench and a jimmy. You'll probably find that the wrench won't fit the nuts but that doesn't matter; while you're pretending to fiddle around with it some one will stop and lend you a helping hand. I had to get stuck in the middle of a swamp in Louisiana before I realized that I had no tools. It took me a half hour to realize that if there were any they would be hidden under the front seat. And if a man promises you that he will stop at the next town and send some one to haul you don't believe him. Ask the next man and the next man and the next man. Keep a steady relay going or you'll sit by the roadside till doomsday. And never say that you have no tools—it sounds suspicious, as though you had stolen the car. Say you lost them, or that they were stolen from you in Chicago. Another thing—if you've just had your front wheels packed don't take it for granted that the wheels are on tight. Stop at the next station and ask to have the lugs tightened, then you'll be sure your front wheel won't roll off in the middle of the night. Take it for granted that nobody, not even a genius, can guarantee that your car won't fall apart five minutes after he's examined it. A car is even more delicate than a Swiss watch. And a lot more diabolical, if you know what I mean.

If you don't know much about cars it's only natural to want to take it to a big service station when something goes wrong. A great mistake, of course, but it's better to learn by experience than by hearsay. How are you to know that the little man who looks like a putterer may be a wizard?

Anyway, you go to the service station. And immediately you come smack up against a man dressed in a butcher's smock, a man with a pad in his hand and a pencil behind his ear, looking very professional and alert, a man who never fully assures you that the car will be perfect when they get through with it but who intimates that the service will be impeccable, of the very highest calibre, and that sort of thing. They all have something of the surgeon about them, these entrepreneurs of the automobile industry. You see, they seem to imply, you've come to us only at the last ditch; we can't perform miracles, but we've had twenty or thirty years' experience and can furnish the best of references. And, just as with the surgeon, you have the feeling when you entrust the car to his immaculate hands, that he is going to telephone you in the middle of the night, after the engine has been taken apart and the bearings are lying all about, and tell you that there's something even more drastically wrong with the car than he had at first suspected. Something serious, what! It starts with a case of bad lungs and ends up with a removal of the appendix, gall bladder, liver and testicles. The bill is always indisputably correct and of a figure no less than formidable. Everything is itemized, except the quality of the foreman's brains. Instinctively you put it safely away in order to produce it at the next hospital when the car breaks down again; you want to be able to prove that you knew what was wrong with the car all along.

After you've had a few experiences of this sort you get wary, that is if you're slow to catch on, as I am. After you stay in a town a while and get acquainted, feel that you are among friends, you throw out a feeler; you learn that just around the corner from the big service station there's a little fellow (his place is always in the rear of some other place and therefore hard to find) who's a wizard at fixing things and asks some ridiculously low sum for his services. They'll tell you that he treats *everybody* that way, even those with "foreign" license plates.

Well, that's exactly what happened to me in Albuquerque, thanks to the friendship I struck up with Dr. Peters who is a great surgeon and a *bon vivant* as well. One day, not having anything better to do—one of those days when you call up telephone numbers or else go to have your teeth cleaned—one day, as I say, in the midst of a downpour I decided to consult the master mind, the painless Parker of the automotive world: Hugh Dutter. There was nothing very seriously wrong—just a constant high fever. The men at the service station didn't attach much importance to it—they attributed it to the altitude, the age of the car and so on. I suppose there was nothing more that they could repair or replace. But when on a cold, rainy day a car runs a temperature of 170 to 180 there must be something wrong, so I reasoned. If she was running that high at 5,000 feet what would she run at 7,000 or 10,000?

I stood in the doorway of the repair shop for almost an hour waiting for Dutter to return. He had gone to have a bite with some friends, never dreaming that there would be any customers waiting for him in such a downpour. His assistant, who was from Kansas, regaled me with stories about fording flooded streams back in Kansas. He spoke as though people had nothing better to do when it rained than practise these dangerous manoeuvres with their tin Lizzies. Once he said a bus got caught in the head waters of a creek, keeled over, was washed downstream and never found again. He liked rain—it made him homesick.

Presently Dutter arrived. I had to wait until he went to a shelf and arranged some accessories. After I had sheepishly explained my troubles he leisurely scratched his head and without even looking in the direction of the engine he said: "Well, there could be a lot of reasons for her heating up on you that way. Have you had your radiator boiled out?"

I told him I had—back in Johnson City, Tennessee.

"How long ago was that?" he said.

"Just a few months back."

"I see. I thought you were going to say a few years ago."

The car was still standing outside in the rain. "Don't you want to look her over?" I said, fearing that he might lose interest in the case.

"You might bring her in," he said. "No harm in taking a look. Nine times out of ten it's the radiator. Maybe they didn't do a good job for you back in Cleveland."

"Johnson City!" I corrected.

"Well, wherever it was." He ordered his assistant to drive her in.

I could see he wasn't very enthusiastic about the job: it wasn't as though I had brought him a bursting gall bladder or a pair of elephantine legs. I thought to myself—better leave him alone with it for a while; maybe when he begins to putter around he'll work up a little interest. So I excused myself and went off to get a bite.

"I'll be back soon," I said.

209

"That's all right, don't hurry," he answered. "It may take hours to find out what's wrong with her."

I had a Chop Suey and on the way back I loitered a bit in order to give him time to arrive at a correct diagnosis. To kill a little time I stopped in at the Chamber of Commerce and inquired about the condition of the roads going to Mesa Verde. I learned that in New Mexico you can tell nothing about the condition of the roads by consulting the map. For one thing the road map doesn't say how much you may be obliged to pay if you get stuck in deep clay and have to be hauled fifty or seventy-five miles. And between gravel and graded roads there's a world of difference. At the Automobile Club in New York I remember the fellow taking a greasy red pencil and tracing a route for me backwards while answering two telephones and cashing a check.

"Mesa Verde won't be officially open until about the middle of May," said the fellow. "I wouldn't risk it yet. If we get a warm rain there's no telling what will happen."

I decided to go to Arizona, unless I had an attack of chilblains. I was a little disappointed though to miss seeing Shiprock and Aztec.

When I got back to the garage I found Dutter bending over the engine; he had his ear to the motor, like a doctor examining a weak lung. From the vital parts there dangled an electric bulb attached to a long wire. The electric bulb always reassures me. It means business. Anyway, he was down in the guts of the thing and getting somewhere—so it looked.

"Found out what's wrong yet?" I ventured to inquire timidly.

"No," he said, burying his wrist in a mess of intricate whirring thingamajigs which looked like the authentic automotive part of the automobile. It was the first time I had ever seen what makes a car go. It was rather beautiful, in a mechanical way. Reminded me of a steam calliope playing Chopin in a tub of grease.

"She wasn't timing right," said Dutter, twisting his neck around to look at me but, like the skilful surgeon, still operating with his deft right hand. "I knew that much before I even looked at her. That'll heat a car up quicker'n anything." And he began explaining to me from deep down in the bowels of the car how the timing worked. As I remember it now an eight cylinder car fires 2,3,5,7 with one cam and 3,4,6,8 with the other. I may be wrong on the figures but the word cam is what interested me. It's a beautiful word and when he tried to point it out to me I liked it still better—the cam. It has a down-to-earth quality about it, like piston and gear. Even an ignoramus like myself knows that piston, just from the sound of the word, means something that has to do with the driving force, that it's intimately connected with the locomotion of the vehicle. I still have to see a piston per se, but I believe in pistons even though I should never have the chance to see one cold and isolate.

The timing occupied him for quite a while. He explained what a difference a quarter of a degree could make. He was working on the carburetor, if I am not mistaken. I accepted this explanation, as I had the others, unquestioningly. Meanwhile I was getting acquainted with the fly-wheel and some other more or less essential organs of the mysterious mechanism. Most everything about a car, I should say in passing, is more or less essential. All but the nuts underneath the chassis; they can get loose and fall out, like old teeth, without serious damage. I'm not speaking now of the universal—that's another matter. But all those rusty nuts which you see dropping off when the car's jacked up on the hoist—actually they mean very little. At worst the running board may drop off, but once you know your running board is off there's no great harm done.

Apropos of something or other he suddenly asked me at what temperature the thermostat was set. I couldn't tell him. I had heard a lot about thermostats, and I knew there was one in the car somewhere, but just where, and just what it looked like, I didn't know. I evaded all references to the subject as skilfully as I could. Again I was ashamed not to know where and what this piece of apparatus was. Starting out from New York, after receiving a brief explanation about the functioning or non-functioning of the thermostat, I had expected the shutters of the hood to fly open automatically when the heat gauge read 180 or 190. To me thermostat meant something like a cuckoo in a cuckoo clock. My eye was constantly on the gauge, waiting for it to hit 180. Rattner, my then side-kick, used to get a bit irritated watching me watch the gauge. Several times we went off the road because of this obsession on my part. But I always expected that some time or other an invisible man would release the trap and the cuckoo would fly out and then bango! the shutters would open up, the air circulate between the legs, and the motor begin to purr like a musical cat. Of course the damned shutters never did fly open. And when the gauge did finally hit 190 the next thing I knew was that the radiator was boiling over and the nearest town was forty miles away.

Well, after the timing had been corrected, the points adjusted, the carburetor calibrated, the accelerator exhilarated, all the nuts, bolts and screws carefully restored to their proper positions, Dutter invited me to accompany him on a test flight. He decided to drive her up through Tijeras Canyon where there was a big grade. He set out at fifty miles an hour, which worried me a bit because the mechanic at the big service station had said to drive her slow for the next thousand miles until she loosened up a bit. The gauge moved slowly up to 180 and, once we were properly in the pass, it swung to 190 and kept on rising.

"I don't think she'll boil," he said, lighting himself a cigarette with a parlor match. "Up here the principle is never to worry until

212

she boils over. Cars act temperamental up here, just like people. It could be weather, it could be scales in the engine box . . . it could be a lot of things. And it mightn't be anything more than altitude. The Buicks never did make big enough radiators for the size of the car." I found this sort of talk rather cheering. More like a good French doctor. The American physician always says immediately—"Better have an X-ray taken; better pull out all your back teeth; better get an artificial leg." He's got you all cut up and bleeding before he's even looked at your throat. If you've got a simple case of worms he finds that you've been suffering from hereditary constriction of the corneal phylactery since childhood. You get drunk and decide to keep the worms or whatever ails you.

Dutter went on to talk in his calm, matter of fact way about new and old Buicks, about too much compression and too little space, about buying whole parts instead of a part of a part, as with the Chevrolet or the Dodge. Not that the Buick wasn't a good car— oh no, it was a damned good car, but like every car it had its weak points too. He talked about boiling over several times on his way from Espanola to Santa Fe. I had boiled over there myself, so I listened sympathetically. I remember getting near the top of the hill and then turning round to coast down in order to get a fresh start. And then suddenly it was dark and there were no clear crystal springs anywhere in sight. And then the lizards began whispering to one another and you could hear them whispering for miles around, so still it was and so utterly desolate.

Coming back Dutter got talking about parts and parts of parts, rather intricate for me, especially when he began comparing Pontiac parts with parts of parts belonging to the Plymouth or the Dodge. The Dodge was a fine car, he thought, but speaking for himself he preferred the old Studebaker. "Why don't you get yourself a nice old Studebaker?" I asked. He looked at me peculiarly. I gathered

213

that the Studebaker must have been taken off the market years ago. And then, almost immediately afterwards, I began talking about Lancias and Pierce Arrows. I wasn't sure whether they made them any more either, but I knew they had always enjoyed a good reputation. I wanted to show him that I was willing to talk cars, if that was the game. He glossed over these remarks however in order to launch into a technical explanation of how cores were casted and molded, how you tested them with an ice pick to see if they were too thick or too thin. This over he went into an excursus about the transmission and the differential, a subject so abstruse that I hadn't the faintest notion what he was getting at. The gauge, I observed, was climbing down towards 170. I thought to myself how pleasant it would be to hire a man like Dutter to accompany me the rest of the way. Even if the car broke down utterly it would be instructive and entertaining to hear him talk about the parts. I could understand how people became attached to their cars, knowing all the parts intimately, as they undoubtedly do.

When we got back to the laboratory he went inside for a thermometer. Then he took the cap off the radiator and stuck the thermometer in the boiling radiator. At intervals he made a reading —comparative readings such as a theologian might do with the Bible. There was a seventeen degree difference, it developed, between the reading of the gauge and the thermometer reading. The difference was in my favor, he said. I didn't understand precisely what he meant by this remark, but I made a mental note of it. The car looked pathetically human with the thermometer sticking out of its throat. It looked like it had quinsy or the mumps.

I heard him mumbling to himself about scales and what a delicate operation that was. The word hydrochloric acid popped up. "Never do that till the very last," he said solemnly.

"Do what?" I asked, but he didn't hear me, I guess.

214

"Can't tell what will happen to her when the acid hits her," he mumbled between his teeth.

"Now I tell you," he went on, when he had satisfied himself that there was nothing seriously wrong, "I'm going to block that thermostat open a little more with a piece of wood—and put in a new fan belt. We'll give her an eight pound pull to begin with and after she's gone about four hundred miles you can test her yourself and see if she's slipping." He scratched his head and ruminated a bit. "If I were you," he continued, "I'd go back to that service station and ask them to loosen the tappets a little. It says .0010 thousandth on the engine but up here you can ride her at .0008 thousandth— until you hear that funny little noise, that clickety-click-click, you know—like little bracelets. I tried to catch that noise before when she was cold but I couldn't get it. I always like to listen for that little noise—then I know she's not too tight. You see, you've got a hot blue flame in there and when your valves are screwed down too tight that flame just burns them up in no time. That can heat a car up too! Just remember—*the tappets!*"

We had a friendly little chat about the slaughter going on in Europe, to wind up the transaction, and then I shook hands with him. "I don't think you'll have any more trouble," he said. "But just to make sure why you come back here after they loosen the tappets and I'll see how she sounds. Got a nice little car there. She ought to last you another twenty thousand miles—*at least.*"

I went back to the big service station and had the tappets attended to. They were most gracious about it, I must say. No charge for their services this time. Rather strange, I thought. Just as I was pulling out the floorwalker in the butcher's smock informed me with diabolical suavity that, no matter what any one may have told me, the pretty little noise I was looking for had nothing to do with the tightness or looseness of the valves. It was something else which

215

caused that. "We don't believe in loosening them too much," he said. "But you wanted it that way, so we obliged you."

I couldn't pretend to contradict him, not having the knowledge of Hugh Dutter to fortify my argument, so I decided to have the car washed and greased and find out in a roundabout way what the devil he meant.

When I came back for the car the manager came over and politely informed me that there was one other very important thing I ought to have done before leaving. "What's that?" I said.

"Grease the clutch."

How much would that be, I wanted to know. He said it was a thirty minute job—not over a dollar.

"O.K.," I said. "Grease the clutch. Grease everything you can lay hands on."

I took a thirty minute stroll around the block, stopping at a tavern, and when I got back the boy informed me that the clutch didn't need greasing.

"What the hell is this?" I said. "What did he tell me to have it greased for?"

"He tells everybody that," said the boy, grinning.

As I was backing out he asked me slyly if she het up much on me. "A little," I said.

"Well, don't pay any attention to it," he said. "Just wait till she boils. It's a mighty smooth running car, that Buick. Prettiest little ole car I ever did see. See us again sometime."

Well, there it is. If you've ever served in the coast artillery you know what it's like to take the azimuth. First you take a course in higher trigonometry, including differential calculus and all the logarithms. When you put the shell in the breech be sure to remove all your fingers before locking the breech. A car is the same way. It's like a horse, in short. What brings on the heat is fuss and bother.

216

Feed him properly, water him well, coax him along when he's weary and he'll die for you. The automobile was invented in order for us to learn how to be patient and gentle with one another. It doesn't matter about the parts, or even about the parts of parts, nor what model or what year it is, so long as you treat her right. What a car appreciates is responsiveness. A loose differential may or may not cause friction and no car, not even a Rolls Royce, will run without a universal, but everything else being equal it's not the pressure or lack of pressure in the exhaust pipe which matters—it's the way you handle her, the pleasant little word now and then, the spirit of forbearance and forgiveness. Do unto others as you would have them do by you is the basic principle of automotive engineering. Henry Ford understood these things from the very beginning. That's why he paid universal wages. He was calibrating the exchequer in order to make the steep grades. There's just one thing to remember about driving any automotive apparatus and that is this: when the car begins to act as though it had the blind staggers it's time to get out and put a bullet through its head. We American people have always been kind to animals and other creatures of the earth. It's in our blood. Be kind to your Buick or your Studebaker. God gave us these blessings in order to enrich the automobile manufacturers. He did not mean for us to lose our tempers easily. If that's clear we can go on to Gallup and trade her in for a spavined mule. . . .

A DESERT RAT

I SIZED him up for a desert rat the moment he sat down. He was very quiet, modest, self-contained, with watery blue eyes and blenched lips. The whites of the eyes were blood-shot. It was his eyes which gave me the impression that he had been living in the blinding sun. But when, in a moment or two, I questioned him about his eyes he replied, to my astonishment, that their condition was due to an attack of measles. He had almost lost his sight, he said, when it occurred to him to try eating butter, lots of butter, a quarter of a pound at a time. From then on his eyes had improved. He was of the opinion that the natural grease which butter provides did the trick.

218

The conversation began smoothly and easily and lasted several hours. The waitress was rather surprised to see me talking to him so earnestly. She had been rather hesitant about placing him at my table—because he was rather shabbily attired and looked as though he might be dirty too. Most of the visitors to the Bright Angel Lodge are decked out in the latest knock-about regalia, the men more so than the women. Some of them go Western when they reach the Grand Canyon and come to table with huge sombreros and boots and checker-board shirts. The women seem crazy to don their pants, especially the fat women with diamond rings on their fingers and feet swollen with corns and bunions.

I must preface all this by remarking that the management of the Bright Angel Lodge seemed surprised that I should remain so long, most of the visitors being in the habit of staying just a day or two, many not even that long, some for just a half hour, long enough, as it were, to look down into the big hole and say they had seen it. I stayed about ten days. It was on the ninth day that I struck up a conversation with the prospector from Barstow. Since I left Albuquerque I hadn't spoken to a soul, except to ask for gas and water. It was wonderful to keep the silence for so long a period. Rambling about the rim of the canyon I caught the weirdest fragments of conversation, startling because so unrelated to the nature of the place. For example, coming up behind an insipid young girl who was flirting with a pudgy Hopi Indian I overheard the following:

She: "In the army you won't be able to. . . ."

He: "But I won't be in the army!"

She: "Oh, that's right, you're going to join the navy." And then she added blithely: "Do you like water . . . and boats . . . and that sort of thing?" As though to say, "because if you do, our admirals and rear-admirals will furnish you with all the water you want . . . good salty water with waves and everything. Wait till you see our ocean—it's real water, every drop of it. And of course there are plenty of cannons to shoot with . . . you know, aeroplanes and what not. It will be quite exciting, you'll see. We have a war every now and then just to keep our boys in trim. You'll love it!"

Another evening, as I'm returning to the lodge from Yavapai Point, an old spinster with a plate of ice cream in her hand remarks to her escort, a seedy-looking professor, as she licks the spoon: "Nothing so extraordinary about this, is there?" It was about seven in the evening and she was pointing to the canyon with her dripping spoon. Evidently the sunset hadn't come up to her expectations. It wasn't all flamy gold like an omelette dripping from Heaven. No, it was a quiet, reserved sunset, showing just a thin rim of fire over the far edge of the canyon. But if she had looked at the ground beneath her feet she might have observed that it was flushed with a beautiful lavender and old rose; and if she had raised her eyes to the topmost rim of rock which supports the thin layer of soil that forms the plateau she would have noticed that it was of a rare tint of black, a poetic tinge of black which could only be compared to a river or the wet trunk of a live oak or that most perfect highway which runs from Jacksonville to Pensacola under a sky filled with dramatic clouds.

The best remark, to be sure, was one I overheard the last evening I spent there. A young girl in the company of three hoodlums, in a voice which seemed to reach clear across the canyon, suddenly says: "Did you see the headline tonight?" She was referring to the San Bernardino crime in which a hunchback figured mysteriously. "It's funny," she said, "I no sooner leave home than my friends get bumped off. You remember Violet? I brought her up to the house once." And she went on in a loud, clear voice, as though speaking through a megaphone, about Violet, Raymond and Jesse, I think it was. Everything struck her as funny, even the stretch one of her friends had done in San Quentin. "He musta been nuts!" she kept repeating over and over. I observed the expression on the face of a society woman in long pants who was sitting nearby, shocked to death by the young girl's casual jocose remarks. "Where do these horrid creatures ever come from?" she seemed to be asking herself. "Really, something ought to be done about this. I must speak to the management." You could just hear her fulminating and bombinating inside, like a choked up engine gasping in the desert at 130 degrees Fahrenheit.

And then there was the son of a curio-shop-keeper who caught me early one morning, thinking I had just arrived, and insisted on pointing things out through a telescope. "That shirt down there, on the pole—it's a rather interesting phenomenon." I couldn't see what was so interesting about it. But to him everything was phenomenal and interesting, including the hotel on the opposite side of the canyon—because you could see it clearly through the telescope. "Have you seen the large painting of the Canyon in my father's shop?" he asked, as I was about to leave him. "It's a phenomenal piece of work." I told him bluntly I had no intention of looking at it, with all due respect to his father and the shop he ran. He looked aggrieved, wounded, utterly amazed that I should not care to see one of the greatest reproductions of Nature by the hand of man. "When you get a little more sense," I said, "maybe it won't seem so wonderful to you. What do I owe you for looking through the telescope?"

He was taken aback. "Owe me?" he repeated. "Why, you don't owe me anything. We're happy to be of service to you. If you need some films just stop in to my father's shop. We carry a complete line. . . ."

"I never use a camera," I said, starting to walk off.

"*What!* You never use a camera? Why, I never heard . . ."

221

"No, and I never buy post cards or blankets or tiny meteorites. I came here to see the Canyon, that's all. Good morning to you and may you thrive in bliss and agony." With that I turned my back on him and continued on my jaunt.

I was fuming to think that a young boy should have nothing better to do than try to waylay tourists for his father at that hour of the morning. Pretending to be fixing the telescope, polishing it, and so on, and then pulling off that nonsense about "man imitating God's handiwork"—on a piece of canvas, no less, when there before one's eyes was God himself in all his glory, manifesting his grandeur without the aid or intervention of man. All to sell you a fossil or a string of beads or some photographic film. Reminded me of the bazaars at Lourdes. Coney Island, foul as it is, is more honest. Nobody raves about the salt in the ocean. One goes there to swelter and stew and be honestly gypped by the most expert gyppers in the world.

Well, to get back to something clean. There was the old desert rat smiling at me and talking about the curse of the automobile. It had done one good thing, he admitted, and that was to break up people's clannishness. But on the other hand it made people rootless. Everything was too easy—nobody wanted to fight and struggle any more. Men were getting soft. Nothing could satisfy them any more. Looking for thrills all the time. Something he couldn't fathom —how they could be soft and cowardly and yet not frightened of death. Long as it gave 'em a thrill, didn't care what happened. He had just left a party of women down the road a ways. One of them had broken her neck. Came around a curve too fast. He spoke about it quietly and easily, as though it were just an incident. He had seen lots of cars turn over in the desert, racing at a hundred and a hundred and ten miles an hour. "Seems like they can't go fast enough," he said. "Nobody goes at forty-five miles an hour, which is the speed

222

limit in California. I don't know why they make laws for people to break; it seems foolish to me. If they want people to drive carefully why do they make motors that run at seventy-five and eighty and a hundred miles an hour? It ain't logical, is it?"

He went on about the virtue of living alone in the desert, of living with the stars and rocks, studying the earth, listening to one's own voice, wondering about Creation and that sort of thing. "A man gets to do a lot of thinking when he's by himself all the time. I ain't never been much of a book reader. All I know is what I learned myself—from experience, from using my eyes and ears."

I wanted to know, rather foolishly, just where he thought the desert began.

"Why, as far as I can make out," he said, "it's all desert, all this country. There's always some vegetation—it ain't just sand, you know. It has brush on it and there's soil if you can bring water to it and nourish it. People seem to get panicky when they get to the desert. Think they're going to die of thirst or freeze to death at night. Of course it happens sometimes, but mostly through frettin'. If you just take it easy and don't fret yourself it won't never hurt you. Most people die of sheer panic. A man can go without water for a day or two—it won't kill him—not if he don't worry about it. Why, I wouldn't want to live anywhere else. You couldn't get me back to Iowa if you paid me to live there."

I wanted to know about the bad lands, if they were absolutely unreclaimable. I had been impressed, on coming to the Painted Desert, I said, because the earth looked like something which had already become extinct. Was it really so—could nothing be done about these regions?

Not much, he thought. They might stay that way for millions of years. There were chemicals in the earth, an acid condition, which made it impossible to grow things in such places. "But I'll tell you," he added, "it's my belief that the tendency is in the other direction."

"What do you mean?" I asked.

"I mean that the earth is coming alive faster than it's going dead. It may take millions of years to notice the change, but it's going on steadily. There's something in the air which feeds the earth. You look at a sunbeam . . . you know how you see things floating in the air. Something is always dropping back to earth . . . little particles which nourish the soil. Now the Painted Desert . . . I've been over a good part of it. There's nothing there to hurt you. It isn't all explored yet, of course. Even the Indians don't know it all." He went on to talk about the colors of the desert, how they had been formed through the cooling of the earth; he talked about prehistoric forms of life embedded in the rocks, about a plateau somewhere in the midst of the Desert which an aviator had discovered and which was full of tiny horses. "Some say they were the little horses brought in by the Spaniards years ago, but my theory is that there's something lacking in the water or the vegetation which stunts their growth." He spoke of the horses with such vivid imagery that I began to see in my mind's eye the original prehistoric beast, the eohippus, or whatever it's called, which I had always pictured as running wild and free on the plains of Tartary. "It's not so strange," he was saying. "You take in Africa, they've got pygmies and elephants and that sort of thing." Why elephants? I asked myself. Perhaps he had meant something else. He knew what an elephant was like, I know, because in a little while he got to talking about the bones and skeletons of great animals which had once roamed the country—camels, elephants, dinosaurs, sabre-toothed tigers, etc., all dug up in the desert and elsewhere. He spoke about the fresh meat found on the frozen mastodons in Siberia, Alaska and Canada, about the earth moving into strange new zodiacal realms and flopping over on its axis; about the great

224

climatic changes, sudden, catastrophic changes, burying whole epochs alive, making deserts of tropical seas and pushing up mountains where once there was sea, and so on. He spoke fascinatingly, lingeringly, as if he had witnessed it all himself from some high place in some ageless cloak of flesh.

"It's the same with man," he continued. "I figure that when we get too close to the secret Nature has a way of getting rid of us. Of course, we're getting smarter and smarter every day, but we never get to the bottom of things, and we never will. God didn't intend it that way. We think we know a lot, but we think in a rut. Book people ain't more intelligent than other folk. They just learn how to read things a certain way. Put them in a new situation and they lose their heads. They ain't flexible. They only know how to think the way they were taught. That ain't intelligent, to my way of thinkin'."

He went on to speak about a group of scientists he had encountered once off Catalina Island. They were experts, he said, on the subject of Indian burial mounds. They had come to this spot, where he was doing some dredging, to investigate a huge pile of skeletons found near the water's edge. It was their theory that at some time in the distant past the Indians of the vicinity had eaten too many clams, had been poisoned and had died in droves, their bodies piled pell-mell in a grand heap.

"Ain't my idea of it!" he said to one of the professors, after he had listened to their nonsense as long as he could stand it.

They looked at him as though to say—"Who asked you for an opinion? What could you possibly know about the subject?"

Finally one of the professors asked him what his idea might be.

"I'm not tellin' you yet," he said. "I want to see what you can find out for yourself first."

That made them angry, of course. After a time he began plying

225

them with questions—Socratic questions, which irritated them still more. Wanted to know, since they had been studying Indian burial grounds all their lives, had they ever seen skeletons piled up this way before. "Ever find any clam shells around here?" he queried. No, they hadn't seen a single clam, dead or alive. "Neither have I," he said. "There ain't never been any clams around here."

Next day he called their attention to the soot. "Would have to bake a lot of clams to make all that soot, wouldn't they?" he said to one of the professors. Between the ash of wood and volcanic ash there's a considerable difference, he wanted me to know. "Wood," he said, "makes a greasy soot; no matter how old it is the soot remains greasy. This soot in which the skeletons were buried was volcanic." His theory was that there had been an eruption, that the Indians had attempted to flee to the sea, and were caught under the rain of fire.

The savants of course scoffed at his theory. "I didn't argue with them," he said. "I didn't want to make them mad again. I just put two and two together and told them what I thought. A day or two later they came to me and they agreed that my idea was fairly sound. Said they were going to look into it."

He went on to talk about the Indians. He had lived with them and knew their ways a bit. He seemed to have a deep respect for them.

I wanted him to tell me about the Navajos whom I had been hearing so much about ever since reaching the West. Was it true that they were increasing at a phenomenal pace? Some authority on the subject had been quoted as saying that in a hundred years, if nothing untowards occurred to arrest the development, the Navajos would be as populous as we are now. Rumor had it that they practised polygamy, each Navajo being allowed three wives. In any case, their increase was phenomenal. I was hoping he would tell me that the Indians would grow strong and powerful again.

By way of answer he said that there were legends which predicted the downfall of the white man through some great catastrophe— fire, famine, flood, or some such thing.

"Why not simply through greed and ignorance?" I put in.

"Yes," he said, "the Indian believes that when the time comes only those who are strong and enduring will survive. They have never accepted our way of life. They don't look upon us as superior to them in any way. They tolerate us, that's all. No matter how educated they become they always return to the tribe. They're just waiting for us to die off, I guess."

I was delighted to hear it. It would be marvelous, I thought to myself, if one day they would be able to rise up strong in number and drive us into the sea, take back the land which we stole from them, tear our cities down, or use them as carnival grounds. Only the night before, as I was taking my customary promenade along the rim of the Canyon, the sight of a funny sheet (Prince Valiant was what caught my eye) lying on the edge of the abyss awakened curious reflections. What can possibly appear more futile, sterile and insignificant in the presence of such a vast and mysterious spectacle as the Grand Canyon than the Sunday comic sheet? There it lay, carelessly tossed aside by an indifferent reader, the least wind ready to lift it aloft and blow it to extinction. Behind this gaudy-colored sheet, requiring for its creation the energies of countless men, the varied resources of Nature, the feeble desires of over-fed children, lay the whole story of the culmination of our Western civilization. Between the funny sheet, a battleship, a dynamo, a radio broadcasting station it is hard for me to make any distinction of value. They are all on the same plane, all manifestations of restless, uncontrolled energy, of impermanency, of death and dissolution. Looking out into the Canyon at the great amphi-

227

theatres, the Coliseums, the temples which Nature over an incalculable period of time has carved out of the different orders of rock, I asked myself why indeed could it not have been the work of man, this vast creation? Why is it that in America the great works of art are all Nature's doing? There were the skyscrapers, to be sure, and the dams and bridges and the concrete highways. All utilitarian. Nowhere in America was there anything comparable to the cathedrals of Europe, the temples of Asia and Egypt—enduring monuments created out of faith and love and passion. No exaltation, no fervor, no zeal—except to increase business, facilitate transportation, enlarge the domain of ruthless exploitation. *The result?* A swiftly decaying people, almost a third of them pauperized, the more intelligent and affluent ones practising race suicide, the under-dogs becoming more and more unruly, more criminal-minded, more degenerate and degraded in every way. A handful of reckless, ambitious politicians trying to convince the mob that this is the last refuge of civilization, God save the mark!

My friend from the desert made frequent allusions to "the great secret." I thought of Goethe's great phrase: *"the open secret"!* The scientists are not the men to read it. They have penetrated nowhere in their attempts to solve the riddle. They have only pushed it back farther, made it appear still more inscrutable. The men of the future will look upon the relics of this age as we now look upon the artifacts of the Stone Age. We are mental dinosaurs. We lumber along heavy-footed, dull-witted, unimaginative amidst miracles to which we are impervious. All our inventions and discoveries lead to annihilation.

Meanwhile the Indian lives very much as he has always lived, unconvinced that we have a better way of life to offer him. He waits stoically for the work of self-destruction to complete itself. When we have grown utterly soft and degenerate, when we collapse in-

228

wardly and fall apart, he will take over this land which we have desperately striven to lay waste. He will move out of the bad lands which we have turned into Reservations for the Untouchables and reclaim the forests and streams which were once his. It will grow quiet again when we are gone: no more hideous factories and mills, no more blast furnaces, no more chimneys and smoke-stacks. Men will become clairvoyant again and telepathic. Our instruments are but crutches which have paralyzed us. We have not grown more humane, through our discoveries and inventions, but more inhuman. And so we must perish, be superseded by an "inferior" race of men whom we have treated like pariahs. They at least have never lost their touch with the earth. They are rooted and will revive the moment the fungus of civilization is removed. It may be true that this is the great melting pot of the world. But the fusion has not begun to take place yet. Only when the red man and the black man, the brown man and the yellow man unite with the white peoples of the earth in full equality, in full amity and respect for one another, will the melting pot serve its purpose. Then we may see on this continent—thousands of years hence—the beginnings of a new order of life. But the white American will first have to be humiliated and defeated; he will have to humble himself and cry for mercy; he will have to acknowledge his sins and omissions; he will have to beg and pray that he be admitted to the new and greater fraternity of mankind which he himself was incapable of creating.

We were talking about the war. "It wouldn't be so bad," said my friend, "if the people who want war did the fighting, but to make people who have no hatred in them, people who are innocent, do the slaughtering is horrible. Wars accomplish nothing. Two wrongs never made a right. Supposing I lick you and I hold you down— what will you be thinking? You'll be waiting for your chance to get me when my back is turned, won't you? You can't keep peace by holding people down. You've got to give people what they want—more than they want. You've got to be generous and kind. The war could be stopped tomorrow if we really wanted it to be stopped.

"I'm afraid, though, that we're going to be in the war in less than thirty days. Looks like Roosevelt wants to push us in. He's going to be the next dictator. You remember when he said that he would be the last president of the United States? How did the other dictators gain power? First they won over organized labor, didn't they? Well, it looks as though Roosevelt were doing the same thing, doesn't it? Of course, I don't think he will last his term out. Unless he is assassinated—which may happen—Lindbergh will be our next president. The people of America don't want to go to war. They want peace. And when the President of the United States tries to make a man like Lindbergh look like a traitor he's inciting the people to revolution. We people out here don't want any trouble with other countries. We want to just mind our own business and get along in our own humble way. We're not afraid of Hitler invading this country. And as for us invading Europe—how are we going to do it? Hitler is the master of Europe and we have to wait until he cracks up, that's how I see it. Give a man enough rope and he'll hang himself, that's what I always say. There's only one way to stop war and that's to do what Hitler's doing—gobble up all the small nations, take their arms away from them, and police the world. We could do it! *If we wanted to be unselfish.* But we'd have to give equality to everybody first. We couldn't do it as conquerors, like Hitler is trying to do. That won't work. We'd have to take the whole world into consideration and see that every man, woman and child got a square deal. We'd have to have something *positive* to offer the world—not just defending ourselves, like England, and pretending that we were defending civilization. If we really set out to do something for the world, *unselfishly,* I believe we could succeed.

230

But I don't think we'll do that. We haven't got the leaders capable of inspiring the people to such an effort. We're out to save big business, international trade, and that sort of thing. What we ought to do is to kill off our own Hitlers and Mussolinis first. We ought to clean our own house before we start in to save the world. Then maybe the people of the world would believe in us."

He apologized for speaking at such length. Said he hadn't ever had any education and so couldn't explain himself very well. Besides, he had got out of the habit of speaking to people, living alone so much. Didn't know why he had talked so much. Anyway, he felt that he had a right to his ideas, whether they were right or wrong, good or bad. Believed in saying what he thought.

"The brain is everything," he said. "If you keep your brain in condition your body will take care of itself. Age is only what you think. I feel just as young now, maybe younger, than I did twenty years ago. I don't worry about things. The people who live the longest are the people who live the simplest. Money won't save you. Money makes you worry and fret. It's good to be alone and be silent. To do your own thinking. I believe in the stars, you know. I watch them all the time. And I never think too long about any one thing. I try not to get into a rut. We've all got to die sometime, so why make things hard for yourself? If you can be content with a little you'll be happy. The main thing is to be able to live with yourself, to like yourself enough to want to be by yourself—not to need other people around you all the time. That's my idea, anyhow. That's why I live in the desert. Maybe I don't know very much, but what I know I learned for myself."

We got up to go. "Olsen is my name," he said. "I was glad to meet you. If you get to Barstow look me up—I'd like to talk to you again. I'll show you a prehistoric fish I've got in a rock—and some sponges and ferns a couple of million years old."

231

FROM GRAND CANYON TO BURBANK

I LEFT Grand Canyon about nine o'clock in the morning of a warm day, looking forward to a serene and beautiful toboggan slide from the clouds to sea level. Now, when I look back on it, I have difficulty in remembering whether Barstow came before or after Needles. I remember vaguely getting to Kingman towards sundown. That soothing noise, as of tiny bracelets passing through a wringer, which is the thing I like best about the engine, had changed to a frightening clatter, as if the clutch, the rear end, the differential, the carburetor, the thermostat and all the nuts, bolts and ball bearings would drop out any minute. I had been advancing by slow stages,

232

stopping every twenty or thirty miles to let the car cool off and add fresh water. Everybody was passing me, heavy trucks, dilapidated jalopies, motorcycles, skooters, teams of oxen, tramps, rats, lizards, even tortoises and snails. On leaving Kingman I saw a stretch of inviting-looking desert ahead. I stepped on the gas, determined to reach Needles at least before turning in. When I got to the foot of a mountain pass, near Oatman, the radiator began to boil over. I had another coke—my fifteenth or twentieth for the day—and sat down on the running board to wait for the engine to cool off again. There was a tremendous glare of fire shooting down through the canyon. An old drunk was hanging about the service station. He got to talking. Said it was the worst spot on Highway 66. Only about twelve miles of it, but pretty bad. I wasn't worrying about whether the road was dangerous or not but whether the water would boil over before I could reach the top of the pass. I tried to find out whether it was a long climb or a short, steep one. "There ain't any part of it you can't do in high," he kept repeating. That meant nothing to me because what other cars do in high I have to do in first sometimes. "Of course it's just as bad going down," he said. "It's only about four miles to the top. If you get over it you're all right." He didn't say *when* you get over it, as one would ordinarily. I didn't like that "if". "What do you mean," I asked, "is it so terribly steep?" No, it wasn't so terribly steep—it was tricky, that's all. People got frightened, it seems, when they found themselves hanging over the edge of the cliff. That's how all the collisions occurred. I watched the sun rapidly setting. I wondered if the one lamp that was functioning would hold out. I felt the hood to see how cool it was. It was still as hot as a furnace. Well, there were eight miles of descent, I figured out. If I could get to the top I might coast down—that would cool her off.

I started off. She was making a terrible racket, a human racket,

233

like some wounded giant screaming with pain. The signs all warned one to go slowly. Instead I stepped it up. I was riding in high and I intended to keep riding in high till I got to the top. Fortunately I passed only two cars. Out of the corner of my eye I was trying to take in the sight below. It was all a blur—just one unending piece of up-ended earth swimming in liquid fire. When I got to the top the gauge read 195 degrees. I had a two gallon can of water with me and no fear of running short. "Now we're going down," I said to myself. "She'll cool off in a jiffy." I guess it was Oatman that lay at the bottom of the pass. It might have been the end of the world. It was a fantastic place and why any one lived there I couldn't understand, but I didn't have time to ruminate on it very long even though I was lowering myself slowly and gingerly. Seemed to me the cogs were slipping. She was in first but she was rolling too fast. I tried working the brakes around the horse shoe curves and down the vertical walls of the town. Nothing held her back properly. The only thing that worked well was the horn. Usually it was faint but now suddenly it had grown strong and lusty. I switched on my one feeble lamp and honked for all I was worth. It was dark. I had descended to some long gentle slope which nevertheless refused to let me race faster than 30 miles an hour. I thought I was flying—when I looked at the roadside—but actually the illusion was that of being under water, of steering some queer kind of open submarine. Despite the drop it was warm, a pleasant evening warmth which invaded the pores and made one relax. I began to feel jovial. It was only the third or fourth time I had driven a car alone at night, my eyesight being rather poor and night driving being an art which I had forgotten to practise when taking my lessons in New York. People seemed to give me a wide berth for some mysterious reason. Sometimes they slowed down almost to a standstill in order to let me pass. I had forgotten about the one light. The

234

moon was out and it seemed to me that it was bright enough to drive without lights. I could only see a few yards ahead, but then that is all I am ever able to see, so everything seemed quite normal.

Nearing Needles it seemed suddenly as if I had come upon a hot house. The air was overpoweringly fragrant and it had become warmer. Just as I came to what looked like a body of water, a lake probably, a man in uniform rushed out to the middle of the road and ordered me to pull over. "Bring her to a halt," he said quietly. I was so groggy that I hadn't noticed that the car was still rolling. "Put your brake on," he said, a little more firmly. It was the California inspection bureau. "So I'm in California?" I said, pleased with myself. For answer he said: "Where did you come from?" For a moment I couldn't think. Come from? Come from? To stall for time I asked him what he meant. "Where did I come from *to-day*— or what?" I asked. He meant this morning, it was evident, by the tone of disgust in which he emphasized the point. Suddenly I remembered—it was the Grand Canyon I had left early that morning. God, I was happy to remember it. These birds can be awfully suspicious when you get a lapse of memory. "You're travelling alone?" he asked. Turning his searchlight on the empty interior of the car he went on to the next question. "Are you an American citizen?" That seemed thoroughly absurd—after all I had been through since morning. I almost laughed in his face, hysterically. "Yes, I'm an American citizen," I said quietly, containing myself, and damned glad that I didn't have to produce a carte d'identité or some other fool evidence of my status. "Born in New York, I suppose?" "Yes," I answered, "born in New York." "In New York City?" "Yes sir, in New York City." Then it seemed to me he asked about insects, cabbage leaves, rhododendrons, stink weeds and formaldehyde, to all of which I instinctively answered No Sir, No Sir, No Sir! It was like a little class in the catechism only it was California and a big

235

lake or something beside the road and the gauge was running up close to 200 again.

"Your light's out, do you know it?" he said.

"Why no," I answered angelically, shutting off the motor and climbing out to have a look at it.

"Where are you bound for now?" he said.

"Needles. Is it very far away?"

"Just a few miles," he said.

"Fine. I'll be hopping along then. Much obliged to you."

I got in and whizzed off with a terrific buzz and clatter. A few yards down the road I was stopped again. A man with a flashlight, a bit drunk, lurching unsteadily, leaned over the side of the car and, holding me by the arm, asked which way it was to such and such a place, a town I had never heard of in my life.

"To the left," I said, without pausing to reflect a second.

"Are you sure about it?" he said, his head swinging over my steering wheel in an amazingly flexible way.

"Absolutely," I said, starting her up.

"I don't want to go back to Kingman," he said.

"No, you can't miss it," I said, stepping on the gas and threatening to decapitate him. "The first turn to your left—just a few yards down the road."

I left him standing in the middle of the road and muttering to himself. All I prayed for was that he wouldn't try to follow me in his drunken gleefulness and run me into a ditch, like a guy I met in Texas one day, near Vega, who insisted that there was something wrong—my generator was gone, he said—and tried to escort me to the next town but in doing so almost wrecked me. What he really wanted was a drink. Funny to be held up in the middle of the night by a thirsty drunkard! Better, of course, than to be run

236

down by a pregnant mother with five children, as happened to a friend of mine.

At Needles I went to bed immediately after supper, planning to get up about five the next morning. But at three-thirty I heard the cocks crowing and feeling quite refreshed I took a shower and decided to start with the crack of dawn. I had breakfast, tanked up, and was on the road at four-thirty. It was coolish at that hour—about seventy-five or eighty degrees, I guess. The gauge read about 170. I figured that before the real heat commenced I ought to be in Barstow—say by nine o'clock in the morning surely. Now and then a crazy bird seemed to fly through the car, making a strange chirping which I had been hearing ever since leaving the Ozarks. It was the kind of music the lugs make when they're too tight or too loose. I never knew for sure whether it was the car or the creatures of the air, and sometimes I wondered if a bird had become a prisoner in the back of the car and was perhaps dying of thirst or melancholy.

As I was pulling out of town a New York car slowed up alongside of me and a woman cried out ecstatically—"Hello there, New York!" She was one of those panicky ones who get an attack of hysteria in the middle of nowhere. They were going at a leisurely pace, about forty-five miles an hour, and I thought I'd just hang on to their tail. I clung to them for about three miles and then I saw that the gauge was climbing up over 190. I slowed down to a walk and began doing some mental calculations. Back in Albuquerque, when I visited that wizard of automotive repairing, Hugh Dutter, I had learned that there was a difference between the reading of the gauge and the thermometer reading. A difference of fifteen degrees, supposedly in my favor, though it never really worked out that way in practice. Hugh Dutter had done everything possible to overcome the heating problem—except to boil out the

237

radiator. But that was my own fault. I told him I had had that done about four thousand miles back. It was only when I got to Joseph City, Arizona, where I met an old Indian trader, that I realized there was nothing to do but have her cleaned out again. Bushman, that was the man's name, was kind enough to ride into Winslow with me in order to put me in the right hands. There I met his son-in-law, another automotive wizard, and I waited four hours or so while the radiator was boiled out, the timing re-timed, the fan belt changed, the points tickled up, the valves unloosened, the carburetor calibrated, and so on. All to the tune of a modest four dollars. It was wonderful, after that operation, to ride into Flagstaff in the heat of the afternoon with the gauge reading 130! I could scarcely believe my eyes. Of course, about an hour later, pulling up a long slope on my way to Cameron, just when it was getting real chilly, the damned thing boiled over. But once I got out of the forest and into the no-man's land where the mountains are wine-colored, the earth pea green, the mesas pink, blue, black and white, everything was lovely. For about forty miles I don't think I passed a human habitation. But that can happen of course most anywhere west of the big cities. Only here it's terrifying. Three cars passed me and then there was a stretch of silence and emptiness, a steady, sinister ebbing of all human life, of plant and vegetable life, of light itself. Suddenly, out of nowhere, it seemed, three horsemen galloped into the center of the road about fifty yards ahead of me. They just materialized, as it were. For a moment I thought it might be a hold-up. But no, they pranced a moment or two in the middle of the road, waved me a greeting, and then spurred their horses on into the phantasmal emptiness of dusk, disappearing in the space of of a few seconds. What was amazing to me was that they seemed to have a sense of direction; they galloped off as if they were going somewhere when obviously there was nowhere to go to. When I

238

got to Cameron I nearly passed it. Luckily there was a gas station, a few shacks, a hotel and some hogans by the side of the road. "Where's Cameron?" I asked, thinking it lay hidden on the other side of the bridge. "You're in it," said the man at the gas station. I was so fascinated by the eeriness of the décor that before inquiring for a room I walked down to the Little Colorado River and took a good look at the canyon there. I didn't know until the next morning that I was camping beside the Painted Desert which I had left the previous morning. I thought only that I had come to some very definite end, some hidden navel of the world where the rivers disappear and the hot magma pushes the granite up into pinkish veins, like geodesic haemorrhoids.

Well, anyway, to get back. Where was I? Somehow, ever since I hit Tucumcari I have become completely disoriented. On the license plates in New Mexico it reads: "The Land of Enchantment". And that it is, by God! There's a huge rectangle which embraces parts of four States—Utah, Colorado, New Mexico and Arizona—and which is nothing but enchantment, sorcery, illusionismus, phantasmagoria. Perhaps the secret of the American continent is contained in this wild, forbidding and partially unexplored territory. It is the land of the Indian par excellence. Everything is hypnagogic, chthonian and super-celestial. Here Nature has gone gaga and dada. Man is just an irruption, like a wart or a pimple. Man is not wanted here. Red men, yes, but then they are so far removed from what we think of as man that they seem like another species. Embedded in the rocks are their glyphs and hieroglyphs. Not to speak of the footprints of dinosaurs and other lumbering antediluvian beasts. When you come to the Grand Canyon it's as though Nature were breaking out into supplication. On an average it's only ten to eighteen miles from rim to rim of the Canyon, but it takes two days to traverse it on foot or horseback. It takes four days for the mail to travel from one side to the other, a fantastic journey in which your letters pass through four States. Animals and birds rarely cross the abyss. The trees and vegetation differ from one plateau to the other. Passing from top to bottom you go through practically all the climatic changes known on this globe, except the Arctic and Antarctic extremes. Between two formations of rock there was, so the scientists say, an interval of 500,000,000 years. It's mad, completely mad, and at the same time so grandiose, so sublime, so illusory, that when you come upon it for the first time you break down and weep with joy. I did, at least. For over thirty years I had been aching to see this huge hole in the earth. Like Phaestos, Mycenae, Epidauros, it is one of the few spots on this earth which not only come up to all expectation but surpass it. My friend Bushman, who had been a guide here for a number of years, had told me some fantastic yarns about the Grand Canyon. I can believe anything that any one might tell me about it, whether it has to do with geological eras and formations, freaks of nature in animal or plant life, or Indian legends. If some one were to tell me that the peaks and mesas and amphitheatres which are so fittingly called Tower of Set, Cheop's Pyramid, Shiva Temple, Osiris Temple, Isis Temple, etc. were the creation of fugitive Egyptians, Hindus, Persians, Chaldeans, Babylonians, Ethiopians, Chinese or Tibetans, I would lend a credulous ear. The Grand Canyon is an enigma and no matter how much we learn we shall never know the ultimate truth about it. . . .

As I was saying, I was just entering the desert that lies between Needles and Barstow. It was six o'clock in the cool of a desert morning and I was sitting on the running board waiting for the engine to cool off. This repeated itself at regular intervals, every twenty or thirty miles, as I said before. When I had covered about fifty miles or so the car slowed down of itself, found its natural

240

rhythm, as it were, and nothing I could do would make it change its pace. I was condemned to crawl along at twenty to twenty-five miles an hour. When I got to a place called Amboy, I believe it was, I had a cool, consoling chat with an old desert rat who was the incarnation of peace, serenity and charity. "Don't fret yourself," he said. "You'll get there in good time. If not to-day why to-morrow. It makes no difference." Some one had stolen his peanut slot machine during the night. It didn't disturb him in the least. He put it down to human nature. "Some folks make you feel like a king," he said, "and others are lower than worms. We learn a lot about human nature watching the cars pass by." He had warned me that there would come a forty mile stretch which would seem like the longest forty miles I had ever covered. "I've done it hundreds of times," he said, "and each time the miles seem to stretch out more and more."

And by God he was right! It must have happened soon after I took leave of him. I had only travelled about five miles when I had to pull up by the side of the road and practice the beatitudes. I got under a shed with a tin roof and patiently twiddled my thumbs. On the wall was a sort of hieroglyphic nomenclature of the engine— the parts that go wrong and make it heat up. There were so many things, according to this graph, which could bring on fever and dysentery that I wondered how any one could ever lay his finger on the trouble without first getting a diploma from Henry Ford's School of Mechanical Diabolism. Moreover, it seemed to me that all the tender, troublesome parts touched on had been treated, in the case of my *charabanc*. Age alone could account for a great deal, it seemed to me. My own organism wasn't functioning any too handsomely, and I'm not exactly an old model, as they say.

Well, inch by inch then. "Don't fret!" that's what I kept telling myself. The new models were whizzing by at seventy-five and eighty

241

miles an hour. Air-conditioned, most likely. For them it was nothing to traverse the desert—a matter of a couple of hours—with the radio bringing them Bing Crosby or Count Basie.

I passed Ludlow upside down. Gold was lying about everywhere in big bright nuggets. There was a lake of pure condensed milk which had frozen in the night. There were yucca palms, or if not yucca date and if not date then cocoanut—and oleanders and striped sea bass from the Everglades. The heat was rippling up slant-wise, like Jacob's Ladder seen through a corrugated mirror. The sun had become a gory omelette frying itself to a crisp. The cicadas were cricketing and that mysterious bird in the back of the car had somehow found its way under my feet between the clutch and the brake. Everything was dragging, including the miniature piano and the steam calliope which had become entangled in the universal during the previous night's underwater passage. It was a grand cacophony of heat and mystification, the engine boiling in oil like an antique instrument, the tires expanding like dead toads, the nuts falling out like old teeth. The first ten miles seemed like a hundred, the second ten miles like a thousand, and the rest of the way just humanly incalculable.

I got to Barstow about one in the afternoon, after passing another examination by the plant, lice and vegetable inspectors at Daggett or some such ungodly place. I hadn't eaten since four in the morning and yet I had no appetite whatever. I ordered a steak, swallowed a sliver of it, and dove into the iced tea. As I was sitting there lucubrating and testifying in all languages I espied two women whom I recognized as guests of the Bright Angel Lodge. They had left the Grand Canyon in the morning and would probably have dinner in Calgary or Ottawa. I felt like an overheated slug. My brain-pan was vaporized. I never thought of Olsen, of course. I was racking my brains to try to remember whether I had started from Flagstaff,

Needles or Winslow. Suddenly I recalled an excursion I had made that day—or was it three days ago?—to Meteor Crater. Where the devil *was* Meteor Crater? I felt slightly hallucinated. The bartender was icing a glass. Meanwhile the owner of the restaurant had taken a squirt gun and was killing flies on the screen door outside. It was Mother's Day. That told me it was Sunday. I had hoped to sit quietly in the shade in Barstow and wait for the sun to set. But you can't sit for hours in a restaurant unless you eat and drink. I grew fidgety. I decided to go to the telegraph office and send a ready made Mother's Day greeting from Barstow. It was sizzling outdoors. The street was just a fried banana flaming with rum and creosote. The houses were wilting, sagging to their knees, threatening to melt into glue or glucose. Only the gas stations seemed capable of surviving. They looked cool, efficient, inviting. They were impeccable and full of mockery. They had nothing to do with human life. There was no distress in them.

The telegraph office was in the railway station. I sat on a bench in the shade, after dispatching my telegram, and floated back to the year 1913, the same month and perhaps the same day, when first I saw Barstow through the window of a railway coach. The train was still standing at the station, just as it had been twenty-eight years ago. Nothing had changed except that I had dragged my carcass halfway around the globe and back again in the meantime. The thing that was most vivid in my memory, curiously enough, was the smell and sight of oranges hanging on the trees. The smell mostly. It was like getting close to a woman for the first time— the woman you never dared hope to meet. I remembered other things too, which had more to do with lemons than with oranges. The job I took near Chula Vista, burning brush all day in a broiling sun. The poster on the wall in San Diego, advertising a coming series of lectures by Emma Goldman—something that

243

altered the whole course of my life. Looking for a job on a cattle ranch near San Pedro, thinking that I would become a cowboy because I was fed up with books. Nights, standing on the porch of the bunk house and looking towards Point Loma, wondering if I had understood that queer book in the library at Brooklyn— *Esoteric Buddhism*. Coming back to it in Paris about twenty years later and going quite daffy over it. No, nothing had radically altered. Confirmations, corroborations rather than disillusionment. At eighteen I was as much of a philosopher as I will ever be. An anarchist at heart, a non-partisan spirit, a free lancer and a free-booter. Strong friendships, strong hatreds, detesting everything lukewarm or compromising. Well, I hadn't liked California then and I had a premonition I wouldn't like it now. One enthusiasm completely vanished—the desire to see the Pacific Ocean. The Pacific leaves me indifferent. That part of it, at any rate, which washes the California shore. Venice, Redondo, Long Beach—I haven't visited them yet, though I'm only a few minutes away from them, being at this precise chronological moment of aberration in the celluloid city of Hollywood.

Well, the car had cooled off and so had I a bit. I had grown a little wistful, in fact. On to San Bernardino!

For twenty miles out of Barstow you ride over a washboard amidst sand dunes reminiscent of Bergen Beach or Canarsie. After a while you notice farms and trees, heavy green trees waving in the breeze. Suddenly the world has grown human again—because of the trees. Slowly, gradually, you begin climbing. And the trees and the farms and the houses climb with you. Every thousand feet there is a big sign indicating the altitude. The landscape becomes thermometric. Around you rugged, towering mountain ranges fading almost to extinction in the dancing heat waves of mid-afternoon. Some of them, indeed, have completely vanished, leaving only the pink snow shimmering in the heavens—like an ice cream cone without the cone. Others leave just a cardboard façade exposed—to indicate their substantiality.

Somewhere about a mile up towards God and his winged satellites the whole works comes toppling down on you. All the ranges converge suddenly—like a publicity stunt. Then comes a burst of green, the wildest, greenest green imaginable, as if to prove beyond the shadow of a doubt that California is indeed the Paradise it boasts of being. Everything but the ocean seems jammed into this mile-high circus at sixty miles an hour. It wasn't I who got the thrill—it was a man inside me trying to recapture the imagined thrill of the pioneers who came through this pass on foot and on horseback. Seated in an automobile, hemmed in by a horde of Sunday afternoon maniacs, one can't possibly experience the emotion which such a scene should produce in the human breast. I want to go back through that pass—Cajon Pass—on foot, holding my hat reverently in my hand and saluting the Creator. I would like it to be winter with a light covering of snow on the ground and a little sleigh under me such as Jean Cocteau used when he was a boy. I'd like to coast down into San Bernardino doing a belly-wopper. And if there are oranges ripening maybe God would be kind enough to put a few within reach so that I could pluck them at eighty miles an hour and give them to the poor. Of course the oranges are at Riverside, but with a light sleigh and a thin dry blanket of snow what are a few geographical dislocations!

The important thing to remember is that California begins at Cajon Pass a mile up in the air. Anything prior to that is vestigial and vestibulary. Barstow is in Nevada and Ludlow is a fiction or a mirage. As for Needles, it's on the ocean bed in another time, probably Tertiary or Mesozoic.

By the time I got to Burbank it was dark and full of embryonic aeroplanes. A flock of mechanical students were sitting on the curb along the Main Street eating dry sandwiches and washing them down with Coca-Colas. I tried to summon a feeling of devotion in memory of Luther Burbank but the traffic was too thick and there was no parking space. I couldn't see any connection between Luther and the town that was named after him. Or perhaps they had named it after another Burbank, the king of soda water or popcorn or laminated· valves. I stopped at a drug store and took a Bromo Seltzer—for "simple headaches". The real California began to make itself felt. I wanted to puke. But you have to get a permit to vomit in public. So I drove into a hotel and took a beautiful room with a radio apparatus that looked like a repository for dirty linen. Bing Crosby was crooning away—the same old song which I had heard in Chattanooga, Boswell's Tavern, Chickamauga and other places. I wanted Connie Boswell but they were all out of her for the moment. I took my socks off and hung them around the knob of the dial to choke it off. It was eight o'clock and I had awakened at dawn about five days ago, it seemed. There were no beetles or bed-bugs—just the steady roar of traffic on the concrete strip. And Bing Crosby, of course, somewhere out in the blue on the invisible ether waves owned by the five-and-ten cent store.

SOIRÉE IN HOLLYWOOD

MY FIRST evening in Hollywood. It was so typical that I almost thought it had been arranged for me. It was by sheer chance, however, that I found myself rolling up to the home of a millionaire in a handsome black Packard. I had been invited to dinner by a perfect stranger. I didn't even know my host's name. Nor do I know it now.

The first thing which struck me, on being introduced all around, was that I was in the presence of wealthy people, people who were bored to death and who were all, including the octogenarians, already three sheets to the wind. The host and hostess seemed to take pleasure in acting as bartenders. It was hard to follow the conversation because everybody was talking at cross purposes. The important thing was to get an edge on before sitting down to the table. One old geezer who had recently recovered from a horrible automobile accident was having his fifth old-fashioned—he was proud of the fact, proud that he could swill it like a youngster even though he was still partially crippled. Every one thought he was a marvel.

There wasn't an attractive woman about, except the one who had brought me to the place. The men looked like business men, except for one or two who looked like aged strike-breakers. There was one fairly young couple, in their thirties, I should say. The husband was a typical go-getter, one of those ex-football players who go in for publicity or insurance or the stock market, some clean all-American pursuit in which you run no risk of soiling your hands. He was a graduate of some Eastern University and had the intelligence of a high-grade chimpanzee.

That was the set-up. When every one had been properly soused dinner was announced. We seated ourselves at a long table, elegantly decorated, with three or four glasses beside each plate. The ice was abundant, of course. The service began, a dozen flunkeys buzzing at your elbow like horse flies. There was a surfeit of everything; a poor man would have had sufficient with the hors-d'oeuvre alone. As they ate, they became more discursive, more argumentative. An elderly thug in a tuxedo who had the complexion of a boiled lobster was railing against labor agitators. He had a religious strain, much to my amazement, but it was more like Torquemada's than Christ's. President Roosevelt's name almost gave him an apoplectic fit. Roosevelt, Bridges, Stalin, Hitler—they were all in the same class to him. That is to say, they were anathema. He had an extraordinary appetite which served, it seemed, to stimulate his adrenal glands. By the time he had reached the meat course he was talking about hanging being too good for some people. The hostess, meanwhile, who was seated at his elbow, was carrying on one of those delightful inconsequential conversations with the person opposite her. She had left some beautiful dachshunds in Biarritz, or was it Sierra Leone, and to believe her, she was greatly worried about them. In times like these, she was saying, people forget about animals. People can be so cruel, especially in time of war. Why, in Peking the servants had run away and left her with forty trunks to pack—it was outrageous. It was so good to be back in California. God's own country, she called it. She hoped the war wouldn't spread to America. Dear me, where was one to go now? You couldn't feel safe anywhere, except in the desert perhaps.

The ex-football player was talking to some one at the far end of the table in a loud voice. It happened to be an Englishwoman and he was insulting her roundly and openly for daring to arouse sympathy for the English in this country. "Why don't you go back to England?" he shouted at the top of his voice. "What are you doing here? You're a menace. We're not fighting to hold the British Empire together. You're a menace. You ought to be expelled from the country."

The woman was trying to say that she was not English but Canadian, but she couldn't make herself heard above the din. The octogenarian, who was now sampling the champagne, was talking about the automobile accident. Nobody was paying any attention to him. Automobile accidents were too common—every one at the table had been in a smash-up at one time or another. One doesn't make a point about such things unless one is feeble-minded.

The hostess was clapping her hands frantically—she wanted to tell us a little story about an experience she had had in Africa once, on one of her safaris.

"Oh, can that!" shouted the football player. "I want to find out why this great country of ours, in the most crucial moment . . ."

"Shut up!" screamed the hostess. "You're drunk."

"That makes no difference," came his booming voice. "I want to know if we're all hundred percent Americans—and if not why not. I suspect that we have some traitors in our midst," and because I hadn't been taking part in any of the conversation he gave me a fixed, drunken look which was intended to make me declare myself. All I could do was smile. That seemed to infuriate him. His eyes roved about the table challengingly and finally, sensing an antagonist worthy of his mettle, rested on the aged, Florida-baked strike-breaker. The latter was at that moment quietly talking to the person beside him about his good friend, Cardinal So-and-so. He, the Cardinal, was always very good to the poor, I heard him say. A very gentle hard-working man, but he would tolerate no nonsense from the dirty labor agitators who were stirring up revolution, fomenting class hatred, preaching anarchy. The more he talked about his holy eminence, the Cardinal, the more he foamed at the mouth. But his rage in no way affected his appetite. He was carnivorous, bibulous, querulous, cantankerous and poisonous as a snake. One could almost see the bile spreading through his varicose veins. He was a man who had spent millions of dollars of the public's money to help the needy, as he put it. What he meant was to prevent the poor from organizing and fighting for their rights. Had he not been dressed like a banker he would have passed for a hod carrier. When he grew angry he not only became flushed but his whole body quivered like guava. He became so intoxicated by his own venom that finally he overstepped the bounds and began denouncing President Roosevelt as a crook and a traitor, among other things. One of the guests, a woman, protested. That brought the football hero to his feet. He said that no man could insult the President of the

250

United States in his presence. The whole table was soon in an uproar. The flunkey at my elbow had just filled the huge liquor glass with some marvelous cognac. I took a sip and sat back with a grin, wondering how it would all end. The louder the altercation the more peaceful I became. *"How do you like your new boarding house, Mr. Smith?"* I heard President McKinley saying to his secretary. Every night Mr. Smith, the president's private secretary, used to visit Mr. McKinley at his home and read aloud to him the amusing letters which he had selected from the daily correspondence. The president, who was overburdened with affairs of state, used to listen silently from his big armchair by the fire: it was his sole recreation. At the end he would always ask *"How do you like your new boarding house, Mr. Smith?"* So worn out by his duties he was that he couldn't think of anything else to say at the close of these séances. Even after Mr. Smith had left his boarding house and taken a room at a hotel President McKinley continued to say *"How do you like your new boarding house, Mr. Smith?"* Then came the Exposition and Csolgosz, who had no idea what a simpleton the president was, assassinated him. There was something wretched and incongruous about murdering a man like McKinley. I remember the incident only because that same day the horse that my aunt was using for a buggy ride got the blind staggers and ran into a lamp post and when I was going to the hospital to see my aunt the extras were out already and young as I was I understood that a great tragedy had befallen the nation. At the same time I felt sorry for Csolgosz—that's the strange thing about the incident. I don't know why I felt sorry for him, except that in some vague way I realized that the punishment meted out to him would be greater than the crime merited. Even at that tender age I felt that punishment was criminal. I couldn't understand why people

251

should be punished—I don't yet. I couldn't even understand why God had the right to punish us for our sins. And of course, as I later realized, God doesn't punish us—we punish ourselves.

Thoughts like these were floating through my head when suddenly I became aware that people were leaving the table. The meal wasn't over yet, but the guests were departing. Something had happened while I was reminiscing. Pre-civil war days, I thought to myself. Infantilism rampant again. And if Roosevelt is assassinated they will make another Lincoln of him. Only this time the slaves will still be slaves. Meanwhile I overhear some one saying what a wonderful president Melvyn Douglas would make. I prick up my ears. I wonder do they mean Melvyn Douglas, the movie star? Yes, that's who they mean. He has a great mind, the woman is saying. And character. And *savoir faire*. Thinks I to myself "and who will the vice-president be, may I ask? Shure and it's not Jimmy Cagney you're thinkin' of?" But the woman is not worried about the vice-presidency. She had been to a palmist the other day and learned some interesting things about herself. Her life line was broken. "Think of it," she said, "all these years and I never knew it was broken. What do you suppose is going to happen? Does it mean war? Or do you think it means an accident?"

The hostess was running about like a wet hen. Trying to rustle up enough hands for a game of bridge. A desperate soul, surrounded by the booty of a thousand battles. "I understand you're a writer," she said, as she tried to carom from my corner of the room to the bar. "Won't you have something to drink—a highball or something? Dear me, I don't know what's come over everybody this evening. I do hate to hear these political discussions. That young man is positively rude. Of course I don't approve of insulting the President of the United States in public but just the same he might have used a little more tact. After all, Mr. So-and-so is an elderly man. He's entitled to some respect, don't you think? Oh, there's So-and-so!" and she dashed off to greet a cinema star who had just dropped in.

The old geezer who was still tottering about handed me a highball. I tried to tell him that I didn't want any but he insisted that I take it anyway. He wanted to have a word with me, he said, winking at me as though he had something very confidential to impart.

"My name is Harrison," he said. "H-a-r-r-i-s-o-n," spelling it out as if it were a difficult name to remember.

"Now what is your name, may I ask?"

"My name is Miller—M-i-l-l-e-r," I answered, spelling it out in Morse for him.

"Miller! Why, that's a very easy name to remember. We had a druggist on our block by that name. Of course. *Miller.* Yes, a very common name."

"So it is," I said.

"And what are you doing out here, Mr. Miller? You're a stranger, I take it?"

"Yes," I said, "I'm just a visitor."

"You're in business, are you?"

"No, hardly. I'm just visiting California."

"I see. Well, where do you come from—the Middle West?"

"No, from New York."

"From New York City? Or from up State?"

"From the city."

"And have you been here very long?"

"No, just a few hours."

"A few hours? My, my . . . well, that's interesting. Very interesting. And will you be staying long, Mr. Miller?"

"I don't know. It depends."

"I see. Depends on how you like it here, is that it?"

"Yes, exactly."

"Well, it's a grand part of the world, I can tell you that. No place like California, I always say. Of course I'm not a native. But I've been out here almost thirty years now. Wonderful climate. And wonderful people, too."

"I suppose so," I said, just to string him along. I was curious to see how long the idiot would keep up his infernal nonsense.

"You're not in business you say?"

"No, I'm not."

"On a vacation, is that it?"

"No, not precisely. I'm an ornithologist, you see."

"A what? Well, that's interesting."

"*Very*," I said, with great solemnity.

"Then you may be staying with us for a while, is that it?"

"That's hard to say. I may stay a week and I may stay a year. It all depends. Depends on what specimens I find."

"I see. Interesting work, no doubt."

"*Very!*"

"Have you ever been to California before, Mr. Miller?"

"Yes, twenty-five years ago."

"Well, well, is that so? *Twenty-five years ago!* And now you're back again."

"Yes, back again."

"Were you doing the same thing when you were here before?"

"You mean ornithology?"

"Yes, that's it."

"No, I was digging ditches then."

"Digging ditches? You mean you were—*digging ditches?*"

"Yes, that's it, Mr. Harrison. It was either dig ditches or starve to death."

"Well, I'm glad you don't have to dig ditches any more. It's not much fun—*digging ditches*, is it?"

"No, especially if the ground is hard. Or if your back is weak. Or vice versa. Or let's say your mother has just been put in the mad house and the alarm goes off too soon."

"I beg your pardon! *What did you say?*"

"If things are not just right, I said. You know what I mean—bunions, lumbago, scrofula. It's different now, of course. I have my birds and other pets. Mornings I used to watch the sun rise. Then I would saddle the jackasses—I had two and the other fellow had three. . . ."

"This was in California, Mr. Miller?"

"Yes, twenty-five years ago. I had just done a stretch in San Quentin. . . ."

"San Quentin?"

"Yes, attempted suicide. I was really gaga but that didn't make any difference to them. You see, when my father set the house afire one of the horses kicked me in the temple. I used to get fainting fits and then after a time I got homicidal spells and finally I became suicidal. Of course I didn't know that the revolver was loaded. I took a pot shot at my sister, just for fun, and luckily I missed her. I tried to explain it to the judge but he wouldn't listen to me. I never carry a revolver any more. If I have to defend myself I use a jack-knife. The best thing, of course, is to use your knee. . . ."

"Excuse me, Mr. Miller, I have to speak to Mrs. So-and-so a moment. Very interesting what you say. *Very interesting indeed.* We must talk some more. Excuse me just a moment. . . ."

I slipped out of the house unnoticed and started to walk towards the foot of the hill. The highballs, the red and the white wines, the champagne, the cognac were gurgling inside me like a sewer. I had no idea where I was, whose house I had been in or whom I had been introduced to. Perhaps the boiled thug was an ex-Governor of the State. Perhaps the hostess was an ex-movie star, a light that had gone out forever. I remembered that some one had whispered in my ear that So-and-so had made a fortune in the opium traffic in China. Lord Haw-Haw probably. The Englishwoman with the horse face may have been a prominent novelist—or just a charity worker. I thought of my friend Fred, now Private Alfred Perlès, No. 13802023 in the 137th Pioneer Corps or something like that. Fred would have sung the Lorelei at the dinner table or asked for a better brand of cognac or made grimaces at the hostess. Or he might have gone to the telephone and called up Gloria Swanson, pretending to be Aldous Huxley or Chatto & Windus of Wimbledon. Fred would never have permitted the dinner to become a fiasco. Everything else failing he would have slipped his silky paw in some one's bosom, saying as he always did—"The left one is better. Fish it out, won't you please?"

I think frequently of Fred in moving about the country. He was always so damned eager to see America. His picture of America was something like Kafka's. It would be a pity to disillusion him. And yet who can say? He might enjoy it hugely. He might not see anything but what he chose to see. I remember my visit to his own Vienna. Certainly it was not the Vienna I had dreamed of. And yet today, when I think of Vienna, I see the Vienna of my dreams and not the one with bed bugs and broken zithers and stinking drains.

I wobble down the canyon road. It's very Californian somehow. I like the scrubby hills, the weeping trees, the desert coolness. I had expected more fragrance in the air.

The stars are out in full strength. Turning a bend in the road I catch a glimpse of the city below. The illumination is more faërique than in other American cities. The red seems to predominate. A few hours ago, towards dusk, I had a glimpse of it from the bedroom

256

window of the woman on the hill. Looking at it through the mirror on her dressing table it seemed even more magical. It was like looking into the future from the narrow window of an oubliette. Imagine the Marquis de Sade looking at the city of Paris through the bars of his cell in the Bastille. Los Angeles gives one the feeling of the future more strongly than any city I know of. A bad future, too, like something out of Fritz Lang's feeble imagination. *Goodbye, Mr. Chips!*

Walking along one of the Neon-lit streets. A shop window with Nylon stockings. Nothing in the window but a glass leg filled with water and a sea horse rising and falling like a feather sailing through heavy air. Thus we see how Surrealism penetrates to every nook and corner of the world. Dali meanwhile is in Bowling Green, Va., thinking up a loaf of bread 30 feet high by 125 feet long, to be removed from the oven stealthily while every one sleeps and placed very circumspectly in the main square of a big city, say Chicago or San Francisco. Just a loaf of bread, enormous of course. No raison d'être. No propaganda. And tomorrow night two loaves of bread, placed simultaneously in two big cities, say New York and New Orleans. Nobody knows who brought them or why they are there. And the next night three loaves of bread—one in Berlin or Bucharest this time. And so on, ad infinitum. Tremendous, no? Would push the war news off the front page. That's what Dali thinks, at any rate. Very interesting. *Very interesting, indeed.* Excuse me now, I have to talk to a lady over in the corner. . . .

Tomorrow I will discover Sunset Boulevard. Eurythmic dancing, ball room dancing, tap dancing, artistic photography, ordinary photography, lousy photography, electro-fever treatment, internal douche treatment, ultra-violet ray treatment, elocution lessons, psychic readings, institutes of religion, astrological demonstrations, hands read, feet manicured, elbows massaged, faces lifted, warts removed, fat reduced, insteps raised, corsets fitted, busts vibrated, corns removed, hair dyed, glasses fitted, soda jerked, hangovers cured, headaches driven away, flatulence dissipated, business improved, limousines rented, the future made clear, the war made comprehensible, octane made higher and butane lower, drive in and get indigestion, flush the kidneys, get a cheap car wash, stay awake pills and go to sleep pills, Chinese herbs are very good for you and without a Coca-cola life is unthinkable. From the car window it's like a strip teaser doing the St. Vitus dance—a corny one.

A NIGHT WITH JUPITER

WELL, where was I? Oh yes, after taking leave of the sidewalk writer I found myself on Cahuenga Boulevard, walking towards the mountains. I was looking up at the stars when a car came up behind me and ran into a lamp post. Everybody was killed. I walked on "irregardless", as they say, and the more I looked at the stars the more I realized how lucky I was to have escaped without so much as a splinter. There was an occasion in Paris when I did some stargazing and damned near broke my neck. I sat down on the steps of a temple, on Ivar Avenue I think it was, and began to muse. About that narrow escape at the Villa Seurat, I mean.

Every once in a while, when I'm riding the crest of a euphoria, I get the notion that I'm immune—to disease, accidents, poverty, even death. I was coming home one night, after having spent a wonderful evening with my friend Moricand, the astrologer, and just as I was about to turn off the avenue d'Orléans into the rue d'Alésia I thought of two things simultaneously: a) to sit down and have a glass of beer, b) to look up and see where Jupiter was at that precise chronological moment. I had just passed the Café Bouquet d'Alésia which faces the church and as there were still a few moments before closing time I saw no reason why I should not sit down on the terrace and enjoy a quiet beer all to myself. There was always a red glow about the church which fascinated me —and at the same time from where I sat I could look at my benevolent planet, Jupiter. I never thought to see where Saturn was, or Mars. Well, I was sitting there like that, feeling wonderful inside and out, when the couple who lived below me happened to come along. We shook hands and then they asked if I would object to their sitting beside me and joining me in a little drink. I was in such a state of elation that, despite the fact that the man, who was an Italian refugee, bored me to death, I said—"Sure, nothing could be better." And with that I began to tell them how marvelous everything was. The man looked at me as though I were a bit cracked, because at that particular moment everything was rotten in the world and he felt particularly rotten about it because it was his business to write about historical events and processes. When he pressed me as to why I felt so good and I told him for no particular reason he looked at me as though I had done him a personal injury. But that didn't deter me in the least. I ordered another round of drinks, not to get high, because the beer was innocuous and besides I was drunk already, drunk with exaltation, but because I wanted to see them look a little more cheerful even if world events did look putrid. Well, I guess I had three beers—and then I suggested we go home. It was a short walk back to the Villa Seurat and in that brief span of time I grew positively radiant. Like an idiot I confessed to them that I was in such a superb state of being that if the Creator himself had willed it he would find it impossible to harm me. And on that note I shook hands with them and climbed the stairs to my studio.

As I was undressing I got the idea of going up to the roof and having a last look at Jupiter. It was a warm night and I had on nothing but my carpet slippers. To get up to the roof I had to climb a vertical iron ladder to the balcony of the studio. Well, to make it short, I had my fill of Jupiter. I was ready to hit the hay. The lights were out but the moonlight came through the long window above the balcony. I walked in a trance to the iron ladder, put my foot out instinctively, missed it and fell through the glass door below. In falling I remember distinctly how delicious it felt to fall backwards into space. I picked myself up and began hopping around like a bird to see if any bones had been broken. I could hop all right but I was gasping, as though some one had stuck a knife in my back. I reached around with one hand and felt a big piece of glass sticking in my back, which I promptly pulled out. I felt another piece in my backside and pulled that out too, and then another in my instep. Then I began to laugh. I laughed because evidently I was not killed and I could still hop about like a bird. The floor was getting rather bloody and no matter where I stepped there was more glass.

I decided to call the Italian downstairs and have him look me over, bandage up the cuts, and so on. When I opened the door I found him coming up the stairs. He had heard the crash and wondered what had happened to me. Previously, while we were at table one day, a rabbit had fallen off the roof and crashed through the sky-light right on to our table. But this time it was no rabbit, he knew that.

"You'd better call a doctor," he said, "you're full of cuts and bruises."

I told him I'd rather not—just find some alcohol and some cotton to wash the cuts. I said I'd sleep it off, it couldn't be very serious.

"But you're bleeding like a pig," he said, and he began to wring his hands frantically.

He woke the fellow up across the hall and asked him to telephone a doctor. No luck. One said, "Take him to the hospital"; another said, "It's too late, I've just gone to bed, call So-and-so."

"I don't want any bloody French doctor," I said. "You find some alcohol and put some bandages over the cuts—I'll be O.K."

Finally they found some wood alcohol and a roll of absorbent cotton. I stood in the bathtub and they sponged me off.

"You're still bleeding," said the Italian, who for some reason couldn't stand the sight of blood.

"Get some adhesive tape and plug the cuts up with cotton," I said. The blood was running down my legs and I didn't like to see it going to waste like that.

Well, they did their best and then they helped me into bed. When I touched the bed I realized that I was full of bruises. I couldn't move. Soon I fell asleep and I guess I must have slept an hour or more when suddenly I awoke and felt something slippery in the bed. I put my hand on the sheet and it was wet with blood. That gave me a start. I got out of bed, turned on the lights and threw the covers back. I was horrified when I saw the pool of blood I had been lying in. Jesus! My own blood and running out of me like a sewer. That brought me to my senses. I ran next door and knocked. "Get up quick!" I yelled. "I'm bleeding to death!"

262

Luckily the fellow had a car. I couldn't put any clothes on, I was stiff and sore and too frightened to bother. I slung a bath robe around me and let him race me to the American hospital in Neuilly. It was almost daylight and everybody was asleep apparently. It seemed hours until the interne came down and deigned to staunch my wounds.

While he was sewing me up here and there and feeling my bones and ligaments we fell into a curious conversation about Surrealism. He was a youngster from Georgia and he had never heard of Surrealism until he came to Paris. He wanted to know what it was all about. Well, it's hard enough to explain what Surrealism means under ordinary circumstances but when you've lost a lot of blood and had an anti-tetanus injection and a man is trying to sew up your rectum and another man is looking at you and wondering why you don't yell or faint it's almost impossible to get the old dialectic working properly. I made a few Surrealistic explanations which I saw at once meant nothing to him and then I closed my eyes and took a cat nap until he had finished his job.

The Surrealistic touch came after we started back in the car. My young friend, who was a Swiss, and a very neurotic one at that, suddenly had an imperious desire to eat breakfast. He wanted to take me to some café on the Champs-Elysées where they had excellent croissants. He said a coffee would do me good, and a little cognac with it.

"But how can I walk into a café in this bathrobe?" I asked. I didn't have the trousers to my pajamas—they had ripped them off, as doctors always do, why I don't know. They rip them off and throw them in the waste basket, when it would be just as easy to pull them off and save them for the laundry.

Arnaud, my friend, saw nothing strange whatever about having breakfast in a bathrobe on the Champs-Elysées. "They can see that you've had an accident," he said. "The bathrobe is full of blood."

"That makes it all right, does it?" I asked.

"It's all right with me," he said. "As for them, *je m'en fous!*"

"If you don't mind," I insisted weakly, "I'd rather wait till we get to our own neighborhood."

"But the croissants there are no good," he said, clinging stubbornly to his obsession like a petulant child.

"Damn the croissants!" I said. "I'm weak, I want to get to bed."

Finally he reluctantly consented to do as I had suggested. "But my palate was just set for those delicious croissants," he said. "I'm hungry. . . . I'm famished."

On the rue de la Tombe-Issoire we stopped at a *bistro* and had breakfast. We had to stand up at the bar. I ate half a croissant and felt like caving in. The workmen dropping in thought we had been on a spree. One burly chap was just about to give me a hearty slap on the back, the very thought of which almost threw me into a faint. Arnaud leisurely devoured one croissant after another. They were not so bad after all, he averred. Just when I thought we were ready to go he asked for another cup of coffee. I stood there in agony while he slowly sipped it—it was too hot to polish off at one gulp.

When I got back to my place I threw the bloody sheets on the floor and laid myself gently on the mattress. The bruises were so painful now that I groaned with pleasure. I fell into a sound sleep —a coma.

When I came to my friend Moricand was sitting beside the bed. Arnaud had telephoned him, he said. He seemed amazed that I was able to talk.

"It happened between one-thirty and two in the morning, did it not?" he asked.

Yes, I thought that was about the time. *Why*, I wanted to know. What was he getting at?

He made a serious face. Then he solemnly extracted a paper from his inside pocket. "This," he said, waving the paper before my eyes, "is the astrological picture of the accident. I was curious, you know. You seemed in such an excellent mood last night when you left me. Well, here it is . . ." and he leaned over to explain the black and red lines which contained so much meaning for him.

"You were lucky not to have killed yourself," he said. "When I came in and saw the blood everywhere I thought surely you were dead. Everything was against you at that hour last night. If you had gone to bed immediately you might have escaped it. Another man would have died, that's a certainty. But you, as I told you often, are very lucky. You have two rudders: when the one gives out the other one comes into play. What saved you was Jupiter. Jupiter was the only planet in your horoscope which was not badly aspected." He explained the set-up to me in detail. It was very much like being walled in. If all the doors had been shut I would have died. He showed me the picture of Balzac's death, an amazing diagram of Fate, as beautiful and austere as a chess problem.

"Can't you show me Hitler's death chart?" I said, smiling weakly.

"*Mon vieux*," he responded with alacrity, "that would indeed give me great pleasure, could I do that. Unfortunately I see nothing catastrophic in sight for him yet. But when he falls, mark my words, he will go out quickly—like a light. Now he is still climbing. When he reaches the top it will be for just a little while and then *Pam!* he will go like that! There are bad days ahead. We're going to suffer a great catastrophe. I wish I had a Jupiter like yours. But I have that infernal Saturn. I don't see any hope . . ."

STIEGLITZ AND MARIN

"THE FIRST task," says Rudhyar, "*is the regeneration of the substance of all arts.*

"The new music sounds ridiculous and meaningless in a concert hall; the new drama calls for a new theatre; the new dance longs for new surroundings and a free relationship to music and dramatic action. Beside this, the conditions of performance, from a social financial standpoint, are tragically absurd. Commercialism has completed the destruction of the spirit of devotion to Art, the spirit of real participation in the performance. The public comes to it in search of sensation rather than prepared *to experience life as an*

266

Alfred Stieglitz

through Art. The greatest need perhaps of the New Art is a new public; the greatest need of the Artists is a consciousness of their true relationship with their public. The Artist has ceased to consider himself a provider of Spiritual Food, an arouser of dynamic Power; he has ceased to consider his position as an 'office', himself as an officiant. He thinks but of expressing himself, but of releasing forces which he cannot handle within himself. Why such a releasing? He does not care to consider. He does not face deliberately and willingly his spiritual duty to the Race. Thus he does not attempt to mould the Race, to gather around his work the proper public for this work. He sells his wares. He is no longer a Messenger of life, attracting by the very example of his own living, human beings to the Message of which he is the bearer."

Often when I let my mind play with the idea of invasion by the enemy I get a recurrent image of Alfred Stieglitz sitting in his "American Place" on the 17th floor of a New York office building surrounded by John Marin's water colors. All his life Stieglitz has been waiting for that public which would celebrate the coming of the artist. His whole life has been one of dedication and devotion— to art. It was Stieglitz who made it possible for John Marin to paint, to continue painting. There is a tremendous story behind these two names. Both Marin and Stieglitz are over seventy now. Marin is still spry enough to hop around and paint more masterpieces. Stieglitz spends most of his time on his back in the cubicle which adjoins the gallery. Mentally he is still as spry as ever, though his heart is giving out. He has alloted himself the minimum of space in "An American Place". Just room enough to move from the cot to the easy chair. If the room were made still smaller I don't believe he would murmur. He can say all he has to say in the space that it requires for a man to stand up or lie down. He needs no megaphone either—just enough voice to whisper his convictions.

And he makes himself heard. Indeed, we will be hearing from him long after he is dead.

I try to visualize the scene. The enemy solidly entrenched within the gates of the city—and Stieglitz still on the job. The door opens and a man in uniform enters the gallery. Stieglitz is in the next room stretched full out on the cot. There are nothing but Marins on the walls. Stieglitz has been expecting a visit of this sort from day to day—he merely wonders why it hasn't happened sooner. The officer takes a quick glance around the room, reassures himself that it is not a trap, then steps briskly to the doorway of the little room where Stieglitz is lying.

"Hello! what are you doing here?" he says.

"I might ask you the same question," answers Stieglitz.

"Are you the watchman?"

"I suppose you might call me that. Yes, I'm a sort of watchman, if that's what you want to know."

"Whose paintings are those—out there?"

"John Marin's."

"Where is he? Why did he leave them here? Aren't they worth anything?"

Stieglitz beckons to the officer to sit down in the easy chair. "I like your questions," he begins. "You get right to the heart of things."

"Come, come," says the officer, "I didn't come here to have a quiet little chat. I want some information. I want to know the meaning of this. Here you are in an empty building and you watch over these paintings—water colors, I see. Why didn't you give yourself up, like the others? How is it we didn't know about this collection?"

"I can't answer all your questions at once," Stieglitz replies in a feeble voice. "I am going to die in a little while. Go slowly, please."

268

The officer looks at him with sympathy, dubiety and suspicion. "An old crackpot," he thinks to himself. He clears his voice. "Well, where is he . . . the owner?"

"He's home painting, I imagine," says Stieglitz wearily.

"What? He's a painter too?"

"Who?"

"Well, who are you talking about?"

"I'm talking about John Marin. Who are you talking about?"

"The man who owns them—that's who I'm talking about. I don't care if he's a painter or a paper-hanger."

"The man who owns them is the man who painted them—John Marin."

"Now we're getting somewhere. Good. What does he value them at?"

"My dear man, that's something we've never been able to determine. What would *you* value them at?"

"I don't know anything about such matters," says the officer huffily.

"Neither do I, to be frank with you. Some people think I'm crazy when I say that. If you like them, name a price and I'll tell you whether you can have them or not."

"Listen, I am not playing a game with you," says the officer.

"I'm absolutely serious," says Stieglitz. "For thirty years now people have been asking me to put a price on John Marin's work. I can't do it. Some say it's very clever and shrewd of me, not to set a fixed price on his paintings. I say very simply: 'How much do you like John Marin's work? How much are you willing to invest to help John Marin continue painting? You spend $2,000.00 for a car, let's say. Well then, how does a Marin compare with a Buick or a Studebaker?' People say that's no way to sell paintings. But I'm not selling paintings. I'm selling John Marin. I believe in him.

I've staked everything on him. Besides, there are people whom I wouldn't let have a Marin for any amount of money. But I'll say this—any man who really wants to own a Marin can have one. Not any one he wants, to be sure, but *a* Marin. I'll fix the price to suit the man's pocket-book. I've never turned any one away who made a genuine offer."

"This is all very interesting, my good fellow, but I am not here to discuss prices and values. I . . ."

Stieglitz interrupts. "It bores me to death too, frankly. I'd rather talk about John Marin." He gets up slowly, with great effort. "Now just come here," he says, taking the officer by the arm. "Here's a Marin that nobody will get until I die. Look at it! Can you put a price on a painting like that?"

In spite of himself the officer finds himself gazing at the work intently. He seems puzzled, baffled.

"Take your time," says Stieglitz, anticipating the officer's perplexity. "I've been looking at that one for twenty-five years and I haven't seen all there is to see in it yet."

The officer slowly turns his gaze away. He talks almost as if to himself. "Funny, I used to paint myself once. I never did water colors, I must confess. It's so long ago—it seems like something that happened in another life." He melts rapidly. Goes on in the same fashion, mumbling his words. Finally he blurts out: "You are quite right—there is something extraordinary about this Marin, as you call him. He's a wizard. I must get General So-and-so to come here —at once. He will be crazy about your John Marin."

"Of course he will," says Stieglitz calmly. "That is, if he has any intelligence. Bring the whole staff up; it will be a pleasure for me to show them John Marin's work."

"You don't seem to be worried about what we might do to you.

270

You talk as if there were no war or anything. You are a strange man. I am beginning to like you."

"Naturally," says Stieglitz unblushingly. "I have nothing to conceal from any one. I don't own anything. I have lived with these paintings all my life practically. They gave me great joy, great understanding. I am almost glad now that my friend Marin wasn't more successful. So is he, I think. You should go to his home— he has a collection there which he keeps for himself. Get him to show them to you."

"But have you thought," says the officer, "that we might carry them off to our country?"

"Of course I have," says Stieglitz promptly. "That doesn't worry me. They belong to the whole world. All I ask is that you take good care of them. You see"—and he takes the officer by the arm again—"there isn't a scratch on these frames. Marin made these frames himself. I want you to keep them that way. Who knows where they will be hanging ten years from now? And fifty years hence—or a hundred? Listen, I am an old man. I have seen lots of things in my time—unbelievable things, too. You think you would like to have them in your country. *Good*—take them. But don't be under any illusions about keeping them. Works of art often survive long after empires crumble. Even if you destroy the paintings you can't destroy the effect they have had upon the world. Even if nobody but myself ever saw them their value would remain and make itself felt. Your cannons can destroy but they can't create, can they? You can't kill off John Marin by destroying his paintings. No, I am not worried about their fate. They have already done something to the world. You could go a step farther and kill John Marin himself—that wouldn't matter either. What John Marin stands for is indestructible. I think he would laugh if

271

you put a revolver to his head and threatened to kill him. He's as tough as an old rooster, you know. Of course you won't want to kill him—I know better than that. You'll probably offer him a good job—that's a subtler way of killing him off. If I were you, I'd just let him be where he is. Don't bother him. He's reached a quiet, serene stage of life now where nothing really disturbs him. See that he has enough to eat, will you? I can't look after him any more, as you see for yourself. I've done all I could. Now it's up to you and the others to come after us. . . . What was that General's name again? Why don't you go and fetch him up here? If he's a connoisseur of art I'm sure we'd have a lot of things in common. Maybe I can disabuse him of some of his notions."

Stieglitz turns quietly on his heels and makes for the cot in the little room. The officer stands in the center of the big room looking vacantly at the Marins on the wall. He pinches himself to make sure he is not dreaming it all. . . .

That's the little comedy I dream of when I think of Stieglitz' last moments. I have an alternative one, which is probably the way it actually will happen. Stieglitz will be standing in front of a Marin, talking in his usual fashion, and suddenly, in the midst of a phrase, he will drop dead. That, I think, is the way the end ought to come. And I'm sure Stieglitz thinks so too.

Stieglitz, who uses the pronoun I so frequently, is about as un-egotistical a man as I've ever encountered. This I of his is more like a rock. Stieglitz never speaks impersonally because to do so would be to deny that he is a person. He is the opposite of a personage, which is to say a personality. Stieglitz is an individual, a unique being. He doesn't put on any show of false modesty—why should he? Would you apologize for using God's name? Everything that Stieglitz says is based on pure conviction. Behind every word that

272

comes from his lips is his whole life, a life, I must repeat, of absolute devotion to the things he believes in. *He believes!*—that's the essence of it all. He isn't giving his opinions—he is saying what he knows to be true, what he, Alfred Stieglitz, has found to be true through personal experience. One can disagree with his views, but one can't refute them. They are alive and breathing all the time, just like Stieglitz himself. To destroy his views you would have to destroy Stieglitz bit by bit. Every particle of him asseverates the truth which is in him. Such men are rare in any epoch. Naturally there is the utmost diversity of opinion about him. *Opinion* again! What does anybody's opinion matter? To answer Stieglitz you would have to be all of a piece. *Are you?* And what answer, finally, is there to make to a man who says: "I believe. I love. I cherish." That's all that Stieglitz is saying. He doesn't ask you to agree with him. He asks you merely to listen to him rhapsodize about the things he loves, about the people he has devoted his whole life to supporting.

People are often irritated with him because he doesn't behave like an art dealer. They say he is shrewd or quixotic or unpredictable —God knows what they all say. They never ask themselves what would have happened to Marin or O'Keeffe or the others if their works had fallen into other hands. To be sure, John Marin *might* have received more money for his work than Stieglitz was ever able to secure for him. But would John Marin be the man he is to-day? Would he be painting the pictures he is painting in his seventy-second year? I doubt it. I have witnessed with my own eyes the process of killing an artist off, as it is practised in this country. We have all witnessed the rise and fall of our great "successes." Our transitory idols! How we love them! And how quickly we forget them! We should thank God that a man like Stieglitz is still amongst us, demonstrating every day of his life the constancy of his love. The man is a perfect marvel of endurance, of fortitude, of patience, of humility, of tenderness, of wisdom, of faith. He is a rock against which the conflicting currents of wishy-washy opinion strike in vain. Stieglitz is unmovable, unalterable. He is anchored. And that is why I have the audacity to picture him sitting in his little office undismayed by the crumbling of the world about. Why should he tremble in the presence of the enemy? Why should he run away? Has he not been surrounded and beleaguered by enemies all his life? Not strong ones, either, but mean, insidious, petty, cunning ones who strike in the dark when one's back is turned. Our own enemies—the worst there can be. The enemies of life, I call them, because wherever a tender, new shoot of life raises its head they trample it down. Not deliberately always, but thought-lessly, aimlessly. The real enemy can always be met and conquered, or won over. Real antagonism is based on love, a love which has not recognized itself. But this other kind, this slimy, crawling hos-tility which is evoked by indifference or ignorance, that is difficult to combat. That saps the very roots of life. The only person who can cope with it is a wizard, a magician. And that is what Stieglitz is, and Marin too. Only Marin operates in the realm of paint, whereas Stieglitz operates in the realm of life. They are constantly fecundating each other, nourishing each other, inspiring each other. There is no more glorious wedlock known to man than this mar-riage of kindred spirits. Everything they touch becomes ennobled. There is no taint anywhere. We reach with them the realm of pure spirit. And there let us rest—until the enemy comes. . . .

I met Stieglitz for the first time last year, shortly after my return from Europe. I never knew him in the days of "291"; if I had met him then, as did so many young writers and painters, the whole course of my life would probably have been altered, as it was through hearing Emma Goldman years before.

"Miracles still happen. I am positive of that—more positive to-day than ever. And I have been positive for a long time." That's what Stieglitz wrote in the fly-leaf of the little book he presented to me on the occasion of our meeting. The book was a compilation of the Letters of John Marin, most of them addressed to Stieglitz.

I feel somewhat guilty now when I think back to that moment. It was my intention then to do a little book on John Marin—and God knows, I may still do it! But I had intended to do it immediately, fired as I was by the sight of all those Marins which I had been waiting to see for so many years.

No matter how many Marins you see, there are always more somewhere. I doubt if even Stieglitz has seen all of John Marin's work. I think Marin works overtime. I think that when he dies we will see a trunk-load of paintings which no one suspected the existence of. It is said that he paints with two hands. I suspect that he paints with both feet also, and with his elbows and the seat of his pants.

Anyway, after seeing as many as I could feast my eyes on, at "An American Place", I had the surprise of my life when I visited Marin at his home in Cliffside. There I saw a great boxful of his New Mexican water colors. I saw Marin too, in a new guise. Marin the man living in a perfectly conventional landscape. A sort of elegant prospector who had returned to the tame, effete East with the nuggets of gold which he had stored away in his garret to look at, fondle, play with in his moments of boredom.

When I say John Marin I always add—"the wizard". The Wizard of Oz, maybe. Anyhow, a wizard. There's no getting round it, the man is a phenomenon. Just as Laotse was intercepted by the Emperor's messenger and ordered to write it all down before disappearing into the blue, so some one has yet to arise who will collar John Marin and extract the last juices before he drops out of sight.

In a letter to Lee Simonson, 1928, Marin writes characteristically:

"I have just received your telegram. Will you please tell me why you asked me to contribute to your magazine? I did not ask nor beg to be a contributor. If my pictures cannot be understood by those of average intelligence, how can you or any one expect my writing to be? You can ask me to alter my pictures to the average intelligence as easily as to ask me to alter my writing to it. Know you too that much of the writings I read are un-understandable to me. So that I may come under the head of lesser average intelligence. . . . Why are you so afraid of the appearance of the Dam fool? Is it that it may be found that he isn't quite the Dam fool after all?"

The emergence of a Marin in a country of mediocrities is something almost impossible to explain. Marin is a freak of nature here. A sport. His would have been the most cruel fate of any artist America has produced—a fate worse than Poe's, worse than Melville's—had it not been for the miraculous *rencontre* with Stieglitz. I hope John Marin will pardon me for saying this, because it might sound as though I doubted his powers, which I don't in the least. I mean simply that America, when it gives birth to a man like John Marin, does its best to kill him off quickly and ruthlessly.

It was Zoler, I believe, who said to me that Marin was as tough as an old rooster, that it was hard to kill him off. An accurate description. For Marin is like a fighting cock, trim, slender, spry, chipper, salty, and always ready with the spurs. That's to say, for those who are looking for a fight. Left to himself, he's gentle, wise, peaceful, considerate and gracious. He says marvelous things, if you know how to draw him out. He prefers not to talk, though. He prefers to illustrate what he has to say with the brush.

In speaking of the "Marin Island" water color, Mr. E. M. Benson says: * "Here finally is a picture that needs no frame to establish its boundaries; whose parts are so finely orchestrated as to create the

* *John Marin, the Man and His Work*—by E. M. Benson.

276

John Marin's painting, "Maine Islands"

illusion of movement *without the fear of chaos*. Our eye is led along the mixed currents of these forms like so many stones skipping over water in a pre-arranged plan. Everything seems to relate to something else, to lead to something else, to be part of a great design, the ebb and flow of a superb pattern. As we look at these forms we are no longer aware of tree, water, and sky in the representational sense, but of abstract symbols for them. It *is the calligraphic signature which we now accept for the fact*: the jagged line for the swift movement of water; the triangle for the tree; the spot of color for the sun or the flower. These plastic metaphors are the body and blood of Marin's art." (Italics mine.)

The calligraphic signature! That is the quintessence of Marin's wizardry, the mark of his soaring achievement. Here Marin joins with the best in Chinese art, carries on the great tradition in that algebra of paint which signalizes mastery. This signature which was explicit in his early work even—the man began to gallop before he had taken but a few steps!—is now recognized as having the validity of a Euclid, a Galileo, a Paracelsus, an Einstein. He is not just another great painter. He is *the* American painter, the blood brother of all the great painters of the past whether in Europe, Asia, South America or Africa. John Marin is our link with the world we seem so fatuously eager to repudiate.

HILER AND HIS MURALS

I said somewhere earlier in this book that the murals in the Aquatic Park Building in San Francisco were the only murals worth talking about in the United States. As a matter of fact, the two things I remember about San Francisco are Hiler's murals and the cable cars. The rest has faded out.

The day I saw the murals I went straight back to the hotel and wrote Hiler a letter about them. I think my letter must have mystified him a bit; it was an hilarious letter to an hilarious painter whom

Note: The reader's attention is called to the book *Why Abstract?* by Hilaire Hiler, Henry Miller & William Saroyan, published by New Directions, which contains an earlier essay on Hiler and his work by Miller.

I always think of with hilarious glee. Hilaire Hiler, the hilarious. He's had a rich life, mostly abroad. He's loved by everybody, including his fellow artists, which is saying a good deal. Every now and then he takes a vacation from paint—to play the piano in a night club, to open a night club himself, to decorate a bar or a gaming room, to write a learned book on costumes, to study the American Indians, to explore the lost continents of Atlantis and Mu, to practise psychoanalysis, to confute the devil and confound the angels, to go on a bender, to find a new mistress, to learn Chinese or Arabic, to write a tract on the technique of painting, to study rug weaving or sailing a boat, and so on. He has a thousand and one interests and he has friends in every corner of the world— good, solid friends who never fail him. Above all he is a comedian. The Irish in him, no doubt. When he gets a bit crocked and sits down to the piano he sings in the weirdest tongues ever heard. What's more, he usually sings his own compositions, which he promptly forgets the next day. It isn't singing, really, it's a sort of cachinnating menopause for drum and zither. His primary obsession is COLOR. I do believe Hiler knows more about color than any man alive. He eats and drinks color. Himself he's the color of color. He's not just colorful, as we say of certain gay and charming birds, but he's color itself. That means that he refracts light extraordinarily well. Sometimes he becomes a veritable aurora borealis. What I am trying to say is that when Hiler tackles a wall he puts into it all that he's lived through, read about, dreamed of and despaired of.

When I got to the Aquatic Park Building I began to laugh—naturally. It was like reading a man's palm. Some people get frightened when they read palms. They see accidents, fiascos, travelogues, disease and dysentery. Well, I looked at Hiler's murals and I saw many things. It was very definitely a sub-aqueous world. It was

279

also very definite that Hiler was at home in it. Not surprising, because he is at home everywhere, just as much with the birds of the air, for instance, as with the monsters of the deep. He's equally at home in psychopathic wards. What delightful hours he spent with the insane at St. Anne's in Paris! What wonderful friends he made there—not with the physicians, God help us, but with the inmates. The saving grace about Hiler is that he permits everybody to collaborate with him. He's democratic in a profound sense.

The murals. . . . Well, there were fish such as I had never seen before, such as perhaps few people have, unless they are lucky enough to enjoy delirium tremens occasionally. Hiler swears that he invented none of them—that they all exist and have a name, and I suppose a genus and a locus vivendi, too. I wouldn't think of questioning his erudition, because it is too vast for me. I know only a few fish, the edible kind mostly, such as sea bass, blue fish, porgy, mackerel, herring, etc. And filet of sole, which is my favorite dish. These are ordinary fish and Hiler probably was bored with them. So he dug up some rare specimens and began recreating their habitat, which is in the mind, of course. The curious thing is that though the décor was distinctly Freudian it was also gay, stimulating and superlatively healthy. Even when the fish became abstract they were tangible and edible and very jocose. Fish you could live with, if you know what I mean. Whereas the Freudian fish are disagreeable, usually poisonous and thoroughly indigestible, Hiler's fish were non-ideological. They were plastic, chromatic, cheerful and recognizable, like Papuans or Patagonians, or snails or slugs. They smile at you, no matter what the weather is. They would smile even if Hitler himself were to look at them. They are unafraid, uninhibited, un-self-conscious. They are like our ancestors, so to speak. And though they are embalmed for all time they have nothing of the museum, the cemetery or the morgue about them. They

A panel of Hilaire Hiler's mural in the Aquatic Park, San Francisco

swim in their own fat and draw their nourishment from the air about them. Hiler made them that way and they are going to stay that way.

Well, I wrote Hiler a letter, as I was saying, and a few months later I got an answer. Here it is, for those who wish to get the esoteric slant on the murals:

". . . While I'm on this subject it might be interesting to give you a few high spots in connection with them (the murals) to see if what I had in mind has anything to do with your reaction and thoughts in connection with them—?

"1. They are primarily a 'flowing arabesque'—color decoration —or design and color plastic. (I hope)

"2. The straight line and right angle, the horizontal and the vertical *had* to be introduced because they had to be architectural —hence Atlantis, *Mu.*

"3. Most of the 'influence' or artistic material came from Asia in or over the Pacific and not from any other direction.

"Much less important and incidental (joli prime cadeau): Water a symbol for birth or rebirth, flood, or belief in religion and myth, biology, psychoanalysis, etc. The mother literally and figuratively. Sub-symbols and surrogates the cowry and spiral—c . . . —gold —shell money—thru Indian Ocean, to Venice, to London, to costermongers' 'pearly buttons', etc. Polynesian influence from Asia to Pacific coast thru Easter Island 'which *was* a mountain on Mu' and cyclic God-Life-Death motive of water birth and water death of a or *the* or our 'civilization' or culture—? Not so far from your Hamlet book as you might think! And we might be convinced that an Asiatic idiom—'Manitou comes out of Asia'—might be more valid in the long run. Whether it came through Bering Straits or across the atolls through indians, or Indians, a trip to the south of Mexico might prove convincing. . . ."

In the same letter he informs me that he is about to open a "Jockey" club in Hollywood,* a *boîte*, I suppose, similar to the one he opened in Montparnasse. I used to pass this latter place every morning, as I was taking my constitutional. What amazed me about the Indians which Hiler had painted on the outside was that the colors remained so fresh and vivid. They always looked as though they had been painted just the day before. It's the same with his canvases, especially that 1920 period during which he painted the immortal *"Parc dans le Midi"*. Often, like the film director Hitchcock, you could find Hiler hidden away in the crowd which he was depicting—usually with his back turned. He wanted to be there with the others, enjoying his own masterpiece—from the inside, as it were. I would give anything to be sitting with him now on a bench somewhere in the Midi. I wouldn't care if it were a plastic, an abstract or an ideological bench, just so long as it would hold us and permit us to do nothing. I've spoken about the American park and how it stinks. These parks of Hiler's belong in "The Absolute Collective" donated to the citizens of the future by Dr. Erich Gutkind. The trees are not natural trees, nor even dream-like trees, but eternal trees whose roots are in the cosmic consciousness of man. They give something more than shade and fruit: they give life. And so, when I think nostalgically of him and his parks, I feel something expanding in me, something like reality itself expanding, and with it the universe, the God concept, the whole infinite panorama of endless life and death, and I feel like jumping up, shaking off the trance, and hugging him in a warm embrace.

(N. B. This is a free ad in lieu of a Guggenheim fellowship.)

* Flash:—A quick flop. Joint closed already.

THE SOUTHLAND

THE SOUTHLAND is a vast domain about which one could go on writing forever. I have said scarcely anything about it and yet the South—and the Southwest, which is a totally different world—are the two sections of America which move me deeply. The old South is full of battlefields, that is one of the first things which impress you. The South has never recovered from the defeat which it suffered at the hands of the North. The defeat was only a military defeat—that one feels very strongly. The Southerner has a different rhythm, a different attitude towards life. Nothing will convince him that he was in the wrong; at bottom he has a supreme contempt for the man of the North. He has his own set of idols—warriors, statesmen, men of letters—whose fame and glory no defeat has ever dimmed. The South remains solidly against the North, in everything. It wages a hopeless fight, very much like that of the Irish against England.

If you are of the North this atmosphere affects you strangely. It would be impossible to live long in the South without being undermined. The climate, the landscape, the manners and customs, the soft speech exert a charm which it is difficult to resist. This world of the South corresponds more nearly to the dream life which the poet imagines than do other sections of the country. Little by little this dream world is being penetrated and poisoned by the spirit of the North. The South is crumbling under the heel of the conqueror. From Rome to Savannah, along the old wagon routes, one can still trace Sherman's march to the sea. It is the path of a vandal, the path of a soldier who said that war is hell and who demonstrated it by the use of fire and sword. The South will never forget Sherman, never forgive him.

At Gettysburg, at Bull Run, at Manassas, at Fredericksburg, at Spottsylvania Court House, at Missionary Ridge, at Vicksburg I tried to visualize the terrible death struggle in which this great republic was locked for four long years. I have stood on many battlefields in various parts of the world but when I stand beside the graves of the dead in our own South the horror of war assails me with desolating poignancy. I see no results of this great conflict which justify the tremendous sacrifice which we as a nation were called upon to make. I see only an enormous waste of life and property, the vindication of right by might, and the substitution of one form of injustice for another. The South is still an open, gaping wound. The new Atlanta, sprung from the ashes of the old, is a hideous nondescript city combining the evil, ugly traits of both North and South. The new Richmond is lifeless and characterless. New Orleans lives only in its tiny French quarter and even that is being rapidly demolished. Charleston is a beautiful memory, a corpse whose lower limbs have been resuscitated. Savannah is a living tomb about which there still clings a sensual aura as in old Corinth. Amidst these embers of the past the Southerner treads his defiant way. Compared to the man of the North, he is a charming, gracious, courteous, dignified, civilized being. He is sensitive and touchy also, capable of violent explosions which to a Northerner are most unpredictable. Some you find living in the pomp and splendor of Jefferson's time; some live like animals, in a condition comparable only to that of the primitive beings in Africa and other remote parts of the world where the benefits of civilization have been imposed by the white man; now and then you find a crumbling mansion occupied by a family of poverty-stricken, half-demented wretches surrounded by the faded relics of the past. There are beautiful regions, such as in the vicinity of Charlottesville, for example, where there seem to be nothing but millionaires. There are mill towns in the Carolinas, for instance, which, like the mining towns of Pennsylvania or West Virginia, fill one with terror and disgust. There are farming regions, in what was once the Old Dominion, where the land assumes a beauty and serenity unrivalled anywhere in the Old World. There are vistas, such as at Chattanooga, Harpers Ferry, Asheville, or along the crest of the Blue Ridge, or in the heart of the Great Smokies, to mention but a few, which instill in the human heart a deep, abiding peace. There are swamps, such as the Okefinokee and the Great Dismal Swamp of Virginia, which inspire an unspeakable dread and longing. There are trees, plants, shrubs, flowers such as are seen nowhere else, and which are not only extraordinarily beautiful but haunting and almost overwhelmingly nostalgic. At Biloxi, Mississippi, there is a row of live oaks planted a century ago by a Greek which are of such staggering loveliness and magnificence as to make one breathless. From the steps of Black Mountain College in North Carolina one has a view of mountains and forests which makes one dream of Asia. In Louisiana there are stretches of bayou country whose beauty is of a nature such as only the Chinese poets have captured. In New Iberia, La., to signal only one example, there is a house and garden belonging to Weeks Hall which constitute in essence and in fact the dream made real.

In Mississippi, near the banks of the great river itself, I came upon the ruins of Windsor. Nothing now remains of this great house but the high, vine-covered Grecian columns. There are so many elegant and mysterious ruins throughout the South, so much death and desolation, so much ghostliness. And always in the fairest spots, as if the invader aiming at the vital centers struck also at the pride and hope of his victim. One is inevitably induced to reflect on what might have been had this promising land been spared the ravages of war, for in our Southern States that culture known as the "slave culture" had exhibited only its first blossoms. We know what the slave cultures of India, Egypt, Rome and Greece bequeathed the world. We are grateful for the legacy; we do not spurn the gift because it was born of injustice. Rare is the man who, looking upon the treasures of antiquity, thinks at what an iniquitous price they were fashioned. Who has the courage, confronted with these miracles of the past, to exclaim: "Better these things had never been than that one single human being had been deprived of his rightful freedom!"

Who knows what splendors might have blossomed forth from such nuclei as Charleston, Savannah, New Orleans! The other day, picking up a travel book, I read with amazement and stupefaction of the dead city of Pagan, the old capital of Burma. "Bleached as bones beneath the moon ahead of us lay the ruins of what had once been Burma's capital city, five thousand stupas, pagodas, temples dating from 108 A.D. and spread over a hundred square miles . . . It is said that in the days of Pagan's glory the pagodas and shrines and monasteries could be counted by the myriad; even now the remains of five thousand can still be traced. The ground is so thickly studded with them that you can scarcely move a foot without touching some sacred object made by the adroit hands of the Paganese." *

It is doubtful if this continent will ever bequeath the world the deathless splendor of the holy cities of India. Only in the cliff dwellings of the Southwest, perhaps, does the work of man here in America arouse emotions remotely analogous to those which the ruins of other great peoples inspire in the traveler. On Avery Island, in Louisiana, I ran across a massive statue of Buddha, brought over from China, which was protected by a glass cage. It was startling to look upon in its bizarre setting. It dominated the landscape which was in itself a work of art in a way that is difficult to describe. Avery Island is an exotic piece of land in the heart of the Acadian country. It has a salt mine the interior of which is like the décor of some fabulous edifice out of the *Thousand and One Nights*. It has a bamboo forest the floor of which reflects a light that suggests the translucent glamour of *Pélleas and Mélisande*. It has a sanctuary for birds which makes one think of W. H. Hudson's purple pages. It is a haven and an ark for all that is exotic in flesh, form and substance. In the midst of a spacious jungle garden, resting immobile and impenetrable on the top of a gentle knoll, is the graven image of Buddha fashioned some eight or nine centuries ago in China. If one suddenly came upon a skyscraper twice the height of the Empire State building one could not be more astonished than by the sight of this silent, graven image which dominates the luxuriant, tangled landscape of Avery Island. An almost oppressive poise and

* *Land of the Eye* by Hassoldt Davis.

287

serenity is emanated by this massive figure of the Buddha. The landscape, for all the care that has been lavished upon it to make it seductive, seems in the presence of this transplanted idol to be almost as fragile as the glass which offers the Buddha a temporal and needless protection. The poise and serenity of the figure evoke the certainty of endless duration. The Louisiana earth seems more than ever restless, agitated, pregnant with life that must flourish and rot. Whatever the angle of the sun, the shadow of the Buddha falls with measure and precision, with gravity and dignity, as if defining with unerring exactitude the utmost limits of hope, desire, courage and belief.

There are thousands of dream places in the old South. You can sit on a bench in a tiny Confederate Park or fling yourself on the banks of a levee or stand on a bluff overlooking an Indian settlement, the air soft, still, fragrant, the world asleep seemingly, but the atmosphere is charged with magical names, epoch-making events, inventions, explorations, discoveries. Rice, tobacco, cotton —out of these three elements alone the South created a great symphonic pageant of human activity.

It is all over now. A new South is being born. The old South was ploughed under. But the ashes are still warm.

ADDENDA

In STARTING on our trip both Rattner and myself had made application for Guggenheim fellowships. We answered all the questions faithfully, submitted the names of persons of good repute who would endorse our request, and in general vouched for the fact we were neither morons, adolescents, insane or alcoholic; we also submitted the necessary specimens of previous work together with projects of work in progress. When the rejections came I found in my envelope a mimeographed copy citing the names of those to whom awards had been made and for what purpose. Believing that the 1941 awards are fairly representative of the Guggenheim tradition I cull a few herewith for the reader's delectation:

Dr. Ernst Cleveland Abbe, Associate Professor of Botany, University of Minnesota: Studies of the bearing of historical, climatic, and geological factors on the vegetation of a heavily glaciated region in the eastern subarctic.

Dr. Solomon E. Asch, Assistant Professor of Psychology, Brooklyn College: The preparation of a book on the formation and change of opinion and attitude.

Dr. Lewis E. Atherton, Assistant Professor of History, University of Missouri: A study of the political, social, economic and intellectual position and influence of the small town and country merchant in the days of slavery.

Dr. Roy Franklin Barton, Teacher of Mathematics, St. Andrew's High School, Sagada, P. I.: The recording, translating and annotating of the Hudhud, a series of epics chanted as work songs and at death wakes by the Ifugaos, a pagan, terrace-building people of the Philippine Islands.

Mr. Wilbur Joseph Cash, Newspaperman, *Charlotte News*, Charlotte, N. C.: Creative writing.

Dr. André Benjamin Delattre, Assistant Professor of Romance Languages, Wayne University: The preparation of an edition of the correspondence of Voltaire with Théodore, François and Jean-Robert Tronchin.

Dr. Paul Theodore Ellsworth, Associate Professor of Economics, University of Cincinnati: A study of the Chilean economy, 1920–1940, in its readjustment to international change.

Dr. Adriance Sherwood Foster, Associate Professor of Botany, University of California: A comparative cyto-histological study of the meristems of buds and of tropical ferns, gymnosperms and woody angiosperms.

Dr. Edward Girden, Instructor in Psychology, Brooklyn College:

A comparative investigation of the neuropsychological determinants of the phenomena of dissociation.

Dr. Aristid V. Grosse, Chemist, Bronxville, New York: Continuation of studies of the products of neutron bombardment of uranium, protactinium and thorium. (Renewal)

Dr. George Katona, Research Psychologist, New York City: Continuation of studies in the field of psychology of learning with special reference to the differences in learning by understanding and learning by memorization and drill. (Renewal)

Dr. William Christian Krumbein, Assistant Professor of Geology, University of Chicago: An investigation of the dynamical processes by which sedimentary particles are abraded, changed in shape, and sorted into the deposits found in nature.

Dr. Clarence Dickinson Long, Jr., Assistant Professor of Economics, Wesleyan University, Middletown, Connecticut: Studies in the history of unemployment in the United States.

Dr. Arthur J. Marder, Research Associate, Bureau of International Research of Harvard University and Radcliffe College: The preparation of a book on British sea power in the dreadnought era.

Dr. Eduardo Neale-Silva, Assistant Professor of Spanish, University of Wisconsin: A study of the Spanish-American social novel, with particular reference to the works of José Eustasio Rivera.

Dr. Eliot Furness Porter, Biologist and Photographer, Hubbard Woods, Illinois: The making of a photographic record, in black and white and in color, of certain species of birds in the United States.

Dr. Dorothy Mary Spencer, Lecturer in Anthropology, University of Pennsylvania: Studies of the Mundari-speaking people in the Chota Nagpur plateau, Bihar, India.

Dr. Harvey Elliott White, Associate Professor of Physics, University of California: A spectroscopic study and analysis of gases of the volcano Mauna Loa.

Dr. David Harris Willson, Associate Professor of History, University of Minnesota: The preparation of a biography of James I, King of England and Scotland.

Dr. Francis Dunham Wormuth, Assistant Professor in Government, Indiana University: Studies in the field of political theory, with particular reference to the doctrine of separation of powers.

A word to the wise: any one who thinks he can make the grade should address himself to Henry Allen Moe, Secretary General of the John Simon Guggenheim Memorial Foundation, 551 5th Ave., N. Y. C.

For complete listing request free catalog from
New Directions, 80 Eighth Avenue, New York 10011

†Bilingual

For complete listing request free catalog from
New Directions, 80 Eighth Avenue, New York 10011

†Bilingu